THE
LOST QUEEN

WILDE JUSTICE, BOOK 2

JENN STARK

Books by Jenn Stark

Wilde Justice Series

The Red King
The Lost Queen

Immortal Vegas Series

Getting Wilde
Wilde Card
Born To Be Wilde
Wicked And Wilde
Aces Wilde
Forever Wilde
Wilde Child
Call of the Wilde
Running Wilde
Wilde Fire

One Wilde Night (prequel novella)

JENN STARK

Demon Enforcers series

Demon Unbound
Demon Forsaken
Demon Bewitched

For Monica
May you achieve your wildest dreams.

QUEEN of SWORDS.

CHAPTER ONE

Huddling in my parka on the relentlessly well-kept sidewalk in the heart of Budapest, next to a building painted the color of buttercream, I questioned my life choices. I was Justice of the Arcana Council, wielder of magic great and small...and I was about to be fleeced of seven dollars and at least a good hour of my time weaving through a tourist trap so stupid, my teeth were grinding.

A hipster about three groups ahead of me elbowed one of his friends, apparently in indignation. "*Blade* was the best," he insisted. "Christopher Lee was a joke." He was a thin, reedy American twenty-something, his skin pale as chalk.

"And you're an idiot," his friend assured him, barely looking up from his phone. The other two guys muttered something about Bela Lugosi. At least their discussion explained why they were here, standing in front of an attraction that promised a peek into the dark history of the original Dracula, Vlad the Impaler. They were doomed to be disappointed. No matter what the placard beneath the ornamental archway said, Vlad had been imprisoned more than a half mile away in the caves below Buda Castle — nowhere near here.

Unfortunately, those caves were now playing host to some creepoid illusionist trying to resurrect the glory days of the Castle Hill labyrinth, in all its bloody detail. There'd been two deaths so far, and I wasn't about to allow a third. From my intel, the illusionist had holed up in the warren of caves below Castle Buda, readying himself for his next kill.

In order to get there, however, I had to start here.

"Dude, Herm Lannister bit it. There goes the next *Fantastic Four* reboot."

A coarse round of snickers and wisecracks followed this touching obituary, and I watched as the other three members of the Gen Z coalition whipped out their cell phones to pay their final respects to whoever Herm Lannister was. Then the four of them crowded inside the door of the attraction, screens glowing, ignoring the glares of the Australian family directly behind them.

"Lantern?" A portly man in an eighteenth-century powdered wig held up a small electric lantern, its bulb casting a cheerful glow. I'd heard him repeat the same spiel five times already. "There are signs below…but *do* be careful," he intoned as he took my cash. Then he handed over the lamp.

I muttered my thanks and stepped into the darkened doorway, feeling dumber by the second. The cave system started almost immediately, right after we were treated with the most hysterically useless wall map—a diagram of the maze so bad, it wasn't even handed out. Well-lit arrows apparently would show folks the way around below, but I wasn't interested in the main attractions of the labyrinth. I simply had to get far enough into it to take a detour to the deeper cavern system.

Setting down the lamp at my first opportunity, I followed the group right in front of me for a good five minutes until they stopped, all of them gawping at what looked like the headpiece of a column that had apparently been wrested from the local history museum and transferred here. We hadn't yet come to the weirder elements of the place—wax figures dressed like the Phantom of the Opera, with canned music floating through the mist—but that was up ahead, I could sense it. If anyone had seen me entering this ridiculous, outrageous, idiotic—

"You always manage to end up in the most interesting locations."

The voice was British, slightly mocking, and so obnoxiously familiar, I pivoted in instinctive reaction, my right hand coming up to deliver a throat punch that'd leave the man choking on his Weetabix for days. Unfortunately, I wasn't fast enough. Nigel Friedman ducked out of the way, pulling me by my parka deeper into the mouth of the next corridor before almost immediately taking a hard right into a section blocked off by a velvet barricade.

"What are you doing here?" I hissed, ignoring Nigel's obvious attempts to be silent. Nigel had been my top bodyguard in my most recent position prior to Justice, when I'd been, albeit briefly, the head of a clandestine quasi-military, quasi-magical syndicate known as the House of Swords. Before that, he'd been one of my top competitors in the artifact hunting trade. So we had history. A lot of history. Which was the only reason I suffered him to be gripping my puffy, down-filled elbow as he felt along the wall with his other hand. He stopped about five yards up as something old and musty gave way.

"I was nearby," he finally answered me.

"Nearby. To Budapest."

9

"Near enough." I could hear the grin in his voice. "I got word your newest case involved Vlad the Impaler, and I thought it was a good time for a holiday."

"You don't need to protect me anymore," I said, but in the darkness, I couldn't help but smile. It was kind of nice, inspiring Nigel's higher instincts.

"I'm not protecting you," he said, his tone still genial. "I'm making sure you don't steal something for the Council that should be in the hands of the House of Swords."

My smile faltered. *What?*

Nigel didn't respond, so I tried the same question out loud. "What?"

He let go of my elbow and waved at me. "A little light would be useful. Just a little."

Scowling, I lifted a hand, and a sputtering marble of fire appeared between my fingers. Way better than a crappy electric lantern, but I'd needed to grab one to keep up appearances. This was one of the many bits of magical ability I'd cobbled together over the past year, most notably when I'd started working with the Arcana Council, a group of powerful Connecteds with a mission to keep Earth's magic in balance. Those abilities were currently in flux, but I could still be counted on to produce a fantastic glow ball.

With its assistance, I could see the Brit more easily. Medium, blonde, and deceptively wiry, Nigel Friedman was an ex-special forces operative of varied and highly useful talents. Now he was grinning at me as he turned sideways and half disappeared into a crack in the cave wall.

Through it, I could hear the haunting melodies of an eighteenth-century concerto starting up, tinny over distant speakers. "You're taking us to the Phantom room?" I asked derisively. "I could've made it there on my own."

"Behind it. The exit to this corridor isn't well marked."

I shrugged, patting my quilted pocket. "That's why I have the cards."

"Oh, we'll be using those soon enough. One more turn, and my intel runs out."

"And here I thought it ran out several years ago."

Still, I followed Nigel into the seam of the wall. The cavern system here was markedly warmer and smelled faintly of sulfur. I was pretty sure I'd read somewhere that the entirety of Castle Hill was riddled with caves that extended all the way down to the Danube River, a subterranean system that had been created by the relentless flow of underground hot springs, and I could believe it. I tugged on my parka, rethinking its usefulness.

"I wondered why you dressed like the Michelin Man," Nigel observed quietly. "We'll go along through here…"

His voice trailed off as we slid through the narrow confines of the corridor, the music on the other side of the wall growing louder, then fainter again as we passed by. I thought about the American boy and his friends, could almost hear his mocking derision. "This place is a joke," I muttered.

"A joke with a very specific purpose." Nigel pulled up short beside me, then made an impatient gesture with his hand. "Ditch the coat. You'll get stuck in some of the narrower passages."

Frowning, I pulled the jacket off. "I'm not going to leave it here. It's cold outside."

"It's not that cold. But no, you're not going to leave it here. Incinerate it."

11

"You know, I'm not a butane lighter you can activate on demand."

"Sara—"

"Fine." With a silent sigh of apology for the perfectly serviceable jacket. I touched my glow marble to it and pulsed the energy to fever pitch. The coat combusted to ash, and the plastic fastenings melted. Nigel kicked the debris aside, spreading it across the floor and beneath a stone ledge.

"Good." He was about to keep moving when I held out a hand. Conveniently, the one pulsing with magic.

"Spill it, Nigel. Why are you really here?"

"We don't really have time—"

"I think we do. I don't know where you got your information, but I'm not here to steal an artifact. I don't do that anymore. You may have missed the memo."

Something in my voice caught him up short, and he turned back to me. His face was wary but curious. "You really expect me to believe you're not here for the Sultan's Cup?"

"I'm not." That said, what the hell was the Sultan's Cup? It sounded way more interesting than the jackwit I was after, for all that he was a particularly deadly jackwit. "I look for people now, Nigel. Not things. Vlad the Impaler is rumored to have returned to this hellhole, using it as a base of operations where he drags unwitting Connecteds into the deep, drains them of their blood, then skewers them. They've been ending up in the Danube with spike holes."

It was Nigel's turn to stare at me. "How is it we don't know this?"

It was a fair question. The House of Swords, where Nigel was still an Ace bodyguard, had been set up in part to protect any mortal souls blessed or cursed enough to have significant psychic abilities. Those humans, known as Connecteds, typically lived in secret on the fringes of society, desperate not to be cast as expendables in a real life X-Men movie.

"You don't know about it because the local constabulary here hasn't put two and two together, that puncture wounds equal Vlad's return," I said. "Especially because the dead haven't been respectable people. They're—whatever the PC term is now for gypsies. And more to the point, they're high-level Connecteds. And though five of them are missing, only two bodies have popped up in the Danube so far."

"You're Justice of the Arcana Council now. You've got bigger fish to fry. Explain to me why you're in the caves of Budapest, handling such a low-level…" Nigel made a face, cutting off his own complaint. "They're kids, aren't they? The victims."

I grimaced. Sometimes it didn't pay for people to know you too well. "You could have asked Nikki what I was doing here. She's ass-deep in old cases, trying to prioritize the backlog of dark practitioners I'm supposed to be icing. But bottom line, I'm here for Vlad, not looking for some stupid cup."

"You really think it's Vlad returned?" Nigel asked, looking around the cavern room as if it would yield any answers.

"No, I don't. The original Vlad wasn't Connected. He was merely morally depraved. That doesn't get you a Get Out of Hell Free card. But the new guy—not the same story. The complaints about him have included illusions, magic spells, and hints of vampirism—once again, not the original Dracula, but the Bram Stoker made-up version. So this new guy is basically using every trick in the Buda Castle playbook and combining them all to lure his mark to him, all under the guise of

Vlad the Impaler, which makes him a prick in the truest sense of the word. And he's targeting kids."

"You say there's still three who could be alive."

"As far as we know. But beyond that, I've also lost all patience for using reincarnation as an excuse for bad deeds. I don't have time for that."

I didn't either. I'd just come off a case where a five-hundred-year-old murderous magician had apparently resurfaced in Venice, all set to butcher a whole new set of victims. So I was definitely tired of the reincarnation schtick. When I brought this once-and-present Vlad to Judgment, he wasn't going to fare well. Everyone in the Connected community needed to know that I planned to treat opportunistic reincarnators with extreme prejudice. Gamon, Judgment of the Arcana Council, whose job it was to judge and then punish the criminals I brought to her, would be more than onboard with the plan. She preferred to treat everyone with extreme prejudice.

Nigel continued watching me. "So a modern-day Vlad... He's operating in the labyrinth?"

"Not this part of the labyrinth." I jerked my thumb behind me. "Way too crowded. My information is that he's underneath the happy castle itself, which is no longer an actual home but a bunch of museums. I could have tried to get in that way, but it seemed too much trouble."

"Why didn't you just..." Nigel wiggled his fingers. "Go there with your mind to suss the guy out? A lot faster, I should think."

I shrugged, in no mood to explain to him that some of my past abilities as Sara Wilde, mercenary artifact hunter, hadn't exactly hung around now that I'd taken on the role of Justice. Especially the ability of astral travel, or the art of traveling with your mind without the inconvenience of your body tagging along. As much as it came with its own raft of side effects, I *missed* that ability. "That process isn't working as well as it used to. So—your turn. Spill on this cup."

He obliged. "Sultan Murad II, then leader of the Ottoman Empire, held Vlad as a hostage starting in 1442, when Vlad was just a boy. Vlad impressed him, but there was a lot more to the son of Dracul than met the eye. He apparently indulged himself with some of the sultan's treasures, including a prized cup. Then, Murad's son, Mehmed II, conspired to have Vlad imprisoned by the king of Hungary, after he'd already started his impaling ways. There are many legends about that imprisonment, but one was that he was held here in Budapest at some point."

"Do not tell me you think Vlad was actually a vampire." What was *with* this place and the Dracula legend? I could understand it in Transylvania—they needed it for tourism—but Buda Castle had been Vlad's unwanted home for barely ten years, and he'd never once so much as bitten anyone here. Impaled them, yes. But not bitten them.

Nigel shook his head. "Not exactly. But the theft of the Sultan's Cup from Murad's palace was discovered a few years after Vlad left. It was never tied to him, that we could tell, but rumors sprang up years later that there was a connection. The cup was supposedly one that provided life-giving benefits to any who sipped from it—and, of course, it was also rumored to drive you crazy."

"Kind of an awkward trade-off." I looked around the cave. "So Vlad gets imprisoned, stripped, and the Sultan's Cup is taken from him. Meanwhile, he may have drunk from it and believed he'd live forever. Big maybe. And...you're thinking that the cup is here, after all this time? Why?"

"The war on magic," he said.

"Right," I sighed. "That."

Not four months earlier, I'd helped stave off some unwanted party guests—the gods and goddesses of the ancients—who'd wanted to come back to Earth. We'd Ubered them back to the other side of the veil where they belonged, but the planet hadn't quite been the same afterward. Demons had popped up in all sorts of unfortunate places, old magic had returned, and in some cases...old artifacts.

Nigel nodded. "Our intelligence at the House of Swords is that previously ransacked tombs are once more filled with gold and magical tools. We're tracking down every rumor we receive, and the Sultan's Cup is on that list. The cup was never found, but Vlad was rumored to carry it on his person, and remember, no one knew its significance at the time of his supposed imprisonment in Buda Castle. It's reasonable that it would have been taken from him while he was here, stashed somewhere by someone who didn't know its worth, and then lost."

"Or it could've been put in the castle's dishwasher and long since forgotten." I narrowed my eyes at him. "There's got to be more to this story than that, for you to be here."

"Well, there is. You. When we realized you were in Budapest, we put two and two together and came up with an artifact we needed to secure."

"How did you know I was here? I've been in Budapest exactly twelve hours."

"You arrived in the Szimpla Kert bar with your hair on fire. Literally. It was noticed."

Yet another part of my new job as Justice I hadn't quite worked out yet. But something wasn't adding up.

"What else am I missing?"

Once again, there was no hesitation. I liked that in my Brits. "You're part of the Council now, and ergo your allegiances are to the Council. Anything they pick up, they get, not us." He said this without any rancor or judgment, and I couldn't help but chuckle. We'd both been mercenaries for too long; we both knew the game.

"You seriously think I'm here to recover an artifact, not a bad guy?"

"I now fully believe you're here to recover a bad guy. I also happen to know that you won't let an artifact pass you by should you happen to stumble across one. And you further have an uncanny ability to stumble across said artifacts." He waved at me. "You draw cards on this yet? Because I have no idea where we go from here. My information stops with this chamber."

"Really." I looked around the room, which appeared to have three entrances, the way we came in plus two chambers that snaked off deeper into the caverns. "Where'd you learn about this room?"

"One of the monks who was imprisoned along with Vlad wrote about it in his papers, which we have in our digitized archives. When we learned you were here, it was five minutes' work to identify how that might…benefit us. Or harm us, depending. Besides, Ma-Singh wanted me to check in on you, though he hadn't heard of the Impaler's return. He worries."

"Ma-Singh." I blinked, sudden and completely unwarranted tears scratching at my eyes as I thought of the big, gruff Mongolian whose life I'd saved multiple times and who'd also attempted to save my life, before he realized I was singularly hard to kill. Ma-Singh had been my general at the House of Swords and was one of very few people I trusted. It was good to know you were loved.

Or it was good to know Nigel was upping his game of manipulation. I pulled out the deck of Tarot cards, one of my trustiest go-tos during my years as an artifact hunter…during my whole life, truth be told. I'd been reading cards since I was old enough to pick up a deck, and they'd never steered me wrong. I might not always understand the message they were trying to give me, but the message was there.

I waved the deck at Nigel. "If you're lying to me, there will be hell to pay, and if you're bringing Ma-Singh into it without his knowledge, I'm taking you straight to Gamon."

"I'm not Connected enough to warrant Gamon's attention."

"She'll make an exception for you."

Nigel looked credibly concerned, and I shuffled the deck, pondering the stone walls around me. Once I'd landed in Budapest, it was the cards that had insisted that the tourist trap of the labyrinth was my fastest way into the Castle Hill cave system. They hadn't told me my journey would involve an annoying Brit, though.

I drew three cards out of the deck and held them out for Nigel to see. Despite him knowing me all these years, he'd never tried to learn Tarot. "King of Swords, Two of Wands, Ace of Cups," he recited. He narrowed his eyes at me. "And you expect me to believe you're not going after the Sultan's Cup?"

"Well, I am *now*," I cracked, though I really didn't care about the missing artifact. But I was more than a little concerned. Up to this point, I'd been pretty consistently pulling the King of Swords to represent the nouveau Vlad the Impaler. But if what Nigel was saying about the cup was true…maybe I really could kill two birds with one stone. Maybe wannabe Vlad had the real Vlad's cup on him and was siphoning power from it. An interesting possibility…

Either way, I had to find him. "We head left," I said, pocketing the cards and pointing to a door. As Nigel turned away, however, I fished out three more cards.

Queen of Swords, Ten of Swords, Ace of Swords.

I stared hard at Nigel's retreating form. I had no idea what the Queen of Swords meant yet in the context of this search, but Nigel was the Ace of Swords, and Ten of Swords almost always meant…betrayal.

Something very bad was about to happen in the labyrinth of Buda Castle.

CHAPTER TWO

"Quiet."

Nigel was a master of subvocalization, but I didn't need the reminder. We'd already traversed a good half mile of the cave system, me leading the way after we changed positions at a wide point in the tunnels. Now he was right on my heels, his breath soft behind me, both of us straining to see what lay around the next corner.

Because something *was* there. A light flickered in the darkness, making me blink hard as my eyes adjusted. Had to be some kind of fire. I could smell the scent of burning wood over the heavy odor of sulfur, so it wasn't a small fire either.

"He alone?" Nigel whispered into my ear, which from any other guy on the planet would have been at least a mild turn-on. But I'd worked too many jobs with Nigel and seen the man naked more times than I cared to remember. Between us, it was all business. And on cases like these, business was good.

I was about to reply when a sob broke through the still air, causing us both to stiffen. That was more than answer enough. The whimper was high-pitched, terrified, and immediately stifled. Whoever had built the fire in the next chamber definitely wasn't alone. A kid was with him, probably more than one of them.

Another childlike whisper sounded quietly over the crackling of wood. "The queen."

I blinked at Nigel, but he was staring ahead, his jaw tight and his body ready to spring forward. Had he not heard it? But I hadn't imagined the slurred words, I knew I hadn't.

"The queen comes. She will save us. The queen comes. The queen, the queen." Same voice. No, correction. *Voices.* There were multiple kids in there.

"What the hell is that?" I growled, and it was Nigel's turn to glance at me, the question clear in his pale blue eyes. He hadn't heard it. The voices weren't in my head, however, and my ears weren't that sharp. The kids were talking on a frequency that Nigel couldn't tap in to so well, which meant only one thing. They were Connecteds.

Nigel had some level of ability — more than he let on, for sure — but I'd leveled up several times over the past year. There was no mistaking that the kids in the cavern chamber were praying...but praying to whom? The queen of England? Mother Mary? Some ancient goddess?

We moved forward as quietly as we could, freezing every few feet whenever the fire ahead of us spit and crackled. As we approached, I could feel the level of magic in the next room pulsing like a living thing. These captured kids were throwing off some of the most powerful energy signatures I'd ever encountered, even for kids, who were known to have purer magic in them than most of their adult counterparts. According to the dossier, the Romani kids had come from a group of travelers making their way through Hungary after a particularly brutal year, so clearly, they were survivors, but that didn't explain the strength I was sensing.

I tried to get a fix on Vlad himself, but I got nothing back through the thick stone.

"The queen lives. She comes, she comes." Again with the children's whispers only I could hear, yet this prayer was more urgent than the last.

"It is ready." A new voice sounded now, unmistakably adult, and one Nigel could hear, if his tensing body language was any indication. We inched closer. The break in the stone was barely a yard away. Light spilled forth into the corridor from the fire beyond, obscuring anything of any relevance dancing in the shadows. Something heavy and metallic scraped across the floor. At intervals, there would be a startled childish yelp, an involuntary gasp. My hands tightened into fists, the fire that burned within me barely banked. Whoever this jackwit was, he was hurting the children every time he passed them in the cave. Five kids had been taken, I recalled. Two had surfaced in the Danube, their wounds consistent with…

I gritted my teeth, not wanting to think of it. The water had blurred any other mortifications of the flesh these children had endured, but I had a feeling the three remaining children in the chamber beyond would have their tale of horror etched into their flesh. I could work with that, though. I could heal them. Their bodies, at least.

But first I had to get to them.

"Slow." Nigel's command was barely audible in my ear. I grimaced, but he was right. It would do us no good if we burst into the room without our bearings. The killer could escape or, worse, the children could be damaged more than they already were. I could heal a broken person. I couldn't bring one back to life.

THE LOST QUEEN

We crouched down to where the rock jutted at an odd angle and created a slight overhang and a blank space beneath. I was in front, and there was only room for one head at a time, so I wriggled forward until my eyes cleared the rock and the room beyond was visible to me.

My breath died in my throat.

The chamber looked like something out of a horror movie. Bones lined the walls, stuffed into niches carved into the rock, a macabre Motel 6 of the dead. I'd heard of the bones when it came to Buda Castle, of course. There was every indication that the castle had been used by the Ottomans for long stretches during their occupation of the area. The discovery of female bones in the pits and wells had given rise to talk that they'd tossed members of their harem into these dark spaces when they were done with them, or had simply walled them up and walked away. There was no way to tell who was stashed in this cavern, whether male or female, but it was the center of the room that riveted my attention.

A pentagram had been carved into the rock floor. Not merely with chalk, though a thick white substance filled the ruts in the stone, but with a spiked tool that could easily have been one of Vlad's execution tools of choice. Now that tool was being wielded by a man hunched over in a long, flowing black robe, only he was drawing a circle with it around the pentagram. At two points of the pentagram stood earthenware jars filled to the brim with a dark liquid I didn't want to guess at. The other three points were manned by kneeling children.

The kids were filthy, their bare hands and feet clearly bound, their eyes screwed shut. Their foreheads were crossed with a long, wicked cut, which caused blood to spill down their cheeks and drip onto the floor.

The wounds looked fresh and doubtless were the cause of the cries Nigel and I had heard moments before. But they weren't the only injuries I could pick out. Similar barely healed cuts marked the children's hands and feet.

My stomach turned, and it was only Nigel's hand snaking out to grab my wrist that kept me in check. I focused on the robed man. He was tall and thin, and I couldn't see anything of his face since it was shadowed by his heavy cowl. There was no doubt this was our guy. If the kids weren't indication enough, the harsh slash of silver at his temple damned him as a marked man. In my role of Justice of the Arcana Council, my mission was to seek out the worst criminal offenders in the world's psychic community. Normally, other than the fact that he was targeting kids, Vlad wouldn't have piqued my interest. But now that I was here, I was beginning to reassess his candidacy for *Justice's Most Wanted*.

Because next to the pentagram, on a stone column beyond the third kneeling child, stood a golden chalice.

The Sultan's Cup.

"The queen will save us, she comes, she comes."

Now that I had eyeballs on the kiddos, I realized they weren't moving their mouths, but the strength of their prayer was hitting me on such a high level, there was no doubt it was coming from them. But what queen were they searching for?

I stared harder, trying to understand what I was seeing, first with my regular eyes, then with my third, which flicked open to take the measure of the energy signatures in the chamber. Everything on this earth emitted energy of one type or another, from the inanimate to the divine, and that held true deep underground as well. It was merely a matter of understanding the nature of that energy.

Plain sight revealed three girls ranged out in a triangle, with the two flanking wings of the pentagram occupied by the pots. Was that on purpose? I searched my memory for the gender of the two children who'd been slain, but couldn't fix on it. It hadn't mattered, at the time — the outrage was the same no matter who the children had been. But now…

My third eye revealed more of the story. The energy currents that ricocheted around this room, along the lines of the pentagram and the newly formed circle, as well as the more tightly drawn triangle of the three children, were completely engorged with power. Another wellspring of energy bubbled from the cup that stood on the stand, and yet more leapt within the man himself. He was no two-bit practitioner, dabbling in powers beyond his ken. He was an extremely strong Connected, a sorcerer in his own right.

The man stood, and the edges of his robe fell open, revealing a heavy belt from which hung a knife and a thick gold coin. My gaze shot to the stand where the cup rested, and sure enough, it wasn't alone. Lying beside it was a long slender wand, the four tools representing the four elements of the arcana as well as the tools of the magician. Not only magicians either, if the pentagram and circle were any indication — but witches.

I knew only one witch reasonably well, but there were many covens that were gradually gaining strength after centuries, even millennia in the shadows. Danae and her coven of deathwalkers had helped me more than once during the war on magic, and now she had taken my place as the head of the House of Swords. The fact did not escape me that here was Nigel, Danae's bodyguard, literally at my back as I witnessed what looked like a summoning where a witch or a queen or a witch queen was being called. Was this some sort of ritual that involved Danae? Or was there another witch in one of the covens of Europe who was being summoned? And regardless, who was the man doing the summoning?

While male witches were not unheard of, covens traditionally were run by women. At least the most powerful ones. Maybe my wannabe Vlad was looking to change that.

Today was not going to be his day.

I rolled to the side and scooted out of the way to give Nigel a look so he would know firsthand what we were running into. The children, though clearly traumatized and suffering from blood loss, looked to be in fairly good shape. Nevertheless, I didn't miss the dark reddish stains on the long spike the male witch had wielded. There was a special place in hell for anyone who harmed children, but there wouldn't be much left of Vlad to experience it by the time Gamon got done with him.

Turning away from the opening to the cave, the man approached the circle, which allowed Nigel and me to cross farther into the opening. At this point, anyone looking our way would notice us. I prayed the children wouldn't see us, or at least would give no indication that we were here.

The man held open his hands, and his voice was rich and full of self-satisfaction as he began to chant. One of the perks of my own recent increase in abilities was that I could easily translate any language. But this wasn't any language I knew. He spoke with more sound than words, a haunting melody of tones that created a reaction in the energy circuits around him. They leapt and whirled, and in the center of the pentagram, a light burst into being.

"The queen will come, the queen, the queen. She will save us. The queen will come!"

The desperate prayers of the children rose up with such power that the man temporarily faltered, and the image in the pentagram roared to life. It was definitely a feminine form, taller than even the man, slender, hair flying in an unseen wind, but the image was completely made of fire. There was no way I could discern the facial features or even anything she was wearing. But I could tell one thing clearly.

The fire spirit's temple was marked with a mirror-bright silver slash.

Oh…crap.

The male witch regained his equilibrium and started chanting again, this time in Romanian.

"Your time has come to stand forth and be counted, Myanya! No more can you hide from your destiny. You must rise as my consort and my slave as is your birthright."

The figure's focus shifted from the children back to him.

I stared at the male witch as he repeated his summons, impressed with his sac for all that his ruthless air of possession and entitlement sickened me. If this Myanya was looking to avoid this douchebag, I gave her mad props, even if the slash of silver at her temple marked her as every bit as dangerous as her summoner was. But there were the children to be considered, and for the first time, I realized their point.

In their blind fear, they were summoning Myanya with every bit as much fervor as the male witch. Even now, she was gradually growing stronger and more real, a scream wrenching from her as her features filled in the barest bit, not enough for identification except for all the wild hair—then dissolved back into white-hot fury, the slash of silver barely recognizable now.

"No," she roared back.

The sorcerer didn't hesitate. He leaned over and yanked up the spike from the ground, turning to the child hunched over nearest to him. He reared back —

"No!"

My voice comingled with Myanya's as Nigel and I rushed into the opening to the chamber. My hands came together to form a ball of blue magic that instantly exploded outward, catching the male witch in its field. I flung him across the chamber, where he clattered into the far wall, sending ancient bones flying out into the room — and the sudden rush of something sharp and metallic shooting down from the ceiling.

The male witch screamed in unholy agony as iron spikes set upon a rail impaled him, pinning him to the floor. The feminine fire spirit laughed in delight, then both she and her damning silver slash winked out of existence.

Out of the corner of my eye, I spotted Nigel breaking the line of the circle. Before I could shout a warning, the entire magical construct erupted in a blaze. Nigel shoved one child, then another away from the fire, rolling them across the floor as they flopped and writhed, helpless in their restraints, and I scooped up the third one. I turned and sent another ball of magic to douse the flames, then prepared to get Vlad off to part two of his very bad day, and —

And realized we had a new problem.

"Um...Nigel?"

"I see them."

He straightened, one of the children slung around his neck, silently sobbing, the other in his arms. I had sliced the bands on the third little girl, who I had perched on my hip, and I stood next to the Sultan's Cup, which was still bubbling over with power, though that was only apparent to my third eye.

28

But facing us over the body of the male witch…were skeletons.

A lot of skeletons. Upright and animated, vibrating with more magic in one concentrated space than even I could safely wield, especially carrying a child, and—

They rushed us.

"*Run*," Nigel yelled.

CHAPTER THREE

We bolted out of the mouth of the cave as the sound of bones on stone followed us, then raced pell-mell into the darkness. I thrust one hand forward, sending balls of light spiraling ahead of us, wishing I could leave Nigel to fend for himself as I turned to lay waste to the skeletal golems behind me. But I didn't trust Nigel to find his way without me, and I didn't trust myself not to blow up the entire cave system of Castle Hill. Sometimes, wielding immense immortal power had its drawbacks.

I didn't have time to read the cards again to find the best way out, but for once, cards weren't really needed. The earth was made up of energy patterns, from rocks to ground to grass to sky. Each of those energy patterns was woven differently depending on the entity it manifested. Rock might beat scissors in the popular hand game, but as far as my third eye was concerned, they were both easily identifiable. Same thing for open and blocked space. Now that I was merely looking for the fastest way to get the hell out of the cave system, my third eye rendered the entire space like a 3D map, showing me the shortest path to sunlight.

Shortest didn't necessarily mean easiest, though.

"Hole!" I shouted, barely in time to turn my head to warn Nigel as I stepped into utter open space, the child clutched to me jerking in convulsive fear as we plummeted down five feet. I wrapped my hands around her and rolled into a quick somersault, protecting her head, then skittered out of the way as Nigel dropped in behind me. He cursed sharply in English as he hit the ground, but he didn't crumple, and any pain he felt from pounding his ankles was likely masked by sheer adrenaline.

We both took off running again, and I heard the skeletons crash into the hole behind us. Easily fifty of them poured through that hole, but the sound of running feet after us sounded…distinctly diminished. Maybe the bones had to be relatively close together to reassemble? I didn't know, but my brain feverishly worked on the problem as we raced through the caves. I couldn't exactly have the streets of Budapest running with skeletons by the time we were done here, but I had to get out — get the children out — and then go back for Vlad. Impaled or not, I had the feeling we hadn't left the guy quite dead enough for him to be useless to me.

The corridor formed a tee in front of us, both paths eventually leading to the daylight if my mental schematic was right, but one of them doing it through increasingly narrow pathways and more drops. The smoother choice was to the right. I whipped around, pulling my head up from the child's bloody neck. "That way!" I ordered Nigel. "Can you — "

I looked down into the face of the little girl I was holding, then jerked my head back reflexively. Her beautiful face was a mask of serenity, for all that she was covered in gore and sweat and dirt, but it was her eyes that stopped me like a punch to the throat. They were milk white, as if she'd been blinded, and her lips stretched into a broad, joyful smile.

"You came, you came. As you must, to bring the dawn," she intoned in an eerily adult voice, speaking in Romanian. I looked from her to Nigel, painfully aware of the skeletons behind us.

"Can you run?" I finally asked the little girl, though how in the name of Christmas she was going to do anything as a blind person, I didn't know. No matter how dark the caverns were despite my glow balls, you needed sight to maneuver around so many tricky corners.

"Sara, *no*," Nigel snapped back at me, clearly reading my mind. Another downside of knowing me so well.

I hugged the little girl a last time, but my gaze pinned Nigel, and I put all the compulsion I could muster in my glare without actually manipulating him magically. From the naked fury on his face, he knew I could go there—would go there—if I had to. "Keep going that way. It's safer, flatter. You'll get there faster. I'll be right behind you," I said, then swung the little girl down.

"I can run!" The child Nigel was carrying wriggled out of his arms. Without hesitation, the Ace of Swords bent down to scoop up the other girl. The third girl, whose hands remained tied, clung to his shoulder, still passed out. I touched her neck and felt a fluttering pulse. She'd survive, but she was injured—far worse than the other two were.

"Come on—come on!" the healthiest child insisted, darting away down the dimly lit corridor.

Nigel clutched the blind girl to him, and, with one last glare at me, he followed his small guide into the semidarkness. As soon as Nigel cleared each of the glowing fireballs, I doused them, then cast another set into the narrower, trickier left-hand path. By now, the skeletons were almost on top of me. I pressed against the wall, hidden in the shadows, and let them pass me by. One — two — twenty — thirty thundered into the narrower tunnel. Crap. Not as many of them had shattered into uselessness as I had hoped, but enough had, I decided. Enough.

I swept up my hands into a fireball and cried out, my voice a high-pitched scream that could probably be heard all the way back among the wax figures in the Labyrinth tourist display. "Stop!" I roared in Turkish, and the jittering skeletons froze.

I grinned. *Good guess.* The Ottomans had been Turkish, at least the ones that'd roamed these halls in the fifteen hundreds. Now the reanimated bones of their dead servants had been pressed once more into service, unknowing of what they were doing, but commanded to obey — much as their human souls had been commanded to obey in life, whether willingly or not.

"Rest." This second command was kinder, gentler, and somewhat of a gamble. But it was a gamble that seemed to work. I stepped back as the skeletons slumped to the floor, their bones dislocating again, with no energy to animate them, their bodies —

I had only the barest second to react as I stepped on a spot in the floor that sounded curiously different, like a metal plate where there should be only rock. It gave way the slightest bit, and I heard the whoosh of metal, exactly as I had with wannabe Vlad in the pentagram chamber. A whoosh of metal that was followed by —

I flattened myself to the floor as a row of spikes shot free of the wall, bolting across the narrow space of the corridor. They passed harmlessly over the skeletons, who'd already collapsed to the floor and clattered against the far wall, but I didn't hesitate. Rolling into a crouch, I lifted my hands again and formed an immense net of protective energy, as tall as I was and three times as broad, and flung it forward. The blue-white mass of magic went soaring through the passageway that Nigel had taken with the kids. It would catch him in time, I prayed, before Nigel or one of his small charges unwittingly tripped any other booby traps Vlad or his modern-day doppelgänger had put in place.

Speaking of...

No way was I going to take the time to pick my way back to Vlad's chamber overtop all the skeletons that had met a bad end, but that didn't mean what I was going to do instead was all that fun. Still, I allowed myself only the slightest pity party...

Okay, maybe a few extra seconds of a pity party.

One of the newest skills I'd developed as Justice allowed me to move through space bodily, as long as I knew my destination. Instant teleportation sounded great, but to make it happen, I needed to destabilize myself, which meant to break down my physical form enough to go poof. There were a number of ways to do this. Unfortunately, I knew of only one that really worked for me.

And it hurt. A *lot*.

A corona of flames burst around me as I focused on the pentagram, the chalk circle, the spikes — and dear old Vlad. A moment later, I'd returned to the chamber, where everything was as I'd left it.

Almost everything.

"Dammit, Nigel..." I muttered. The Sultan's Cup had been taken from its stone perch, though how the wily Brit had managed that while he was scooping up children, I had no guess. This was why he'd been my number one nemesis back in the glory days of artifact hunting, I supposed.

But those days were done. I glanced back at the stone pedestal, gnawing on my bottom lip. Mostly done, anyway.

I stepped over to where the earthenware jars had been knocked over, their contents seeping across the stone floor. Blood stained the rock, mingling with the salt that had been so carefully poured into the carved stone. At least now I knew what those thick white lines had been. I squatted, laying my fingers gently against the nearest pool. I could still feel a burst of vitality in that blood, but there was nothing I could do to recall it to life. I couldn't put it back into the bodies of the children who'd been pulled from the Danube. I couldn't undo the murders committed by faux Vlad.

Not for the first time, I regretted that I had no skill to bring back the dead. I was pretty sure that not even Death, one of the more powerful members of the Arcana Council, had that ability. And perhaps it was unfair for me to want to restore to this life a soul that had suffered so terribly upon this earth. I couldn't help but think about all those I'd already lost, and all those I was destined to lose, simply by not being enough. Every time I thought that my powers had finally brought me to a place where I could ensure the safety of those around me, I was reminded how foolish a desire that was.

"Unnghhh."

The man on the floor captured my attention, and I refocused on the problem at hand. The spikes remained in a pretty line along his body, but only half of them had impaled him. He would have a nice set of puncture wounds along his right torso and shoulder, but all in all, he'd escaped what should've been far worse damage.

Good. More for Gamon to work with.

I also couldn't help but notice how much wannabe Vlad resembled the Ten of Swords. Sometimes, the cards really did have a sense of humor.

Interrogations weren't my strong suit, but this one, I couldn't avoid. I ambled over to the felled magician and crouched beside him. The mark of Justice gleamed bright silver at his temple. I only knew the most recent of his crimes, and those would be more than enough to condemn him to a date with Judgment. Still, I had a few questions.

"Yo." I tapped the man on his shoulder, the one that was spiked into the ground, and his eyes flared open as he barked a short, agonized yelp. Then his eyes focused on me, and he shut up. Fast.

"You know who I am?" I asked, speaking in Romanian.

"Justice." His voice was garbled, rough, and I thought back to his ululating cry. That probably was hell on your karaoke career. "I have no quarrel with you."

I burst out with a harsh laugh of my own. "Well, that's really kind of you, but I have a quarrel with you. In fact, you're marked."

I tapped his temple, and the man had the bad grace to look totally surprised. He opened his mouth, obviously to protest, and my blood pressure leapt.

"You killed two children, you asshat. You used three others for your little summoning game, and now they're barely alive. I should have shackled you with my bright shiny cuffs of Justice, but you went ahead and saved me the trouble by getting gutted by your own booby trap. I appreciate that."

"Those children were Promised," Vlad said, clearly still mystified. "They are sworn to my service."

"They are human children, and as such, they are sworn to no one's service," I snapped. Something in my voice must have penetrated Vlad's entitlement, because he zipped it before I incinerated him to ash. "They're safe, no thanks to you, and whatever is left of your worldly possessions will go to the families of those you killed."

"My…" He nearly strangled himself trying to keep silent as his brain knit together the meaning of my words. I kept going while I still had him conscious and focused.

"Who exactly was it you were trying to summon in that little pentagram of yours? Because that sure as hell wasn't a demon. I've met a few."

To my surprise, the male witch had the gall to glare at me, his look turning mulish. I reached out and rattled the nearest spike that was currently pinning him, and he yelped again.

"Do you even know who I am?" he demanded.

"Well, right now, you're looking like Vlad the Impaled," I said, grinning at my own joke. He didn't seem impressed with my humor. Everyone's a critic.

"I am a descendent of the house of Dracul," he growled, curling his lips back from his teeth. I was impressed with his dental work. His canines had been carefully polished down to sharp points, giving him a definite edge in any Halloween costume parties. "These caves are as known to me as the back of my hand. My family owns them far more than the denizens of the castle ever have or ever will."

"Yeah, I saw your handiwork back there with the Indiana Jones adventure ride. What about the skeletons? That you too?"

His smile was frosty. "My power is great. The male witches of my house command all that rests in this place."

"Uh-huh. You do that with your little cup of power? Because that's missing now too. I don't know where it could've gotten to."

"It will return to us," Vlad said, with impressive confidence for a man spiked to the ground. "It always does."

Interesting—and something to look up, once I tracked down Nigel and his nicked tumbler of doom. "And when you say 'us,' who do you mean, exactly? In case I need to notify your next of kin."

His sudden silence made me realize he'd successfully distracted me, and I sighed. I was worse than a puppy at the dog park.

"Back to the pentagram," I said. "Who was she?"

The pronoun definitely got his attention. "My wife," he said. "My rightful consort."

"Really. She didn't seem to share the attraction."

"She has no choice. The witch who responded to my call is the designated vessel for the scarred queen. She is destined to be the consort of the most powerful male witch on earth—and that is me."

I couldn't help it. I reached out and rapped on the spikes again, making Vlad vibrate in pain. "Who is she in real life? A mortal? Or is she actually a demon after all?" I asked, looking back at the pentagram. There were female demons, sure, but most demons manifested as males on this earth. It was just their schtick.

On the floor, however, Vlad coughed. This time, a little blood came up. "She's no demon," he sneered. "But don't be fooled. She commits horrific crimes whenever she emerges, all in the service of whoever succeeds in dominating her. The howls of the afflicted rise and writhe whenever Myanya takes form. But in the end, she is not what's important. Her consort is."

"So you've mentioned," I said drolly. "Seems to me she was the one in control here. Where'll she go now that she's toasted you?" I didn't like the idea of a fiery spirit like Myanya hanging around getting ready to strike again, and that silver mark at her temple was as much of a red flag as I was going to get.

"Myanya's spirit will retreat into her vessel, where she will stay until I claim her once and for all," Vlad said. "Who she kills until then is immaterial. They were meant to die."

Great. Myanya had officially become my next target, whether I secretly sided with her in the case of Myanya vs. wannabe Vlad or not. "So she's dangerous."

"She is *nothing*," Vlad insisted. "Without her consort, Myanya is a filthy, sniveling spirit resurrected once a generation, whose destiny is to be subjugated and reviled by the one who owns her, like the pathetic whore witch whose body she inhabits. She has no choice but to kneel in utter obedience at my feet and—"

And…that did it. This pompous, delusional, insufferable man totally deserved a lot of alone time with Gamon, and I was happy to help him get to it.

I grabbed his collar tight, and we both disintegrated into flames.

CHAPTER FOUR

Two days later, I sat back on my heels in a rare open space within my office's impressive library, surrounded entirely by boxes, scroll tubes, and books. Around me hung four faint glow balls, the strongest I could conjure inside this heavily warded chamber. The wards weren't mine, unfortunately, or I would simply have switched them off. Instead, the best I could do was flip them off.

"These are all the old cases involving witches?" I asked.

"This is the lot." Mrs. French, the diminutive caretaker of the library of Justice, stood between two towering columns of boxes. She kept her eagle eyes trained on a young boy who looked no older than ten, but was in fact far older, as he hauled three more awkward scroll tubes to the pile. "You can set those right there, Ned, there's a good man. Now off with you to breakfast, eh? I've put yours off to the side, with an extra surprise, for helping us."

"Thank you, Mum!"

Ned scurried off down the corridor, not in the direction of the main door to the office, but to a point deeper in the library.

I watched him curiously. "There's a kitchen back there somewhere?"

"More than a kitchen, an entire dormitory for the boys." Mrs. French straightened, brushing her hands on her skirts. "We had it put in right after Justice Abigail opened the office, and it's changed very little over the years. There never was much of a need to alter anything, you see." Her smile slipped a little, and she looked toward the back of the library too. We could no longer hear Ned's retreating steps. "Of course, that will change now. But change is good."

"It won't change all that fast." The boys who assisted Mrs. French had remained children for two hundred years. Their fortunes had changed once I'd become Justice. Hopefully for the better. They'd at least start aging normally, anyway.

I self-consciously rubbed the small scar in the center of my right hand, where the residual of the Nul Magis toxin I'd gotten struck with a few weeks earlier still remained etched into my skin. Though that toxin had allowed me to reset the boys' biological clocks, it'd also been my first major injury sustained in my new job. I wasn't at all sure what my Workers' Comp was like. Something to take up with the big boss.

"No, it surely won't," Mrs. French agreed. She turned her attention to the pile around me. "You're sure you don't want to bring these into the main office where we have proper light?"

"I'll get there eventually. I want to weed out at least some of these cases immediately." I surveyed the huge pile with some dismay. "I didn't think there'd be so many of them. I thought witches were...I don't know. Quieter."

"You can be as quiet as you please and still come to the attention of Justice." Mrs. French sniffed. "We've more than two hundred official covens worldwide, and thousands more than that who call themselves covens but don't adhere to the proper codes. What you see here are cases that involve witches or initiate witches in the traditional sense, plus anyone *claiming* to be a kitchen witch, hedge rider, hoodooist, Jewitches, or Gardnerian. I stopped short of the Feri witches. Once you involve the Fae, your troubles increase exponentially." She gave a delicate shudder.

"Yeah, I don't think that's what we're dealing with here." I also didn't think we'd be dealing with outlier covens. The male witch I'd delivered to Gamon two days earlier had been firmly entrenched in his entitlement and didn't have any other information of use. He didn't know who Myanya's vessel witch was, specifically. He'd merely summoned her, and, after several tries, she'd picked up his call. He was a member of a Romanian coven, as ancient as it was powerful, though said coven was, of course, disavowing any knowledge of his attempt to summon Myanya. I'd poked around a little after resettling the girls with their parents, doing what I could to heal those who'd been injured and ease the pain of the families whose sons had died.

Alas, I hadn't learned much else about the witch spirit who'd been summoned to Vlad's side, and that bothered me. Even without the silver slash at her temple, Myanya reeked of trouble. But with it…she was now my newest, biggest problem.

She also hadn't saved the children who'd prayed to her for deliverance, which I considered a significant mark against her. I frowned, thinking of the parents' faces as Nigel and I had returned the lost children and shared the barest details about those who had died. Healing of the heart was a tricky thing. All too often, pain was a necessary reminder of the loss, and to take away that pain would be to diminish the importance of the loss. Humans were...complicated.

Of course, travelers weren't the kind of people who went in much for formal therapy, but I'd been assured that the children's emotional needs would be met. If anything, the fact that they had been singled out by one of the more powerful male witches in Hungary was a strange sort of balm to their traumatized community.

I refocused on Vlad. Though he'd been clearly willing to kidnap his helpers from the fringes of society, he wouldn't be targeting his bride in that social sphere, I decided. I got the impression he was aiming high. Still, I really didn't care about Vlad's social network. I wasn't in Budapest to mediate a meet-cute gone wrong, I was there to take out an asshat magician who was killing kids for his own gain.

Even as I thought that, however, a new question formed in my mind. Had I really only gone after Vlad because of the children? Or had his case called to me so strongly because there was a bigger problem here I simply wasn't seeing yet?

Looking at the pile of witch complaints that had come in over the centuries but had never been addressed by Justice, I strongly suspected the latter. Which could prove...complicated. But, no rest for the weary.

"Myanya," I said out loud, testing the name out. "I've never heard of her."

"I certainly couldn't find that name in the files, and you would think I would have." Mrs. French humphed. "Mistress Danae will be visiting at ten o'clock, as you requested. She wanted to come here, which I thought was rather nice of her. She even asked for a tour of the library."

"Not gonna happen." Until I'd offered her the job as Mistress of Swords, Danae had been living quite happily as the head of one of the oldest covens in North America, a group of witches based in Chicago known as the deathwalkers. These were witches with no aversion to summoning both demons and the dead, which was a practice that some of the more modern sects had begun to avoid. She and her coven were very good at it, for all that her ranks had taken a direct hit during the recent war on magic. The deathwalkers were already rebuilding, however, and Danae's role with the House of Swords was no doubt aiding in her recruitment efforts. She didn't need the added benefit of a library card to a place where there were a whole lot of dead criminals. "What did you find about any deathwalker cases, specifically? Especially during Danae's tenure?"

"So far, they appear to be encamped on the high road. No open cases with them going back at least two hundred years. Not to say that they were always pure as the driven snow, but they've done their level best to make it seem that way."

"All right. Go ahead and get ready for her visit. She strikes me as a tea drinker this early in the day."

"Then she's a good sort, right there." Mrs. French hesitated, eyeing me with concern over the top of her wire-rimmed glasses. Today she was wearing a deep-blue muslin dress with a frilly white lace collar, her white hair swept back in a neat chignon, and she looked exactly like a genteel librarian should. At least if that librarian had been shelving books since the Victorian Age. Unlike her library assistants, Mrs. French hadn't been bespelled into undead service. She merely was a Revenant—a race of mortals that were exceptionally long-lived. She'd been a young girl when she'd begun working in the library, and I suspected she had many, many secrets of her own.

"I will say, I'm not too fond of leaving you back here alone, Justice Wilde," she continued. "You're sure you'll be all right? There's...well, there's the unpleasantness that can be found in some of these boxes and tubes, and there's simply no telling where it might crop up. If it would be anywhere, it'd be here."

She waved her hand over the piled-up containers. I grabbed the nearest one, a scroll tube, and shook it experimentally.

"I'm pretty sure this one is safe," I said casually enough, though I set the tube down without opening it. I waved off Mrs. French. "Go."

I waited until she left and then cast another glance over the boxes. My reason for having Mrs. French out of the way and keeping the majority of these boxes in the library of Justice was twofold. First, I *was* actually capable of a little bit of magic within this warded hall. My predecessor, Abigail Strand, had worked as Justice for approximately three years back in the 1850s. Along the way, she had slowly lost full control of her exceptional mental faculties, until she met an early demise, hastened in part by her inability to keep her fractured attention focused on her own safety. Abigail had been a relatively high-level Connected, but beyond grappling with multiple aspects of her identity that would come to the fore at various times when she was threatened, she'd clearly been frightened of those Connecteds who were more powerful than her. As a result, she had deadened the library to all magical abilities, even those of a future Justice, which would be me. While I appreciated her zeal, I needed to break through those wards. Otherwise, I was never going to be able to get through all these cold cases, as well as deal with the influx of new jobs that were piling up every day.

Secondly, despite what I'd said to Mrs. French, I *was* concerned about the rumor, misbelief, superstition, or whatever it was that said that part of Abigail's deteriorating condition had resulted from the cases themselves. That every few cases, she would open a box, tube, or arcane file folder that quickened her mental decline. There had to be a way of identifying which of the containers were problematic, and I didn't really want that process to be spied on by outside eyes. Because in its way, this supposed plague was a safety mechanism of the library. And as such, there had to be a reason for it.

Where better to learn what that reason might be than to start with an embarrassment of witches?

Lifting my hands, I allowed my third eye to flicker open. As I suspected, the containers before me immediately responded to being viewed through the perspective of a magical lens. The energy currents zipped and shivered along their surfaces, and they all pulsed with a power invisible to the naked eye.

In fact...

I turned and surveyed the library around me more closely, as far as my third eye could see. I'd done that before, but now, with the benefit of focus and stillness, I realized that the library wasn't quite the labyrinth of crazy I had at first supposed it to be. The jobs that had come in for Justice were ordered by type and year, a rough approximation anyway, but there was a secondary layer to their organization as well. The more potent the cases, the higher up in the shelves they were positioned. By the time you reached the very top tiers of the library, the ceiling glowed with a virtual constellation of power.

I stared at that ceiling, dumbstruck. Had Abigail realized that the most intense cases were hanging out above her? Talk about a sword of Damocles... Every time she entered the library, there must've been unconscious heaviness from above that settled over her, weighing her down, jacking up her crown chakra. If she hadn't had the ability to identify what was happening, was it any wonder that she'd begun to doubt her own mental faculties? There had been some indication that Abigail Strand had suffered from a dissociative identity disorder, but a new theory suddenly presented itself to me. What if there were identities, aspects of her personality, that were simply drawn forth in the presence of so much latent power hovering above? What if they weren't called out merely to protect Abigail in a general sense, but to battle a very specific threat?

Either way, it gave me an idea for the containers before me.

Focusing all my energy, I breathed out and extended my hands, the crackling of my blue fire barely skittering past my own fingers. But it wasn't my magic that I wanted to direct. Not this time. The way these books and boxes and scroll tubes were shelved hadn't been the result of Mrs. French and her helpers' mad organizational skills. They hadn't been able to intuit where the cases should go. In fact, I already knew from personal experience that where the young librarians thought they'd stored particular items wasn't always where they were eventually found. They were close — the same section, the same set of shelves — but some were higher than the boys had remembered them, some lower. The assistants hadn't figured out the movement because they hadn't known what they were looking for.

I did.

"Order yourselves," I murmured. "By your own rightful power."

Nothing happened. I kept my hands stretched wide, energy crackling between my fingers but serving as little more than additional lighting, and watched the containers before me. They quivered and glowed, and some seemed to shift ever so slightly, but they mostly remained in place.

"Come forward, greatest among you, or be judged for your weakness," I tried again.

Still nothing. I wasn't pulling on the right trigger. In my mind's eye, I considered the library as some sort of fell hierarchy of power—the more banal the Connected issues, the lower the shelves. But that seemed too easy. In any given moment, the most boring case in the house could end up being the one of crucial importance, and it wasn't sophisticated enough to simply say "look up" to find all the cases of any merit.

Unless…

Unless Abigail truly had feared not only what was in her head, but also above her head. Thus, because magic often fed on emotions, the most powerful and dangerous of the cases in the library of Justice had followed her unwitting direction. Grinning down at her like gargoyles, their power and their anonymity enhanced by their safety in numbers. After all, these cases weren't exactly accusing the Girl Scouts of the Connected world. Why wouldn't they be as cunning in their traps as they had been during the execution of their crime?

I needed to cut to the chase. I'd assembled all these containers bearing complaints from or about the witch community because I suspected I'd find the fiery resurrected spirit of Myanya at the center of at least a few. And if I could learn what she'd done in the past, I

48

could perhaps understand what she was doing now. Because I knew beyond a shadow of a doubt she was doing something.

"I am Justice of the Arcana Council," I murmured. "Myanya, your time has come. Defy me if you dare."

That did the trick. The energy leapt in the cases, shimmering forth, and several of the boxes visibly slid toward me. Willing to take their chances, or…maybe they knew something I didn't. Either way, progress. But progress wasn't success.

I tried again. "Myanya, your time has come. All must be known. All must be shown. I am Justice of the Arcana Council, and you are in my house. Show yourself!"

The pressure in my head suddenly exploded in a burst of bright white light. My eyes widened—all of them—as the library around me was transformed. Instead of the gloomy, crowded labyrinth of twisting stacks and shifting scaffolding, it was awash in colors, but no less a trap. And in the middle of the trap, I saw Abigail. Running for her life, a malevolent coiling fiery spirit twisting after her—Myanya, it had to be. Abigail looked over her shoulder, and I realized that I was seeing her for the first time—her open, expressive face, her delicate chin and high cheekbones, her large, terrified eyes. Her deep auburn hair was down around her shoulders, and her slender body was stretched to the utmost, until finally she smashed into a shelf in front of her. She threw her arms in a protective cross above her head, crying out with horror as the light came crashing down—

I blinked, my eyes refocusing.

Five containers sat in front of me, the rest of them gone. I glanced quickly to the stacks around me, and could identify them all—glowing like tiny stars throughout the room. Some on the bottommost shelves, some higher up, many, many more still in the upper rafters of the library, winking down at me like mini strobe lights. There were many containers that held powerful crimes sent to Justice to solve, but only five that apparently held Myanya or whatever she'd been in previous incarnations—incarnations strong enough to go toe to toe with Justice of the Arcana Council.

Five, I could handle.

I stood up, keeping my mind carefully blank, and bundled the five containers into two large sacks, wrapping each in the bits of cotton cloth that I found at their bottoms. There were more than enough cloth rags for the containers, and I wondered at that. How many containers did Mrs. French think I'd exit with?

Slinging the bags over my shoulder, I made my way back toward the front of the library, to where the main offices of Justice Hall waited. I could feel the pressure of all the crimes I left behind as I walked, and I once again marveled at how real and immediate that pressure was. Abigail had been all alone, facing it without proper preparation. These five cases, had they unraveled while she was Justice, might well have overtaken her.

But I wasn't Abigail, and I'd eventually learned that doing things completely alone was not only unnecessary…but stupid.

I wasn't going to be facing Myanya's past crimes alone.

Danae would be facing them too.

CHAPTER FIVE

I emerged from the library to find Danae already seated in the lobby of my office, her gaze riveted on me the moment I exited the door. She made to stand, but I waved her off.

"Danae, please, stay seated. I'm sorry I made you wait."

"It was no trouble. No one in my coven was even alive the last time Justice came calling. The tales of your office and your library are all that we have." She smiled with dry amusement. "It appears nothing at all has changed."

I thought of the pneumatic tube system in my office and noted that that door was open to the lobby as well, the better for Mrs. French to overhear, I was sure. No doubt Danae got the limited tour of my office and its case-delivery system, as well as a quick look at whatever cases had come in today. I didn't mind. The more cases piled up, the more I thought I wanted someone—anyone else other than me—to know about them. It seemed inappropriate to let them wait on my convenience, but I was only one person. There was only so much I could do.

Right now, however, I wasn't alone in my efforts. As usual, Danae was stunningly beautiful without even trying, her long, glossy fall of black braids cascading over her shoulders, her dark skin accentuated by high cheekbones and chiseled features. Her nearly black eyes flashed with curiosity as I set the bags filled with cold cases down on the coffee table in front of us.

She set her teacup down in its dainty saucer, her inquisitive gaze moving from the bags to me. I settled into a chair opposite her as Mrs. French bustled out of the office once more. She poured coffee into a mug that looked like the roller derby skating cousin to Danae's teacup, and doctored the brew for me while breezily making conversation.

"Three new cases have arrived, Justice Wilde, all set up for you on your desk, once you've finished your meeting. Mistress Danae, would you care for more hot water? Fresh tea?"

Danae murmured something noncommittal, and Mrs. French buzzed around us, resupplying us with water, napkins, and a plate of what I suspected were scones, that she no sooner set down, then whisked up again, her gaze on the shopping bag.

"Oh!" she breathed out. "So few of them. Did you expect to be bringing out so few?"

Something in her voice tugged at me, and I narrowed my eyes. "Did you think I'd be bringing out more?" I asked as nonchalantly as possible.

"Oh! Well, no, not at all. Not precisely. It's only that—there were so many. Cases, I mean. Involving, ah…"

Mrs. French stumbled to a halt as Danae shifted her cool gaze over. A strange energy skittered between the two women, and I frowned. "Do you two know each other?" I asked.

Mrs. French shook her head. "No, no, nothing like that."

"Not precisely," Danae agreed, and lifted her cup to her lips, taking an experimental sip. "Oh, that is lovely. I thank you for it."

"Of course! Of course," Mrs. French said. She stood for a moment more, nervously wringing her hands together, until I figured out she was waiting for me to say something.

"We're good here," I said, knowing it was the right thing when Mrs. French nodded several times, then bobbed a quick and nervous curtsey.

"Right-o, then. I'll just pop back to the office and manage anything new that comes in, but do call on me if you need me. I'll be here right away."

"Of course," I echoed as Mrs. French dropped another curtsey, this time to Danae, and scurried out of the room. I stared after her a moment before turning to Danae.

"What was that about?"

Danae's response was sotto voce, low enough that even the most intrepid librarian couldn't hear it. "Your Mrs. French is no stranger to my coven, though we haven't had a reason to speak with her since the late 1800s."

"Really?" I asked, equally quiet. "How do you know that you had interaction then?"

"I looked up any shared history between Justice and our coven after she contacted me this morning. She was so...nervous. But when she reached out to us then, we weren't based in Chicago but London, and we were headed by a high priestess who was also a well-known medium."

"Aren't you all mediums to some extent?"

"To some extent, yes," Danae agreed. "But our title as deathwalkers was affixed with our work in the late 1800s. It was that work that made clear the benefits of moving to another location. Eventually, we became too well known in London, too popular among people who could not suffer the dead to rest. We needed a city that wasn't quite as aware of who and what we were."

"Why Chicago?"

"Primarily because it wasn't New York. There wasn't quite the level of sophistication, nor especially the deep understanding of the old ways that sometimes led to an uncomfortable amount of scrutiny. But as I said, when Mrs. French called upon us, we were still based in London." Her gaze shifted to me. "She wanted a session. A call beyond the grave."

I grimaced. Every Revenant eventually had to face the dying of their non-Revenant friends and loved ones. It wasn't surprising that Mrs. French had lost someone she loved who wasn't as exceptionally long-lived as she was. "Well, what she asked of your coven is certainly none of my business—"

"There were two calls, actually," Danae went on. "The second was for a child that she thought would have grown up by the time she requested it. The first was for Abigail Strand."

I paused with the mug halfway to my mouth. "When?"

"According to our records, in 1857. Today I asked her when Justice Strand had passed, and she said 1853. I gave no indication that I had any record of her contacting the London coven to request our medium services, and immediately moved on to other topics. Her fluster left her shortly thereafter, but as you can see, it hovers barely below the surface, ready to come spilling out."

"And do you have records of those services?" I asked, curious despite myself. "Was your coven able to summon Justice Strand?"

"Interesting you should ask. The records on the case stop abruptly after the record of the request." Danae said, setting down her teacup. "And begin again shortly thereafter. It would seem that the exact details of our encounter on behalf of Mrs. French were purged from our files."

My brows drifted up. "Why?"

"An answer I have yet to determine to my satisfaction," Danae said. "But I suspect it is not the primary answer you want from me today anyway." She nodded to the bag.

"First things first," I said, settling back in my seat. I was willing to take a pause on the question of Mrs. French's interaction with Danae's coven, mainly because Mrs. French was in the next room. I didn't want her to overhear anything that would cause her distress.

Besides that, I had bigger problems than a distraught young woman seeking solace in a connection with the spirit of her former boss. In many ways, I trusted Danae implicitly. I'd tapped her as head of the House of Swords, and I knew her dedication to the Connected community was paramount.

That said, none of us always stuck to the high road when it came to managing the mysterious and the arcane in this world. And I suspected Danae kept an E-ZPass to the dark side close at hand.

I launched right in. "What happened with the Sultan's Cup in Budapest? Don't think I didn't miss the fact that Nigel spirited it off with the children from that cave."

Danae was watching me carefully, no doubt reading the play of emotions across my face.

"It's safe," she said. "The cup of Murad II is authentic, insofar as carbon dating shows that it was constructed around the time of the sultan's rule during the Ottoman empire, and we are now gathering any information we can, anecdotal or otherwise, to identify the exact properties of the chalice." She smiled thinly. "The Magician of the Arcana Council was generous enough to offer to examine the cup himself and give us whatever information we might need."

"In exchange for?" I'd been one of Armaeus Bertrand's top artifact hunters when I'd first come to Vegas. I knew how the Magician worked.

So, apparently, did Danae. "In exchange for his unlimited access to the piece, as well as a guiding say in its eventual disposition. It would appear that the Magician is not terribly keen on this particular chalice being exposed to rank-and-file Connecteds, but we don't know why. Is it mere snobbery, or is there something more to his reticence?"

With Armaeus, it was hard to say. Once upon a time, he'd been all about "that balance of magic," which had translated to the Arcana Council hoarding magical artifacts. Since the war on magic, however, he'd paid less attention to the world outside his spectral fortress. I wasn't sure that was such a good thing, now that I thought about it.

Danae's gaze flashed to meet mine. "It would perhaps be very useful if we could divine what the Magician is thinking, without having to accede to his demands."

"That's…potentially doable," I said, grateful that I'd become used to keeping my mental barriers up against the Magician. It wasn't that I didn't love the man. Demigod. Whatever he was. It was more that I had a healthier appreciation than most of exactly how duplicitous his ways were. And to this day, a part of me felt he was running a dangerously long game that I needed to understand more fully, to better interact with him. If not on an emotional level, then on a professional one.

"And are you the one to potentially do it?" Danae prodded.

"Maybe." I redirected her. "What else did Nigel tell you about the male witch Vlad?"

"Not nearly enough," she acknowledged ruefully. "Nigel is uniquely capable in many ways, but he does not have your grasp of Romanian, it would seem. He was unable to decipher most of what the male witch said. Plus, he was notably absent when you went back to interview Vlad yourself."

"Yeah, well, he had more important things to do at the time. But bottom line, Vlad was summoning a witch—a witch queen, specifically. Know anyone using that title?"

"There are many coven heads who style themselves as queen," Danae allowed cautiously. "It's an older practice, though, and a largely hidden one."

As she spoke, I pulled open the mouth of the nearest bag and removed the case files, continuing the process until all five containers were positioned on the table. Instead of leaning forward with interest as I expected, Danae carefully sat back in her seat. She set her teacup down on the table beside her and positioned her hands in her lap, her fingers lightly touching as her lips twitched with a prayer I could not discern.

"You know what these case files hold?" I asked.

"Two of them," she said, her position remaining defensive, protective. "The black box and the jeweled case bear the seal of my coven."

I blinked down in surprise. Mrs. French had said none of the cases could be laid at the feet of the deathwalkers, yet out of the top five finalists, there were two? "They do?"

Danae waved a hand, and an inscription appeared in the top corner of both boxes.

I scowled at the containers. I could see energy signatures, perceive 3D maps of booby-trapped labyrinths, and envision the atomic composition of human beings. Yet rudimentary glamours fooled me? Seriously?

"You know, I'm kind of a big deal. I would've thought I could see past a basic locking illusion."

"Perhaps, something else to ask your Magician," Danae said mildly. "But the wrongs my coven surreptitiously sought to have Justice address remain locked within those files, and happened well before my time. One of them is even before the time of the last Justice." She pointed to the jeweled case. "I'm not sure how much that helps you."

"Maybe a little, maybe a lot," I hedged. "I need to know about a witch queen who apparently is fated to serve a stronger male."

Danae's lips twitched. "There's not a lot of that in our practice. It's a large reason why our practice exists."

"Well, this one did, and she's apparently a big deal. The children were praying to her to show up and save them. And she did. More interestingly, Vlad with the pointy spikes was pretty sure she owed him the favor of hooking up with him. In fact, he was pretty rude about it."

"Did he have a name?"

I nodded. "He called her Myanya."

With an audible crack, all five of the containers flew open and the door to my office slammed shut, the pressure in the lobby almost overwhelming. In an instant, Danae was flung backward and pinned against the far wall, her eyes bugging out, her arms outspread.

"Danae!" I gasped. I jumped up and turned to face her fully, ignoring the maelstrom of energy behind me, fury lighting my nerve endings. *This is my office, dammit. No one overrules me here.*

I brought my hands together, and a ball of blue flame crackled for only a moment before bursting forth toward Danae. My eyes widened with surprise as for half a second, the barrier pinning Danae seemed merely to absorb the energy, neutralizing it, until I focused harder and the barrier shattered in a million crystalline shards. My own energy pulled those shards away from Danae, keeping her safe, and as she stumbled to the floor, rage radiating off her, I turned back to the case files.

The energy surrounding the files was fraught, intense, but it wasn't shaped into a figure like I'd immediately supposed it would be, the white-hot witch in the pentagram in the Buda Castle caves. Instead, the pages of all the cases were caught up in a cyclone about three inches above the table, shifting and tumbling as if they were caught in a wind machine. I stared in wonder at the self-contained twister as Danae stepped up beside me, breathing hard.

"Who the hell is this chick?" I demanded.

We both flinched as a loud pounding sounded at the door to Justice Hall. The pages all collapsed to the table.

"Yo! What's a girl gotta do to deliver donuts these days?"

CHAPTER SIX

Nikki Dawes swept into the reception area of Justice Hall, holding aloft a distinctive white-and-orange pastry box. As usual, the food took second chair to her virtuoso clothing performance. Nikki was my right-hand everything and had been almost since the moment I'd first stepped foot in Vegas, all six-foot-four fabulous inches of her, the truest friend you could ever meet from the tip of her varying shades of hair to the heels of her size-thirteen stiletto pumps. She was also a woman whose entrances defied the laws of physics, and today was no exception.

"I come bearing manna from heaven," she announced.

Mrs. French burst through the door from my private office and hurried across the room, her keen eyes not missing the chaos of the coffee table.

"Oh my, oh my, oh my," she murmured, the words almost a mantra as she opened the main door wide. "Oh!" she said, stepping back. "My."

Nikki grinned. "Francine, your face makes this corset worthwhile, and let me tell you, that is saying something."

Nikki sashayed forward in a gown that looked like it could have been bought in the London shops of Bond Street back in the eighties — the 1880s. With a high frilled collar that plunged down her neckline, the gown was essentially two pieces in one, a dark cream satin underdress bordered by a black and tan striped jacket of sorts. The jacket extended from collar to hem of the gown and was cinched at the back by a corset tied with heavy black cord. The wide skirt was ruched up at the knees to reveal a black crinoline beneath, the style allowing easy viewing of the heavy buckled platform boots that graced Nikki's glorious feet.

"Nikki," Danae greeted warmly.

"Danae! I did not know we would be seeing you today, but thank God I got extra cream-filled," Nikki chortled, her laughter sending her piled-up hair — today a mass of jet-black ringlets — bouncing in jovial delight. Her coiffure added a good eight inches to her height, and it was pierced with what looked like knitting needles holding clocks, gears, and even a small owl. She swept across the room and eyed the mess on the table with interest, then set the box on the side table. She opened it. Immediately, the delicious smell of overprocessed carbohydrates flooded my senses.

"Those are all for us?" Danae asked dubiously, flipping a few strands of her braids over her shoulder.

"All of them, and I'm praying that our French connection has…Oh! excellent." Nikki grinned as she saw the pot of coffee. "I figured if I was going to go steampunk, the least you all could do was provide the steam."

Despite her ongoing delight at Mrs. French's name, I knew that Nikki had already fallen for the diminutive librarian and her unceasingly fussy ways. Mrs. French, for her part, never knew exactly what to do with Nikki. Which wasn't at all unusual.

Now Mrs. French stepped forward, mesmerized by Nikki's outfit. "I've never seen anything quite like that. What *is* that material?"

"None of it as authentic as yours, I can tell you that." Nikki sighed. She reached out to Mrs. French's tiny form, her long fingers catching the puffed shoulders of Mrs. French's gown. "I don't even know how that was made. The costumer had nothing like it, at least not in my size. I was devastated."

"Hmpf," Mrs. French managed, but Nikki took her thin-lipped disapproval in stride with a broad wink and turned back to us. Her gaze zipped to the open library door, the containers on the table and all their scattered papers, Danae, and a twittering Mrs. French in rapid succession, taking it all in. Prior to coming to Vegas to ply her trade as a psychic, Nikki had served as a beat cop for years, facing punks and thugs and the kind of violence she never really talked about, but which had marked her all the same. Her Connected intuition had served her well in that role, and it had only gotten keener in the years since she'd hung up her shield and begun advancing her own psychic skills. She'd also been fully briefed on my dustup in Budapest, so she was up to speed.

"I take it that's the new case?" she asked, pointing to the mess on the table.

"Cases," I amended. Danae had already begun picking through the pages, matching them up by their style and paper. "Five different crimes over the past...I don't know how many years, all of them dealing with the witch prophecy Myanya."

"Whoa, whoa, whoa." Nikki held up a hand. "She sounds like a bubblegum pop singer. Who's Myanya?"

"Not a who, a what," Danae corrected, shaking her head. She stretched out her hands, palms forward, as if she was going to catch the swirl of papers like a big bouncing volleyball of energy. "A prophesied spirit who returns every twenty-eight years, usually to a coven that's positioned in a place where witches most need to command magic at the highest level. Her energy is entirely female, but her curse is that she is chained to the male energy that coexists and balances the female. That male energy does not have to be housed within a male, of course, but it usually is, and he's usually a Connected of impressive ability."

"That word 'chained' doesn't sound like it's a real positive connection for this Myanya," Nikki observed.

"It's not," Danae agreed. "The female witch who hosts Myanya's spirit becomes extraordinarily powerful once the prophecy is fulfilled. But the path to that power is an exceedingly dark one. In most cases, she must first be betrayed or suppressed, stripped of her magic by her consort, and ground down almost to nothing."

I grimaced. "And she lets that happen?"

"The spirit embodied in the prophecy does, yes. Myanya flies in the face of the traditional balance of power in the covens. She emerges on this earth in the body of a witch who is in the full flower of her abilities. But, as the legend goes, as Myanya builds toward her incarnation of ultimate strength, she renders her vessel witch vulnerable to attack from an aggressive outside force, usually in the form of a male witch. It's in this conflict that the sacred energy of the world is reborn, and it is a conflict Myanya cannot avoid. The fire is ready to be lit, and all her rage, all her strength, all her outcry of the oppressed is the sacrifice. And so she goes to war with those who would claim her, loses, and rises again as the scarred warrior. She then leads her coven for twenty-eight years, and their strength increases tenfold under her influence. Then the cycle starts again."

I studied the papers, thinking about that. "Twenty-eight years," I muttered. "What are the odds she'd strike again right after the war on magic? Will that make her even more powerful?" A witch on a rampage was never a good thing, but now? If the psychic abilities of whatever vessel witch Myanya chose had been recently amped by the war, this newly reborn Myanya could be seriously bad news.

Danae began sorting through the papers. "Well, the prophecy is due to strike this year, but it hasn't been fulfilled in two or three cycles. I honestly thought it had run its course. I researched it as part of my training to become high priestess of my coven, but there was no movement among the most powerful covens during the most relevant anniversary in 1990. No covens reported Myanya returning."

"They could have been lying."

She shrugged. "They could have. More likely, Myanya failed in her attempt to take over a witch and bend her to her will. It is not an easy prophecy to endure. Once the subjugation is complete and the prophecy of the scarred warrior fulfilled, the witch quite often turns on her oppressor, killing him if he's not strong enough."

I stared at her. "She kills the guy who's just put her through hell?"

"It's happened. It's not talked about, but...it's happened."

"Right." I thought back to Vlad on the floor of the cave. He'd wanted to marry Myanya, demanded it as his right. Did he have any idea what kind of honeymoon he was setting himself up for? "So how does that work, exactly? Vlad summoned Myanya, but she was a spirit, not a person. How do you oppress a spirit?"

"If he'd had time to complete the ritual, he would have entered the pentagram and traveled through it to wherever the vessel witch resides," Danae explained. "The vessel witch is human and can be physically and psychically overpowered by the aggressor. Once broken, the Myanya spirit must submit to her consort and do whatever he asks. He owns her."

"But there are crimes against Connecteds in these files," I said, pointing to the boxes. "Presumably Connecteds who aren't either the witch who Myanya chooses as her vessel or the witch who goes all Lord and Master on her. These are innocent Connecteds filing a grievance. Otherwise, they wouldn't have shown up in my library."

As it turned out, petitioning for the aid of Justice was easier than filing a police report. All any afflicted Connected had to do was verbally summon me—me, specifically, not a divine being of any stripe. Then, through a means I hadn't yet had time to fully explore, the summoner's request was translated into a written case file. That file was sent to my attention through a delivery system that hadn't been updated since Abigail Strand had held the office, but which still worked impressively, and depressingly, well.

"You have to understand," Danae continued. "The energy of Myanya has not developed for the good of witches. It's evolved to benefit Myanya. In her fury to escape her destiny or in the aftermath of her degradation, she kills, she destroys. Though she normally does not act on such a large scale, she's capable of burning down entire cities or sending tsunami waves crashing down on the unsuspecting, if she believes one of them might chain her down. She knows she is doomed to die and rise again, smoking from the ashes of her last humiliation, but that humiliation is deep enough to be intolerable, so she fights with the fury of the damned."

"Well, I hate to break it to you, but I think she's out there right now," I said.

"If what you're telling me is true, she is," Danae agreed. "Only this time, it's worse."

Nikki leaned forward. "Worse how?"

"Because the prophecy begins when Myanya is claimed by the male witch, her power is overmatched, and she is subdued, sent down into the long tumult of the soul before she emerges the scarred warrior. But she has *not* been claimed. The male witch you encountered in the cavern of Budapest failed, and Myanya returned to her vessel witch, now stronger. Worse, we don't know if this Vlad is the first male witch who's attempted to set the prophecy in motion."

We digested that along with another round of donuts, until Danae finished sorting through the containers and papers. "These case files date from the earliest in 1542, to the most recent in 1906. We've no idea when the Myanya prophecy began, but it didn't generate a complaint before the fifteen hundreds, at least."

"They were dealing with the plagues." Nikki snorted. "A crazy witch prophecy probably didn't seem all that bad." She picked up the topmost page that rested in a jeweled case and handed it to me. "What is that, Turkish?"

"Yep." I read down the document until I reached the relevant part. "In this complaint, Myanya took over the body of a young girl who was promised into...some sort of harem, it looks like. A dozen women were with her when her power was challenged, though it doesn't go into detail as to challenged how."

"It usually doesn't," Danae said, her tone dark. She bit into a second donut. Sometimes your problems were too big for one donut.

I ignored the siren call of sugar and fat for the moment, as well as Danae's cryptic comment. "Apparently, the witch laid waste to the harem — the wives, the servants, I assume the guy in charge of the harem as well, whatever you want to call him. Husband doesn't quite wash, given that these people were essentially slaves."

Nikki sat back. "So she blew up the entire house? Then what happened? She simply walked free?"

Danae supplied this information. "The pattern is always the same in the end. The vessel carrying the Myanya spirit is enslaved by another more powerful opponent, her body and will broken in service to her oppressor. Then, after a period of subjugation, she emerges triumphant but scarred and takes up her mantle as a warrior for her coven. The coven with the warrior queen Myanya becomes the most powerful of its era, for either twenty-eight years, or as long as the queen lives after the challenge. Sometimes that isn't very long."

"What do you mean?" I looked over my third donut. "I thought the whole point of this was that she wins the gold ring of awesome and rules for twenty-eight years. Lather, rinse out the blood, repeat."

"That's true," Danae said. "But some trials are harsher than others, and the scars can run more deeply in the mind than in the flesh. Far too many of the warrior queens go mad after the trauma they endure."

Nikki blew out a long breath. "That really doesn't seem like a job I'd be trying all that hard to get."

"We have no record of Myanya taking form since 1934," Danae said thoughtfully. She had set her donut down on the tray, only half-eaten. I didn't know if I should admire her restraint or accuse her of anti-Americanism. "As to where she could be targeting now…we'd have to look to the strongest covens. We'll need to make a list."

"Oh! A moment, please, a moment. I have just the thing for this." Mrs. French sprang up and hustled into the next room, and a moment later, a tall, slender, flat object came wheeling out of my office, Mrs. French clucking along behind it. "Miss Dawes, you'll be so pleased, I hope."

"Francesca! You're a gem!" Nikki said, standing and striding over to pull the rolling whiteboard the rest of the way. She moved it around so it faced Danae and me. "You honestly can't have an investigation without a whiteboard," she announced. "I personally prefer a corkboard and pins, but Mrs. French overruled me."

"The boys would have a field day with acres of string and pushpins," Mrs. French put in, with the world-weary tone of a woman who'd seen it all…and had cleaned up afterward. "Trust me on this one."

"But a whiteboard gives us most of what we need and get this." Nikki picked up a small metallic-looking cube from the pen tray and tossed it toward the pristine white expanse. It stuck. "Magnetic," she crowed.

"Well, you did ask me to find you one," Mrs. French said, bemused.

"It's so great." Nikki sighed contentedly as she tossed three more cubes against the surface of the white board, chortling when they also stuck. Then she picked up a dry-erase marker and turned back to us.

"So who've we got?" she asked, pen poised. "Who are the bigs in witch world?"

Danae nodded. "The Dubai coven is very strong right now, but I can't see Myanya trying to get a foothold there. It's one of the few male-centric covens in the world. Bali is a possibility too, as well as Istanbul. And, of course, the Moscow coven. Myanya targeted them in 1962. It was the last time I have record of her, because the prophecy was denied."

"Denied?" That was the first I'd heard that term applied to Myanya. "You mean someone died in the process?"

"In a manner of speaking." Danae leaned forward and looked at the whiteboard. "I don't think Myanya is that far from us, though. Again, the strongest coven right now in the northern hemisphere is mine, and we haven't had any activity of this sort. I would know."

"You would? That's how this works? As the head of the coven, you know everything going on? Because I was head of the House of Swords, and I wasn't always as looped in as I wanted to be."

"Were you to become the head of a coven, you would know, yes. It would take a very powerful witch to keep such a thing hidden from you, and you would have had ample warning that one of your own was building such a power."

"Right," I said. "Good thing I'm not a witch."

"Well…" Danae sighed. "About that."

CHAPTER SEVEN

I looked at her sharply. "That sigh sounded less than ideal."

"Well, there's a lot about you that's less than ideal," Danae replied, "and by that I mean — dangerous. You've escalated in your abilities every time you've faced a new and different challenge — the Council, the gods and goddesses you encountered in the war on magic —"

"Mommy Dearest," Nikki put in.

"And then the senate of magicians in Venice. Nikki told me about how your body assimilated the toxin of Nul Magis."

I shot Nikki a dirty look. "Seriously?"

"I worry," she protested. "Magic and spells are not really my thing, but they are Danae's."

"And if Armaeus hasn't already told you this, you shouldn't have been able to hold the Nul Magis within you as a living toxin. It should have either withered to nothing within you or been forcibly removed by one of the members of the Council."

I pulled my right hand into a fist, the Nul Magis a tiny speck in my palm, but not an inanimate one. It pulsed in indignation at Danae's words. "I tried to heal myself," I grumbled. "It wouldn't take."

"It didn't take because you were meant to keep that power. You leveled up to accommodate it, and you don't even understand what you have accepted into your energy field."

"Is there a point to this?"

"The point is this: I am concerned that any confrontation you have with Myanya will result in a similar power crisis."

I rolled my eyes. "I don't think I'm the one having the crisis here."

"You know what I mean," Danae said coldly. "You rush into situations without any preparation. You make decisions on the fly based on little more than how you feel in the moment or, worse, the turn of a Tarot card—"

"I'll have you know I trust my cards more than I trust most people," I shot back. "I'm not getting the underlying concern here. Are you worried about me? Because if I haven't proven it ably enough, I can take care of myself."

I didn't speak the words calmly, though I wanted to. But the truth was, Danae was seriously cheddaring my cheese. I hadn't asked for the abilities I was manifesting and developing. Nevertheless, they were mine. Still, I was getting doubters. I'd had my abilities dismissed when I'd been an artifact hunter, when I'd unexpectedly become the head of the House of Swords, and when I'd commanded a team of the other heads of the Houses—who would never have come together except for me. Now, I was Justice of the Arcana Council, and I still had my doubters.

Danae was watching me closely, and I didn't like the look in her eyes. She lifted a hand as another surge of irritation rippled through me.

"I am *not* one of your doubters, Sara."

My brows lifted. Could Danae read my mind? Or was I that transparent? Probably the latter.

She kept going. "The respect you crave is closer than you think, but it doesn't start in the world around you."

"That's beautiful," I said drily. "Since taking this job, I've had enough self-improvement mumbo jumbo to fill a dozen Tony Robbins seminars. I've got it. Think positively, manifest what you want, be the you that you most want to become. I've got all that."

"I'm afraid my warning is a little more specific than that," Danae said, not losing her calm demeanor. "You need to be more cognizant not only of the abilities you can currently manifest, but of your propensity to sponge up the abilities of those around you."

"Except my exceptional sense of style," Nikki pointed out.

Danae inclined her head gracefully. "Except for that. Otherwise, you are at risk of absorbing more magic than you can completely process in a given moment."

"And that's bad why?"

She shrugged. "I said you're not exactly like a witch, yet you display many of the same characteristics of a witch coming into the full flush of her powers. A witch in that state who becomes overwhelmed, goes into stasis. She freezes, in a sense, until she can absorb the spell being cast or the influx of power. If you find yourself opposite Myanya, know that she has been working with witches since the dawn of recorded history. You cannot afford that sort of stasis."

I considered her words, then glanced at Nikki. "I'm not asking this out of cockiness but genuine curiosity. Have you ever seen me freeze up?"

Nikki tilted her head, her gaze scanning the ceiling. "You've been hurt bad. You've been legit frozen," she said, as if she was ticking off a To-Do list. "You've caught fire more times than I can count. Oh—there was that time when the Gods' Nails pierced your hands. Whatever happened to them?"

"Focus, Nikki."

"Right...okay, you've been electrocuted, skewered by the weapons of Atlantis... That sucked. Nearly drowned on a couple of occasions, and you kind of exploded that one time. But—no. I don't actually remember you not being able to function when magic hit you. You always seemed to, I don't know, already have the magic there. It was simply sort of flipped on."

"Flipped on," Danae murmured. "I can see that."

"So is that a good thing or a bad thing?" Nikki pressed, but Danae shook her head.

"It's neither and both. It's merely something to be aware of. If you freeze, she is a powerful spirit, and she will use that weakness to take you."

"Yeah?" I cracked. "I'd like to see her try."

Danae remained serious. "You may well get your chance."

"Back to the issue at hand." Nikki rapped the whiteboard. "What covens do we have in the Americas we should be worried about?"

"The Peruvian and Guatemalan covens are currently at war with each other, or they'd be more of a concern," Danae said thoughtfully, "although the energy of war might well attract Myanya."

"But war doesn't allow you a lot of downtime." I made a mental note to do some research on the South

American covens. Witches at war didn't seem like a really great idea, ancient prophecy or no.

"What about closer to home?" Nikki asked. "Mexico? The US? Um… Are there covens in Canada?"

"There are," Danae said. "And they get healthcare."

A clattering noise sounded from the inner office, the sound of a case about to shoot through one of the pneumatic tubes no doubt, and Mrs. French perked up. The woman was truly never happier than when she could do her job. I admired that in her. I admired that in anyone, honestly, which might explain my issues with interpersonal relationships.

"I'll get that," she said cheerfully, picking up a stray plate and extra napkins. I didn't miss the fact that the plate contained a completely untouched bear claw. Mrs. French might not eat a donut in front of us, but even she was not proof against their magic.

"In the US, there are fewer covens of power than you'd expect. Many of them are underground, especially in the Midwest and South, while those in the major cities must walk the line between who they truly are and who the media makes them out to be. Most of the time, the media treatment is a lot more exciting than reality, though not always. Nevertheless, far too many witches today are more easily found clubbing than paying attention to the ancient rites."

"Do you tell them to get off your lawn too?" Nikki deadpanned. When Danae flicked an irritated glance in her direction, Nikki rapped the board. "Coven locations, Danae. In the US."

"Los Angeles, Memphis, New York. Chicago, of course, but we haven't been targeted."

"As far as you know," I said, which earned me a stink eye from Danae. She gave excellent stink eye.

"As far as I know," she conceded. "The New Orleans coven went dark with Katrina, and by dark, I don't mean radio silent. If they're the target of Myanya's prophecy...that would be bad."

"Right," Nikki said. She wrote down the name and underlined it. "I always did like New Orleans. Maybe we head there first."

"One more thought, it can't hurt to check the Istanbul covens," Danae said. "The 1906 crime indicated among your cases would be a matter of record, though I'm sure no one would have laid it at the feet of a witch. There are two primary covens currently remaining in Istanbul, but again, this was over a hundred years ago. Whoever is in power now is not necessarily from the coven who was in power then. I'll need to do the research to see what covens were in existence when Myanya last arose." She shrugged, gazing at the whiteboard. "But it honestly could be any of them."

"So that leaves us where?" I asked. "I mean, do we know for sure that this current energy spike truly is Myanya? Wouldn't there be other indications?"

A second rumbling sounded in the inner office, and Mrs. French squeaked. I hid my smile. When it rained in pneumatic tube land, it usually poured.

"There are always signs," Danae admitted. "Nigel said the pentagram in the cave was girded by a circle, both of them filled with salt?"

"Yep. Which is why my first thought was demon."

"But it was a female figure who came through, and human in nature, not animal-like, clawed, snouted?"

I shook my head. "It looked like a woman—long hair, elongated body, arms with hands at the end, not paws or claws. She reacted to Vlad's voice as if she knew him."

"The descendant of Vlad the Impaler," Danae said thoughtfully. "As I said, he would have the lineage to declare his right to be her consort."

"Yeah, he was all sorts of full of himself. I don't have the full, ah, report on his recovery either. But I think his wounds were self-inflicted—his own trap went south."

"Not necessarily his fault," Danae said. "The trap could have been sprung by Myanya. Even within the pentagram, she wields great power. She couldn't harm him directly, but if she knew the trap was there, ready to be sprung, she could weaken its restraints, prime it to drop."

"Doesn't that sort of defeat the purpose of a pentagram?"

Danae's smile was cold. "Not for a male witch wise to the ways of a warrior queen. For an ignorant one? Well, he gets what he gets."

Another banging racket sounded from the office, and Nikki stood, brushing crumbs from her costume. "I think maybe we should—"

"Justice Wilde!" Mrs. French appeared at the door, her arms full of containers that were carefully wrapped in the same linens she'd served with the donut and coffee. "We... I don't think we need to worry too much about where to find Myanya." She held the pneumatic canisters higher. "We've now four different unfortunate souls summoning you who've found her for us."

"Where?"

Mrs. French's expression faltered. "Well, that's where it starts to get tricky. The first is Cairo, the second, London. The third is Bangkok, and the fourth..." She held up a canister. "Well, it's here."

Nikki scowled. "That's one hell of a remote this Myanya has a hold of."

"It's more than that," Danae said, sitting straighter. "These attacks are far too close together to be a mistake. This is no ingénue crippled by the power growing within her. It's someone channeling that power to create as much destruction as possible before she's sucked into the next stage of her journey. This lost queen isn't trying to be found."

"Well, she's throwing a party on the wrong turf," I took the canister with the local case and cracked it open, then scanned the topmost page. "You want to tag along? Because it looks like someone's luck just ran out in Vegas."

CHAPTER EIGHT

I always get to drive you to the nicest places," Nikki said, cleaning her sunglasses on the hem of her shirt as she rested behind the wheel of the limo. When I'd first come to Vegas two years earlier as a mercenary artifact hunter for the Council, Nikki'd been assigned as my chauffeur. It remained her favorite way to travel with me. Probably because there were no flames involved.

"This is nicer than most, I gotta admit." I leaned forward in the back seat, peering at the sun-blasted 1970s-era sign announcing Mister Mephistopheles's Magic Emporium of Mystery and Mayhem, and breathed in the smell of cheap alcohol and fast food. The brand-new complaint from the local male witch had led us deeper into downtown Vegas, away from the glitz and glamour of the Strip...but not quite as far as the worn-down nostalgia of the Golden Nugget and Fremont Hotel, which was where I expected we'd end up when I saw the address of this magic shop.

No. Mister Mephistopheles's emporium was located in the wasteland of cut-rate hotels and apartment complexes advertising the quality of their background checks, sandwiched between a youth hostel and a meat and grocery market that offered a permanent "you buy, we fry" offer for their returning clientele.

"Ten to one the place isn't even open," Nikki hazarded as we finally emerged from the car into the warm, sunny day. There was no shade to be found in this area of town, and during the summer, the streets would be vibrating with heat. But it was March in the desert, which was ridiculously pleasant. In fact, almost a little too pleasant.

"You picking that up?" I asked.

"Yep." Nikki scanned the street, shifting her stance to allow her easy access to her concealed gun. For this recon trip, she'd changed out of her steampunk costume and into something a little more understated—black tank, leather jacket, camo pants, heavy boots, and aviator shades beneath an eye-popping fall of cherry-red curls. As usual, Nikki put the special in special ops.

"Temperature drop of about ten degrees." I peered at the front door of the emporium. "No one seems to be taking advantage of it, though."

Nikki snorted. "It's eleven a.m. on a Thursday morning. Anyone with a job is already at it, and those who don't have it are still sleeping off discount night at the casinos. Add to that the fact that this particular cry for Justice came in less than an hour ago, this may be the queen of all fresh crime scenes."

"Noted." Other than the milder temperature, the building didn't seem to indicate that any sort of foul play had taken place, though the case in question had been succinct. "Guy knew I was in town, though."

"He knew Justice had an office here, definitely. Your personal location, maybe not." Nikki recited the details of the complaint as we strolled up the street, but there was no way we were inconspicuous. We were the only foot traffic in a three-block area. "Vic reported the initial attack took place at oh-three-hundred in his basement magician man cave, part of his residence beneath his place of business. He should still be there."

"Wasn't there a fire?"

"He said there was." Nikki side-eyed the building. "Though not so's you'd notice it out here."

We reached the building and tried the front door—which was our first confirmation that something definitely wasn't right at the emporium. It was unlocked, in an area of Vegas that never remained unlocked for longer than it took a customer to cross the threshold.

"Cameras," Nikki warned. I lifted a hand, my pulse of energy scrambling the circuits of electricity in the shop long enough to give us safe passage. The video equipment would keep recording. It simply wouldn't see or hear us as more than murmurs of static and some unexplained smudges on the feed.

We stepped into the cool, musty room, and I rubbed my arms. Despite my long-sleeved shirt, gooseflesh prickled my skin at the intense chill in the small space.

Mister Mephistopheles's Emporium looked exactly as expected, a low-end Party City for all things magical. There was an entire row of shelves given over to costumes and accessories, two more that held the equipment for common magic tricks, and another one devoted to trick card sets. Positioned in permanent displays against the wall were boxes with saws sticking out of them, dry ice, and lighting sets, and even a *Prestige*-style water box, fortunately empty at the moment.

"How'd this guy stay in business?" Nikki muttered, poking at a can of silly string. "He's got way more crap in here than he can possibly sell."

"Register." I pointed to the back wall, where a large countertop fronted a wall full of screens, all of them showing vantage points of every corner of the store. The sign "Smile, You're on Camera" surmounted this impressive digital display, and the cameras were definitely still recording. Two of the screens at the lower end of the display, however, were blank.

"You think there's anything worthwhile on the feed?" I asked.

"Probably only on those two—they're unlabeled." Nikki gestured to the blank screens. "Gotta be basement access."

"Yup." We moved around the counter and tried the door into what I suspected would be a standard office—but it was locked. I frowned at the doorknob. "Why keep the access door locked if you're going to leave the front of the building wide open?"

"Looking to create an attractive nuisance?" Nikki suggested. "If you've got a lot of lookie-loos in the area, especially with that hostel up the street, you might want to encourage walk-in business, even when the store isn't manned."

"That seems a little dangerous."

"Or a little too comfortable," Nikki agreed, turning around to scan the room again. "We got nothing here but magic trinkets, nothing really for sale of any use, even for a reseller looking to feed a drug habit. There's just not a lot of market for exploding dice."

I tapped the screens. "This system doesn't suck. The electronics would go for something."

"Cameras are too high up for easy access." Nikki shook her head. "Plus, anyone trying to nick the screens would be recorded. I get the feeling Mr. Mephistopheles isn't a guy who deletes his vids. I think we'll find thirty years of footage in that basement of his, going all the way back to when video cameras were first made."

"Maybe."

The two right screens flickered on, cutting off the conversation.

"Motion sensors," Nikki said, shifting to the right. "Not sure what triggered it. Though for reals, dude's man cave is hard core."

She wasn't kidding. The first camera view showed a basement rec room, its concrete floor painted with several different sections of symbols. The most dramatic symbol was a large pentagram slightly off the center of the space, bright white against the dull gray of the concrete. In exactly the same manner as the pentagram in Budapest, the five-pointed star was bordered by a white circle of what looked to be salt. Unlike the circle in Budapest, however, this circle had already been broken in several places before we got here.

Most notably by the man sprawled across its edge, desperately trying to crawl away.

"Door," Nikki snapped. I didn't hesitate.

A blue ball of fire coalesced between my fingers and immediately shot out as I lifted my hand, hitting the doorknob and blasting the door backward. A bevy of red lights sprang to life above the door, and an urgent high-pitched alarm sounded. Fantastic.

There was nothing for it, however. Nikki and I bolted through the door. It opened not into an office but a short corridor with two additional doors. The one to the right yielded a small utilitarian office, completely empty. The one at the back of the corridor, also unlocked, opened onto a set of steep stairs—too steep for ordinary building codes by far.

"Bunker," Nikki called back as she led the way down the stairs, answering my unasked question.

Understanding zipped through me. This place had been built in the 1950s, I was pretty sure, during the era of nuclear bomb testing not all that far away. It wasn't unreasonable that an underground bomb shelter had been built back in the day, maybe even one that'd been expanded as the building above took shape.

We reached the bottom floor a few seconds later, then raced past a bedroom, kitchen, and storage closets until we reached a final door that led into a remarkably wide space of about twenty square feet. These people meant serious business with their bunkers.

The room opened up to exactly the same scene we'd seen on the screens upstairs. Various sections of arcane script, dominated by the pentagram in the center of the room. Not to mention the near-dead male witch sprawled out on the floor.

"Help me," he managed.

I stared down at him hard, surprised to see not the slash of silver across his temple that I expected, which would indicate that he was marked for Justice, but a corona of purple-white light radiating around his entire body. This was also an indication that someone needed Justice, but of an entirely different sort. This man needed my help.

He didn't have to ask me twice. I moved forward, my third eye snapping open, and immediately saw a problem. In the center of the pentagram spun a vortex of energy that served as the equivalent of a sucking hole of quicksand. The mage, a slight man of no more than a hundred and forty pounds, including his voluminous velour robe dusted with silver stars, was losing the battle. Though not visible to the regular eye, the quicksand held another horror too. More spikes waited at the bottom of the pit the vortex was sucking the man toward. If he got pulled into that, he would have a future as Swiss cheese and little else.

As Nikki lurched to my right, grabbing for the man's shoulders, I reached down as well. Together we hauled him away from the sucking maw of death. This was harder than I would have expected, at least at the beginning. The magic of the vortex redoubled with an impressive fury as we attempted to save Mr. Wizard. With a final heave, we broke free of the clinging magic.

We sprawled on the floor, the man immediately scrabbling away from us, his eyes wild with...fury?

"Who are you?" he demanded. "You're not my consort! How dare you interrupt my spell!"

I stared at him as Nikki snorted. "This job keeps getting better and better," she said.

"Mordechai Jones, birth name Harold, one of two owners of the shop," she continued, meeting my gaze above the magician's sputtering as she reported what she'd learned in the flash of time she'd had hold of Mr. Wizard's body. Nikki's most advanced Connected ability wasn't that of reading minds so much as memories. It had proven more than useful during her years on the police force. Memories weren't always as reliable as fact, but they yielded far more interesting information about their subjects than dry details alone. "He considers himself the more successful one, the white magician, whose patient and caring execution of the Wiccan Rede has allowed him to become the supreme magician in the family. Long estranged from the local coven along with his brother, Robert."

At the sound of his brother's name, Harold glared at Nikki, then up. "Malachi," he roared, his thin white face apoplectic. "Show yourself."

"You're a blasted fool!"

Dumbfounded, Nikki and I turned to see another man burst into the room. He was shockingly pale, which made all the blood covering him that much more startling.

"She wasn't yours! She was mine, you know she was mine, that you hadn't the strength or the power to hold her, yet you wouldn't leave it alone." He whirled as Nikki started forward.

"Don't you touch me." The mage apparently named Malachi straightened to his full height, and my eyes narrowed on him. This guy was yin to Harold's yang, without question, complete with the slash of silver at his temple instead of the purple glow of the brother in need of aid. I didn't know what Malachi's crimes were, but he had them. In spades.

He also seemed to be a glutton for punishment. "You interrupted my spell," he accused me, echoing his brother. "I had her exactly where I wanted, the sniveling cow."

"Whoa, whoa, whoa—" Nikki's hands flew up, and my own hackles rose. What was with the disrespect being shown to Myanya, a witch spirit of clearly superior powers? This didn't make any sense.

From the floor, Harold-slash-Mordechai began to sputter again. "You know nothing about her, Malachi. That's why you failed. She is pure light and formless energy. She deserves to be ruled by a master who will treat her with respect!" Mordechai's face was now mottled red, and spit flew from his mouth as he screamed. My head swiveled from one to the other, and I was getting more confused by the second. Malachi might have been a bastard in his own right, but Mordechai was clearly no prize.

My gaze went back to the gnashing maw of spikes in the center of the pentagram, beyond the vortex of quicksand. Maybe I should've let them both be eaten.

"First things first," Nikki snapped, her cop voice penetrating the outrage of both men. "Which one of you summoned Justice?"

"You summoned *Justice*?" The blood-soaked Malachi turned on his brother, who promptly curled up in a ball like a pill bug, huddling in his own robes. "You know you are giving me a death sentence, you fool."

"You were dying," Mordechai wailed, scooting behind Nikki and me. "You were covered in blood."

"*Her* blood." Malachi spread his hands wide. "The witch spirit has grown lax in all the years since last she suffered. She's no longer as vigilant as she once was. I knew her weaknesses, studied them. As the city's most knowledgeable magician, I know all, and I see all."

"Most knowledgeable." I couldn't help the skepticism in my voice. "I think there's maybe another Magician in the city you're forgetting."

"You! You of all people should respect a magician's might." Malachi turned on me, his face now a fetching shade of purple. "I warned Armaeus he was a fool to allow you to ascend to any of the seats of the Council, but would he listen? No, he would not. And *Justice*. That was the biggest mistake of all."

Anger is a funny thing. Sometimes it can creep up on you, slowly build until you find yourself all wound up in its grasp.

Sometimes it moves a lot faster than that.

Mordechai wailed in fright as Malachi's robes lit up with spectral fire, burning straight off him until he was dressed in nothing but his baggy trousers and faded white T-shirt.

86

"Um, Sara—" Nikki's voice was drowned out by the pounding in my brain. I advanced on Malachi.

"You've got a date with Judgment, Malachi, and if you've been doing your careful reading of the Mystere Arcanum, I think you know what that means. You can go now, or you can go later, or you might get lucky and not go at all, but you will owe me *big* for that. You understand that?"

"Sara," Nikki said, more urgently this time.

"You have no *right*," the two-bit magician cried. His face looked pale beneath all the blood. I didn't care. I'd had it up to here.

"You get one chance," I offered him, but I could tell he wasn't going to take it. I was almost glad. Gamon could sprinkle hot sauce on this Cheez-It and tell me later what she found out from him. I reached out and grabbed the wailing Malachi by the shoulder, feeling my fury kindle along my nerves as fire licked to life around me and my cells began to destabilize—

"*Sara!*" It wasn't Nikki's voice that roared behind me this time, but one even more familiar. "What in the *fuck* is going on here?"

Enter Brody Rooks, detective for the Las Vegas Metropolitan Police Department.

CHAPTER NINE

I want my lawyer," Mordechai whined, slumping in the conference room at the precinct house.

"No, you don't," I corrected him. Brody sighed. "Sara. You're supposed to be helpful here."

"I'm the soul of helpfulness." I stared down Mordechai and his brother as they glared back at me across the table. We were in a conference room, not an interview room, which explained why I was even allowed to join this party of idiots. The brothers Grimm weren't being questioned in relation to any crime they might have committed. They were barely being questioned at all and had only agreed to come down to the station because Brody had assured them they'd get special treatment if they made their statements in person on the premises. I'd further explained to the brothers that Mordechai was going to be turning their little bunker into a permanently solo bachelor pad unless he and Malachi played ball. Now it was time for them to start playing.

"What happened?" I prompted.

"What happened was that two complete and utter strangers to us broke into our place of business and entered our private residence without permission,"

Malachi retorted. He shot another gaze to Brody. "You should be arresting them."

"That would be negative," I said, raising a hand. "You summoned Justice. Justice showed up."

"I didn't summon you," Malachi grumbled, and Mordechai threw up his hands in exasperation.

"You were covered in *blood*. You still are!" Mordechai complained. "You were being summoned into the arms of Myanya and, like it or not, you were not ready. She really wanted me."

"Don't even think you have either the mortar *or* the pestle to handle something like Myanya. You of all people know she craves the strength of the destroyer. You can't even destroy a bridge hand."

"You are completely—"

"Gentlemen," Brody broke in, his cop voice sharp enough to make the brothers jerk to attention. "You're here because your alarm system triggered a status with your security company to call the paranormal investigations division of the LVMPD to your business."

I smirked, turning to him. "Seriously? You have a paranormal investigations division?"

"We do now," he said levelly, sounding none too appreciative in my book. Brody and I went way back, all the way to Memphis, Tennessee, more than ten years ago, when he was a rookie cop and I was a teenaged card reader with a penchant for finding the lost. He'd gotten stuck with me as part of the department's commitment to community outreach, and we'd forged an unlikely partnership. Up until recently, we'd tended to work on opposite sides of the law, but Brody always tried to make the relationship work. Mainly because it helped him close his cases that much sooner. I wasn't sure if there seriously was a paranormal investigations division, but given the amount of crazy the LVMPD had to manage with the Arcana Council in their backyard, I wouldn't be surprised.

Brody redoubled his focus on the Jones brothers. "It's illegal to tell police a crime has been committed when it hasn't, gentlemen. And according to these two witnesses, you invited them onto your premises and they entered in good faith."

"They broke the *door* down," Mordechai spluttered.

"After observing you in distress on your own security camera," Nikki drawled. "Next time, don't look like you're about to get eaten by a magic trash compactor."

"You had no right to barge in on us like that," Malachi growled. "We had the problem contained."

"The problem that resulted in you being covered in blood. You understand this is a concern for us." Brody leaned in. "I could reasonably get a warrant right now to search your home and business for an injured party, or test you against all the known rape and assault cases we currently have in the precinct. That's going to take a while."

"No." Malachi's eyes widened. "I don't have time for that. I have to reassert my case to Myanya, work my advantage before some other suitor usurps my position."

Brody's jaw tightened, and Nikki took pity on him.

"Why don't I bring us up to speed? The Jones brothers aren't merely magicians but witches. As such, they have a whole slew of rituals, history, and beliefs that are unique to their practice of magic. One of those beliefs is the prophecy of the scarred warrior, which is a witch who endures trials at the hands of an oppressor only to emerge triumphant. These two," she pointed at the brothers, "were auditioning for the role of the oppressor."

"That's not even remotely an accurate representation of the glory that Myanya will experience at the hands of her consort. It is through the consort that she achieves her true role of scarred warrior, and her suffering is required for her eventual victory," Mordechai said, ever so breathlessly.

"That's both deeply disturbing and borderline enough for me to throat-punch you," Nikki said, and Brody held up a hand again.

"This Myanya is a real person? You've injured her?"

"I have drawn first blood," Malachi confirmed, pride rolling off him in palpable waves. "But she cut herself. I invoked the rite of Furorem, and she willingly took part to strengthen her abilities."

"Okay, you just went full-on Harry Potter, buddy," Nikki said, squinting at Malachi. "Explain that."

He preened. "Myanya is a vessel, and she must receive her trials from an outside hand. Most rightfully, her consort, but not in all cases. Her nemesis can take any form, though the male dominance of the consort is most traditional."

"Malachi Jones, let me be clear here. Are you confessing to aggravated assault?" Brody snapped, but Mordechai chimed in, his voice ringing with excitement.

"If the consort is strong enough, he can deepen Myanya's power before he takes her for his own and subjugates her to his will," he said, his high-pitched voice trembling with the force of his words. "So by enacting the rite of Furorem, the consort demonstrates that his confidence is supreme."

"Or his stupidity," I pointed out. "Because from what you're telling me, this little trick you pulled has only served to increase Myanya's power, yet you didn't actually claim her."

"I was interrupted," Malachi fumed. "And then betrayed."

"You were bleeding from the eyeballs," Mordechai insisted. "And you were already inside the pentagram."

Malachi turned on him. "I was not."

"The circle was broken—it was. You were screaming and waving your arms—I entered and shoved you out, then I…" His face took on a look of wonderment. "Then I saw Myanya myself."

Finally, we were getting someplace. I leaned forward slightly, not missing Brody's glance toward me.

"And what did you see, Mordechai?" I prompted.

"Sheer, unclaimed beauty," he gushed, which wasn't exactly helpful. "The vessel of the feminine, set forth to receive the seed of—"

"No. Dude. I mean, what did she look like? Height, weight, eyes, hair?"

He blinked at me but wasn't quite knocked out of his thrall. "She was long and slender, then short and round, her hair cropped short, then flowing," he said in unabashed wonder.

"Oh, for the love of Christmas," muttered Nikki, and I tried again.

"How did you know it was Myanya? If she keeps changing form, how do you know this wasn't another witch trying to take her place? To usurp the rightful position of your consort?"

"They would not dare," Malachi said, righteous indignation dripping from his old-man voice. "No witch can take the place of the sacred vessel of Myanya."

"According to…?"

"It isn't *done*." This time, it was Mordechai who was doing the insisting, but at least his tone had grown more reflective. "The witch chosen to be Myanya, the scarred warrior, is often unaware of the transition taking place until it is already upon her. It's not a choice, to take on this energy. Though the outcome as scarred warrior will ensure the strength of the witch's coven, it can be quite difficult for the vessel."

"The vessel," I said dryly. "You mean the young woman who has to be subjugated by the forces of oppression that she neither seeks out nor deserves?"

"It's an honor," Malachi put in.

"*I'm* going to throat-punch you if you say that one more time," Brody said, his voice mild as he sat back in his seat. Malachi blinked at him, but Brody's attention had already shifted to me. "So this leaves us where, exactly? These guys can't help us identify this victim, unless…" He glanced back to the brothers. "Is she local?"

"Hardly," Malachi scoffed. "The most powerful witch in all the covens wouldn't be found in Las Vegas. The Arcana Council is here."

That made me sit up straighter, and Nikki caught it too. "The Council?" she asked. "Why should that matter?"

"Because the witch must be allowed space to grow, to become, to take on her full power," Mordechai said. He focused on me with greater interest now. "Wait. You're seeking the identity of Myanya *now*, before she takes her full power? Why? The prophecy is one of great strength for the covens and will ensure whoever harbors the scarred warrior full dominion over their enemies. You all — " He stopped as his glance took in Brody, then he nodded. "You all are Connected. Surely you can understand the value of a fellow Connected wanting to better herself to the point of ensuring she and her people are safe?"

"Well, of course we can," I said reasonably. "Except for the fact that she's killing people."

"No, that's not possible," Malachi dismissed. "The only individual strong enough to challenge the energy of Myanya is another witch. Witches cannot kill each other. They can force submission, but not kill."

"Really. According to who?" Something I needed to check with Danae about.

"It simply isn't done," Mordechai said again. "'Do what thou wilt and cause harm to none' isn't merely a handy mantra, it's our way of life."

"Except for the part where you subjugate another person to your will?"

"That's the fulfillment of the prophecy," Mordechai protested. "There's no true subjugation involved, merely allowance as part of the natural order."

"Natural order for who?" Nikki drawled. She subtly flexed her biceps, and the two men didn't miss the gesture. She could snap either one of them like twigs, and despite their impressive sense of entitlement, they knew it.

"Right," I said, drawing their attention back. "So let's say for the sake of argument that whatever witch has been graced with the energy of Myanya sees the writing on the wall and realizes that her future is a very nasty short term for a questionably appealing long term. Maybe she's not down with sacrificing herself for her coven, or maybe she's not down with licking someone's boots to get there. What are her options?"

Mordechai blinked at me. "Options?"

"Can she reject the prophecy?"

"Absolutely not," Malachi blustered, and even Mordechai shook his head.

"I do see what you're saying," Mordechai said. "That if a woman—and yes, the spirit of Myanya only inhabits a female—rejects the prophecy, can she also reject Myanya? And the answer to that is—no. The power of the witch covens must be rejuvenated over time, and Myanya is one of the most potent tools to do so. She must occupy a vessel. The cycle must be completed. That's why we were summoned."

"Who notified you?" Brody interrupted, startling us both. His arms were folded now, his expression flat and hard. "We have a missing victim whose blood you're wearing, Mr. Jones. Where is she, and who alerted you to her whereabouts? Did you guys get some sort of memo that the prophecy was about to be fulfilled, so you should get your subjugation robes on, some sort of Tinder for assholes?"

Malachi's lips pulled back in a snarl, but Mordechai merely nodded. "That's a crass way of putting it—"

Brody snorted. "It's kind of a crass prophecy."

"But in a manner of speaking, yes," Mordechai continued. "The prophecy of Myanya on the cusp of fulfillment is a message shared with the most powerful witches in all the covens, particularly the male witches, as they traditionally are the triggering event for her power."

"And you got that information, how? A text message? Email?"

"More a sense of knowing." Malachi's voice was regulated, as if he was coming down from his douchebag high, and he spread his hands out, eyeing the specks of blood that still dotted them. "The prophecy must be fulfilled. If it isn't, the witch queen's power will grow unabated, demanding a challenger until one destroys her. She needs her consort as much as he needs her."

"Uh-huh," I said. "I think that's still open for debate, but to your point—what are we looking at in terms of a timeline? When did you get your PSA that the prophecy was about to be fulfilled?"

Mordechai and Malachi looked at each other, transferring communication in the way brothers could. "A week?" Mordechai asked.

"Less than that. A week ago was the ren fest in Reno. We came back Sunday night, and we didn't know before then, or we would've spent the weekend preparing."

"Right, right." Mordechai lifted his knobby hand and rubbed his jaw. "Three days, then. Monday. After we watched the DVR of *Elementary*. That night."

"Yes," Malachi nodded, satisfied. "That was it."

"Three days," I said. It'd been two days ago that I'd unimpaled Vlad from the spikes of his own trap. "And you didn't try contacting her until now?"

"Oh, we tried. Or I tried." He side-eyed Mordechai. "I didn't even know you were going to challenge her as consort."

"I wasn't planning on it originally," Mordechai sniffed. "I was merely making sure she didn't turn you into ham loaf. That's *not* all her blood."

"No, it's not." Malachi looked back to me. "But to your question, we prepared for a full day, then began the ritual of connecting. It took another day and a half for us to gain the ascendant queen's attention and — well, you know what happened after that."

"Wait a minute," Brody said. "It's been three days since notification went out. What was she doing up to that point?"

He glanced out the conference room window as several people crowded around one of the televisions flickering in the bullpen of the precinct. He narrowed his eyes, then shook his head.

"Whatever they're looking at, it's not local," he said, focusing back on us.

"Not local but — yo, that was a *Kardashian* talking to reporters or I'm Celine Dion. Hold one second." Nikki bounded up and out of the room, making a beeline for the TV.

Brody turned back to the Jones brothers. "So what was she doing?"

"What she'll continue to do until the prophecy is fulfilled," Malachi said, shrugging one bony shoulder. "Answering the challenges of the male witches who seek to destroy her, body and soul...until one gets the job done."

CHAPTER TEN

When I left the precinct house, Brody still needed to talk with the Jones brothers about the source of all the blood on Malachi, and Nikki was in a heated discussion over whatever had happened on TV to one of the celebrities she followed. I didn't know if the terrible car wreck depicted on the screen was real life or reality TV, but apparently, that didn't seem to matter — to either Nikki or the cops on duty.

Strange days, indeed.

I hailed a car and gave the driver the destination of the Luxor Casino, allowing myself a rare minute to sit back and simply watch the Vegas skyline pass by as the car turned onto Las Vegas Boulevard all the way at the end of the Strip, near the Stratosphere. The great casinos of Vegas soared into view within a few stoplights, and I leaned forward, looking up — and up still farther. These were the residences that would never appear on a postcard but were as much a part of the landscape as the strip shows and carnie barkers luring people through casino doors into a world of glittering lights.

Las Vegas was the home of the Arcana Council, the most powerful wielders of magic on the planet.

THE LOST QUEEN

First up was the Stratosphere, which served as home to the most mercurial of Council members, Nikola Tesla, or the Hanged Man. His residence, not surprisingly, had evolved into a complex blend of intricate geometric shapes, along which electrical currents zipped and skittered twenty-four hours a day. Several blocks up was my own domain, Justice Hall, which looked exactly like its inspiration from the DC comic books, complete with the impressive domed façade. The fact that I didn't live in my ethereal residence notwithstanding, I was glad to have some official real estate on Arcana Alley. Across the street from me, soaring atop Treasure Island, was the thick white monolith that marked the tower of Michael the Archangel, or the Hierophant. Like Tesla, Michael was the kind of guy who annoyed you more the longer you got to know him. Both of them could stay inside their respective towers for the next decade for all I cared.

Then came Caesar's Palace, with its empty stone fortress. To my knowledge, none of the Council members lived there, yet it refused to dissolve into glitter like a good little abandoned residence. I'd thought potentially Gamon would choose it as her home on the Strip, but she didn't appear to be a fan, either.

The next inhabited pair of casino-topping residences pulled more of a smile from me: the Foolscap glass menagerie atop glittering Bellagio Casino, and the sensually spinning lava lamp of a residence atop the legendary Vegas hotel, the Flamingo. Simon, the Fool of the Arcana Council, lived above Bellagio with his troupe of Mongolian bodyguards, while the Flamingo's skyway was the home of Aleksander Kreios, aka the Devil. The last I'd seen of the Devil was in Venice a few weeks ago. Since then, crickets. I know I'd been busy, yet…nevertheless.

Next up was yet another study in asshat-ery, the Emperor, Viktor Dal, who lived atop Paris Casino in a jet-black tower that pulsed with energy, day and night. I wasn't a fan of the Emperor either, and the animosity was mutual. Some might say our differences were water under the bridge, but it was particularly toxic water and the bridge had been blown up. Fortunately, Viktor was keeping a fairly low profile of late. I frowned. Actually, most of the Arcana Council was keeping a low profile, it seemed. Was that on purpose? Or had I missed a committee meeting already?

Across from Paris and further along the Strip, was the Excalibur Hotel and Casino, and atop it rested a lonely hut on a high platform: the home of the Council's Hermit. I'd rarely seen Willem of Galt in his humble home, which wasn't too surprising. First off, he was the caretaker of the veil between the worlds, and secondly...he was my dad. So many unresolved issues there, so little time.

Then there was the last fortress on the Strip, and by far the most impressive. The Magician's residence might easily have served as the hall of the mountain king in a Wagnerian opera, all soaring spires and arches and turrets lifting into the heavens. There, buried somewhere deep within that complex labyrinth, was Armaeus Bertrand, the leader of the Arcana Council. There were other Council members, of course. Eshe, the High Priestess, had made her home on the Strip mostly by couch-surfing her way through Armaeus's million-and-one rooms. Death and Judgment preferred off-campus housing, and the recently ascended Lovers — the one-time gods Zeus and Hera — hadn't stopped fighting with each other long enough to sign a spectral lease. But right now, the thing that struck me most about the Magician's abode was the same thing I'd noticed in the other homes of the Arcana Council...namely, how quiet it was.

When it came to the Council, quiet didn't necessarily mean good.

I paid my Lyft driver and made my way into the lobby of the Luxor hotel, struck as I always was by the almost breathtaking level of glitz and kitsch the place maintained. The tourists streaming from the hotel to the casino didn't seem to pay attention to how over the top the lobby was, barely stopping to look up before disappearing into the wall of noise that marked the casino proper. Old, young, tall, short, every size and every description, some with the earnestness of penny slotters, some with the slick strut of black jack and craps players. Even at two p.m. on a weekday, there were bachelorette parties and early spring breakers, conference attendees sneaking out of sessions and die-hard regulars whose skin had turned the faintest shade of green after a long winter hunched over the machines.

These were the people who made up Vegas, their belief fully staked on the next turn of the card, the next roll of the dice, the next spin of the roulette wheel, or the next tug on the arm of a slot machine. Their magic was what had pulled the Arcana Council to Las Vegas in the early forties, when the mob was still king and Bugsy Siegel built the Flamingo, and their magic was what kept the Council anchored in power today.

Sometimes, it merely took having enough people who believed in possibility to make all the difference in the world.

I crossed the lobby of the hotel and easily saw the elevators to the Magician's domain, Prime Luxe, hidden alongside the bays of the Luxor. No matter how many times I visited the hotel, I never tired of entering the

Magician's lair this way. Though I could now technically scramble my cells long enough to poof into Armaeus's office with my hair on fire, there was something old world about going up in an elevator cage to meet the most powerful man on the planet.

The most powerful, and the most inscrutable.

A few moments later, when the elevator doors snicked open, I knew that the Magician had picked up on my mood. Which was good, since I'd been telegraphing it for that exact purpose. No matter how much I loved the man, he had one fatal flaw. He didn't share his toys. Ordinarily, this wouldn't bother me, except when those toys were the information I needed to do my job.

"Miss Wilde. How good of you to join me."

I braced myself for seeing Armaeus, because no matter how many times it happened, it was always a revelation to me. Sometimes, like today, I needed that revelation more than others.

The Magician of the Arcana Council stood at the far wall of his office, silhouetted by the bright sunshine and surrounded with the view of the sprawling city far below. A city that extended in one direction past towering skyscrapers and the constant movement of the Strip, and in the other, out into what looked from this distance to be a vast and formless desert, where very little lived and even less moved. It was the dichotomy of living in an oasis in the desert, and it suited the man who had lived above it for nearly eighty years...after living elsewhere in the world for going on nine hundred years.

Armaeus Bertrand was holding up pretty well, I had to say.

Tall and elegant despite his powerful build, today the Magician wore what passed for him as casual clothes—a tailored blue silk shirt, open at the collar, dark trousers, thousand-dollar loafers. He boasted a heavy platinum watch on one wrist, but otherwise, no jewelry adorned his burnished bronze skin, the rich coloring a testament to his French-Egyptian birth. His dark hair flowed in thick waves past his collar, framing a face distinctive for its chiseled cheekbones and jaw and his flashing, dark, black-gold eyes. The very first time I'd met the Magician, he'd been a voice in my mind. And it was the voice that continued to draw me back, year over year. Our relationship had never been easy, and it hadn't always been good, but it was powerfully addictive, I had to admit.

It also wasn't the point of me being here today, I reminded myself.

"You're angry with me." Armaeus observed mildly as I crossed the room. He'd arranged the chairs in the seating area of his office to invite conversation, but I was too keyed up to sit.

I sighed. "Angry is perhaps overstating it. Call me…dismayed. Confused. Uncertain. You know what's going on with this Myanya, this witch prophecy that's taking over the covens, and you didn't tell me."

"You didn't ask."

"I didn't know it was happening," I protested. "How can I ask you about something if you don't give me a heads-up that it's even going to be a thing? I'm not you. I don't sit around and consider the probabilities of every possible situation transitioning into the next situation, time without end."

Armaeus regarded me speculatively as I neared him, and I tried not to let that rattle me either. As much as I knew the Magician cared for me, it didn't stop him from being endlessly intrigued by my progression in my Connected abilities. If he were forced to choose between a relationship with me and continued study...I might not like the answer he'd give.

His lips quirked. The Magician also had the ability to read my thoughts unless I carefully shielded them from him. At this moment, if he really wanted to shuffle around in my mental file cabinet, I didn't care what he saw.

He tilted his head, his eyes gleaming more darkly, and the tiniest frisson of apprehension skated across my nerves. Okay, so I mostly didn't care what he saw. The Magician had a way of taking everything I was willing to give the moment I gave it, before I could change my mind.

"You acknowledge that I've been alive for hundreds of years, but you don't truly understand what that means, Miss Wilde. I assure you, it changes your perspective. The study of your emerging power is a far more potent and compelling topic than you give yourself credit for."

"Uh-huh," I smiled. "So what you're telling me is, you're dating me for my mind?"

"Far from it. In fact, that's something I need to speak to you about—later."

At the deep, rolling insinuation in his voice, every one of my nerve endings perked up and turned Armaeus's way. "Later as in when?" I prompted.

"That depends on what information you have to share with me regarding the return of Myanya. I have been distracted with my own studies these past several days and only realized the prophecy had been triggered when I picked up your thoughts today."

That surprised me, and maybe mollified me a little too. Maybe I needed to stop assuming the worst when it came to the Magician holding out on me. Despite his tendency to throw me into the fire and assume he could heal my scorch marks later. "You were that deep in the Fortress of Solitude?" I took a moment to look a little more closely at Armaeus, but I couldn't see anything different about him. Devastatingly gorgeous? Check. Insufferably arrogant? Check. Practically steaming with magic? Check. "What gives with that?"

"There is a season to all things, Miss Wilde, including for me," Armaeus said, dismissing my question. Another small tremor of concern skated across my awareness.

He kept going. "But no, I wasn't aware the spirit of Myanya had returned. Her last known incursion was in 1934, and she made another attempt in 1962, which failed, as it was a time of great unrest among the covens. The energy she brought was not well received, for all that it would eventually strengthen the coven who harbored the scarred warrior queen."

I screwed my face up, because I could feel a math coming on. "So, that would have brought her back—when? 1990? I think Danae mentioned that date."

"Perfect numbers." Armaeus nodded. "We have no record of the prophecy being fulfilled in 1990, or even attempted. That year, my focus wasn't on the covens as heavily, but on events of a decidedly more mundane nature."

I lifted my brows. "I don't remember anyone mentioning you at the Berlin Wall."

Armaeus flicked his gaze over my shoulder, fixing on a distant spot in the universe where he stored his imaginary calculator. "Earlier this year, I considered the possibility of her return, but discarded it as there was no data to be found that the prophecy had been fulfilled in 1990. With the prophecy going unfulfilled twice, it would have taken an act of the covens working in concert to resurrect Myanya's energy, which was unlikely given the negative consequences to the witch in question. Like so many other prophecies, it should have been consigned to ash. But here we are."

"Clearly. So where is she?"

Armaeus blinked, his eyes once more sharpening their focus on me. "What do you mean?"

"I mean, Myanya's starting to issue invites to wannabe oppressors, only she's flipping the tables. Bigtime. According to the complaints that have come into Justice Hall, I've got three dead guys already, another guy who should be dead except for his fast-thinking brother, and an impaled descendent of Dracula who insists Myanya simply needs to give him another chance. I'm laying that one at her doorstep too, and I have a feeling there are others. According to Danae, a bunch of dead guys is not at all the way the prophecy is supposed to start."

"It's not how it's transpired in the past, but—the spirit evolves. Myanya evolves." Armaeus frowned pensively. "The secrets for her success now likely lie in the evidence of her failure in the past."

"We don't even know where she made the attempt in 1990, or if she did," I said. "That's not going to help us."

"Not in 1990, no," Armaeus said. "But 1962 was a different story. The failed attempt of the scarred warrior prophecy took place in Moscow, Russia, in the shadow of St. Basil's Cathedral."

"A cathedral. In Moscow. Not exactly where I would expect a coven of witches to hang out."

Armaeus smiled. "You should never underestimate the power of true believers."

"Okay, great," I said, making a "give it to me" gesture. "So what happened? Myanya killed her vessel witch? Or did she simply ice her suitors like she's doing now?"

"Neither. The vessel witch who Myanya had chosen to fulfill the prophecy allowed her to take hold—and then banished her. The prophecy cycle ended almost as soon as it started."

I frowned. The Jones brothers had said…then again, I needed to consider the source of that particular piece of intel. "I didn't think that was possible."

"Ordinarily, it isn't. And it wasn't without great cost to the vessel witch in question."

Something about this wasn't tracking, but I was willing to go along. "Okay, so where and when did that happen, and should I head there now? Or is it something we need to see together?"

A strange shadow passed over Armaeus's face. "You will need to see it in person, but I can't go with you. I can't leave here, in fact. Not yet. There's still…too much to be done."

My brows lifted. "Is there something going on with the Council I need to be aware of?" I asked, but Armaeus shook his head.

"No. But time is of the essence now. I suggest you collect the inimitable Miss Dawes and be on your way."

I thought of Nikki in the streets of Moscow and couldn't help but smile as well. But I also could tell Armaeus was giving me the brush-off. "And what about you?"

"Your focus should be only on the lost queen, Miss Wilde. And defeating her." The Magician's beautiful lips quirked up in a half smile. "It's important for you to close this case."

I frowned at him. "Why? In case you didn't notice, I'm lousy with cases back at the office. Why does this one matter any more than they do?"

"When you answer that, you'll be much further down the path toward unraveling the mystery of the lost queen, my dear Miss Wilde...and many other mysteries as well."

Then he disappeared in a shatter of smoke.

CHAPTER ELEVEN

I t only took me the length of the elevator ride down from Armaeus's penthouse to decide I wasn't going to play the game his way anymore. Something was going on with the Magician, something important, and I needed to understand it. I couldn't keep getting angry at him withholding information from me if I wasn't willing to go after that information myself. If Armaeus wanted to keep something from me, he would. If he was willing to let me see it with my own eyes if I sought it out...

Then I needed to take my own action.

"Figure it out, Sara," I muttered, striding out once again into the lobby of the Luxor. There were almost the same people there that had been wandering the space every time I'd visited — different clothes, different hairstyles, even different skin color, but the same people.

I wasn't the same person, though. I had changed these past several weeks and months. It was time for me to start acting like it.

Stopping in front of the gift shop, I stared hard at the window, my gaze running mindlessly over the trinkets that lined the shelves. There were faux gold statues of every description, miniature King Tuts and Queen Nefertiti masks, and ankhs in sterling silver and pewter along with the gold plate. Not for the first time, I considered the poetic justice of Armaeus living above a pyramid-shaped homage to his mother's native land, when he'd barely ever returned to Egypt while I'd known him. And when he *had* hit the land of the pharaohs, it hadn't gone so well for him. The ancient crypts lying beneath the shifting sands had been a trap designed to ensnare him, and, being the Magician, he'd at least had some inkling of the possibility that such an eventuality could…

Happen.

I frowned more fiercely, staring at nothing. Armaeus was the Magician, arguably one of the most powerful one-time humans on the planet, and he'd said more than once that I was potentially going to grow in strength to rival him—or even surpass him. Was that what was going on here? Was he trying to level himself up to prepare for me?

Or was it something else? Time and time again, when the Magician had seemed to thrust me into danger without concern for how damaged I might end up, he'd done so knowing that he'd be there to catch me when and if I stumbled. That he could always take care of me, always protect me.

Or, failing that, he could always heal me after the worst had been done.

But what about now? I was Justice of the Arcana Council, and I'd already learned that some of my abilities had transferred, some were brand-new, and others had vanished, never mind that they'd been the most useful ones. Had the dynamic between Armaeus and me changed as well? He'd appeared to love me as much as or more than he always had, but upstairs just now, our vibe had seemed completely different.

I scowled into the plateglass window, hard enough it began to vibrate. Was I seriously one of no less than a hundred other women in the city at this exact moment, standing alone in the lobby of a Vegas casino, wondering if my boyfriend simply wasn't that into me?

I dissolved into my own crackling hiss of smoke. I knew Armaeus's domain, dammit. I didn't need a freaking road map to find him.

A few seconds later, I flared back into existence, surrounded by shelves as large and looming as the ones in the library of Justice, but decidedly neater. Now, however, I looked at Armaeus's library with new eyes.

"The Mystere Arcanum," I murmured, remembering what the Jones brothers called it, Malachi and Mordechai. The repository for all that was mystic and magical, the grimoires of ancient magicians.

I'd known Armaeus had amassed this library, at least tangentially. When I'd first started working for him as an artifact hunter, a good quarter of the items he'd wanted me to find were exclusively so that he could store them away in his own little museum, hidden from the prying eyes of mortals who didn't understand the artifacts' power or potential. And I was more than a little bit convinced that he'd been the guy behind the burning of the Library of Alexandria, an act of vandalism so breathtakingly awful, I hadn't wanted to examine it too much. But the Magician had long been more about the balance of magic on Earth than about the preservation of magic itself. It wasn't completely unbelievable that he'd set fire to the greatest compendium of knowledge in the ancient world.

I looked around the shelves, each of them stacked floor to ceiling with ancient, dusty tomes and scroll cases and boxes. It also wasn't completely unbelievable that Armaeus had stolen what he needed from the Library of Alexandria, then merely set what was left on fire.

A sound from the back of the room drew my attention. Not because it was subtle either. It was a two-parter. The first the hissing sound of something moving through the still air at great speed, then connecting with something soft and fleshy.

The second was the sound of a deep and throaty scream.

Armaeus.

My first instinct was to race through the library at full speed, balls of fire at the ready, but I forced myself to move carefully and cautiously forward. Armaeus was not your average Magician. His power derived from ancient practices that stretched all the way back to the founding of Egypt and were deeply rooted in the first chakra, the seat of ultimate life-giving power and sex magic. Those practices that had gained renewed traction in the mid-1600s when John Dee and Edward Kelley had gotten wind of them from a few of their chattier angels. Then there was another resurgence during Aleister Crowley's tenure in the early 1920s, where things took on another layer of crazy. Armaeus tended to keep his practice to himself, but approaching him now, when he was apparently in the process of being flogged, might not be the negative that it would be if I was under the lash.

"Ungh!" Then again, I wasn't a big fan of anyone getting the crap beaten out of them, even if they ostensibly liked it.

I moved more quickly through the maze of shelves, not missing the fact that the deeper I got into Armaeus's lair, the older and more dilapidated the library became.

Had it been this way the last time I was in here, when Nikki and I had found the Magician hunched over a cauldron of fire, attended only by the Devil? I couldn't remember, and I didn't have time to parse the details, as I came around the last bookshelf and skidded to a stop, my breath dying in my throat thankfully before I could release it in a scream.

Instead, I clapped my hands over my mouth. *Armaeus!*

The Magician didn't move from where he lay slumped forward, hanging from what looked like Olympic rings, suspended by a cross beam high above him. His hands were bound to the rings but his feet and knees reached the floor, and now buckled beneath him. Behind him was a massive wall of smoke, and through that smoke hissed curling firebrands that lashed out at odd intervals.

Another one raked across Armaeus's back, laying open his flesh in a river of fire. As I watched, horrified, Armaeus closed the wound with a grunt of exertion, the skin knitting together in time for an equal and opposite lash to strike him from the other side.

Unable to contain my mind the way I could contain my voice, my thoughts screamed out again. *Armaeus, what are you doing?*

"You should not be here."

To my surprise, Armaeus's voice didn't sound in my mind as I'd expected it to, utilizing the telepathic connection he'd established with me more than two years ago. And it certainly wasn't coming from his mouth. As I watched, the Magician hung forward, his head and hair drenched in sweat, blood pooling beneath him from the wounds he'd already healed. His skin was scored both black and white from the effects of the lash, and sparks of electricity danced across his arms as they strained to maintain hold on the Olympic rings. He looked like a man who was completely spent, not someone who'd been in casual conversation with me not fifteen minutes earlier.

I narrowed my eyes, then spoke aloud. Loudly. "How long have you been here playing Hurt the Magician? Because that's way more blood than you could produce with ten minutes' worth of honest exercise."

"Miss Wilde—"

"Don't you *Miss Wilde* me. You want to hook up with a bunch of nymphs in a magic six-way, that's your business, but since when is self-mortification your kink?"

The laugh that sounded was long, deep, and decidedly dark—and it still didn't come from Armaeus's slumped body, but from somewhere high above me in the chamber. "There is much that you know about the Magician of the Arcana Council, and much that he has yet to share with you."

My brows went up. It sure as heck sounded like the Magician talking to me, but he didn't typically refer to himself in the third person. "Can I assume it's not Armaeus I'm talking to?"

"I am merely one aspect of Armaeus. The clinician, you could call me. I watch. I observe. I track. I record."

"Yeah, I know that part of him. It's the same aspect that tends to stare at me like I'm a bug he's about to pin to a foam core board like a kid at a science fair. For the record, you're one of the dickier aspects of the guy."

Against the Olympic rings, Armaeus convulsed in a laugh—a laugh that ended in a tortured groan as another lash of fire struck out, this one flaying open the meat of his arm.

"Will you stop that?" I demanded.

"Why?" This voice came from the other side of the space, and the sound was little more than a seductive purr. "What is it about the pain you see, the agony, that upsets you so...Miss Wilde?"

The sound of my name spoken in the bodiless voice that was Armaeus and yet not Armaeus, not all of him, was unnerving. As I squared my shoulders, the second voice started up again, this time with a long and mocking laugh.

"The Magician spends a great deal of his time protecting you. You think that he is protecting you from all outside horrors of this world. Occasionally, you think that he's protecting you from himself. But the Magician knows far more about you than you realize, Miss Wilde. He knows that he is protecting you—"

"No!" With what seemed like a gargantuan effort, the corporeal Armaeus gathered his feet beneath him and stood, easing the strain on his arms as he grasped the Olympic rings with fingers drenched in sweat and blood. He swung around toward me, his eyes naked with pain.

"What are you doing here?" I gasped, and this time, I did move forward. Not all the way, though. Armaeus had inscribed a circle around him that contained both his little torture stand as well as the billowing smoke from which the snaking fire lashes emerged. "What is this test?"

"Not—what you think," Armaeus managed, but the test apparently wasn't finished yet. Another lash of fire slashed out of the wall of smoke, catching him across the upper shoulders and driving him back to his knees. I pursed my lips together, feeling tears surge up within me. Armaeus was a demigod. He'd lived with and worked his magic for hundreds of years before I'd been born. It wasn't my place to judge him for what he felt he needed to do. It also wasn't my place to try to stop him from his magical practice simply because I couldn't bear to see him suffer.

"Not — what you think," Armaeus growled again. He was looking at me and so didn't see the enormous cat-o'-nine-tails that burst out from the smoke until it was practically upon him, raking over his head and back. He threw back his head and howled, and my third eye snapped open...then blinked.

The Magician's entire body had been fractured into a dozen different entities. He was there, in the center, glorying or wallowing in as much pain as I'd ever seen him endure. But at the same time, his mind manifested its varied aspects all around Armaeus. There was the clinician, the seducer, the teacher, the student, the tyrant, and the healer, and nearly a half-dozen more. All of them roared up to the heavens like they were in a battle with the gods themselves, and then —

And then the gods roared back.

The thunderclap of power had the effect of a sonic boom, dropping me to the floor as Armaeus flopped forward, his body bouncing off the mat beneath his feet and springing forward again, like a child strapped to an out-of-control swing. I staggered back up to my knees, but the pressure pummeling me was enough to take my breath away. Standing took tremendous strength, and I lunged forward, desperate to reach Armaeus as he hung lifeless in the rings. With each step, a reverberation of the sonic boom pushed its way up my legs, rattling my bones, until by the time I reached Armaeus's side, I'd lost all sense of balance. I flung myself at him, sliding down his body, both of us now drenched in his gore and sweat. He was speaking, but it was a language so ancient, I couldn't translate it, and it sounded more like he was repeating a mantra over and over again.

Eventually, the words pieced themselves together in my mind.

"The many become the one. The one, the many. The scattered becomes the whole, the whole, within each of the scattered."

I had no idea what any of that meant and focused on loosening Armaeus's hands from the heavy rings. When I finally got one wrist unhooked, he sagged forward, seeming to break from his thrall.

"You...shouldn't be here," he gasped, and I snorted, my focus on the other ring.

"Then you shouldn't do such a bad job of projecting your illusion to take a meeting with me. I totally knew you were faking it. I didn't expect to find you faking it for torture porn."

He half coughed, half gasped, and the next strike happened so fast, I reacted on pure instinct. The lash of power struck out from the billowing smoke like electric fire, and I swung Armaeus out of its range.

It was too late for me to form a fireball with my hands. Instead, I did what any red-blooded woman with her back up against a wall, her weapons useless, staring an honest-to-gods alien in the face would do.

I screamed full and bloody murder.

CHAPTER TWELVE

T ruly, there are moments when I feel you're wasted
on the Magician, no matter how much I love him.
And verily, I do love him so."

I opened one eye, though there was no need for me
to do so. I was surrounded in utter darkness, with
nothing to indicate that the Devil of the Arcana Council
was beside me except for the rich, mocking sensuality of
his voice. But I knew immediately he wasn't alone.
"Who's with you?" I gasped, my voice ragged.

"I am," Danae said quietly from the darkness. "I was
the one who alerted Kreios to the danger you were in,
and he helped me get you out."

That made me pause for a second. I'd been in
danger? I mean, sure, there was the whole tentacle flog
monster thing that had rushed me after I'd thrust
Armaeus out of the way, but…danger?

And how had Danae known I was in trouble?

"What happen—" I swallowed hard, wincing
against the pain. "What happened?"

"You shouldn't be able to enter the Magician's lair
when he's invoking spells at that level. The fact you did
so without even working that hard is something that
will be occupying Armaeus's next round of studies for,

I suspect, at least a century or two. Fortunately, he'll have a significant period of time to study that."

"Is he okay?"

"Of course," Kreios said, sounding amused I'd even ask. "If you were to question him, he would say it was merely one of a myriad of potential outcomes for which he was eminently prepared."

"He didn't look all that prepared to me. What was he doing?"

Kreios moved beyond the pentagram. "He didn't give me his protocol. Can you describe what you saw?"

"He was hanging on some sort of sports apparatus, like Olympic rings, and getting the crap blasted out of him by something beyond a wall of smoke. Tentacles would come out and grind him up or cut him clear through to the bone, and then he'd heal himself."

"And then?" Kreios pressed.

I pursed my lips, remembering. "And then he started talking to me with different voices, and after that, he sort of…" I let my own words trail off, my mind racing ahead. "I think I might have blacked out for a minute there."

Fortunately, neither Kreios nor Danae had the kind of mind-reading abilities that Armaeus did, and my mental barriers were more than enough to keep them from following my thoughts. But the reality was, Armaeus had broken into multiple personalities. That was exactly what I'd seen in his lair. And who else had recently been the subject of a dissociative identity disorder? None other than Abigail Strand, the last Justice of the Arcana Council.

Was Armaeus doing research into what might happen to me, if I followed the same path that Abigail had? Or was he pursuing some other random curious path?

I shook my head, trying to clear it of dread. "Where is he now?"

"He reached out to me once your presence left him. He was in no position to follow you. However, he knew the energy to pull you free most likely came from Danae." I could almost hear Kreios's lips quirk into a smile. "Though you were unaware of the forces working on your behalf, I assure you, Armaeus was very focused on your safety, even in the face of his own distress."

"So he knew how…I got here? And he allowed it?"

"He didn't have a choice," Danae drawled. "That's how weak he was, no matter what Kreios would have you believe."

A match was struck, then another, and soon I was surrounded by five thick pillar candles, each at the far ends of a pentagram — with me squarely in the middle of it.

I froze, looking at the deeply etched lines of chalk.

"Exactly where am I?" I asked carefully. "And why am I in one of your little Etch-a-sketches?"

"I took precautions," Danae said simply. "When I saw you in your office. I gathered items you had touched, several strands of hair. Items from your desk."

I lifted my brows. The tour Mrs. French had given Danae took on a whole new meaning. "You know that's super creepy, right? It's only because I trust you that I'm not completely freaked out right now. But I may be freaked out later, I'm warning you."

"I've been working on a theory about you, Sara," Danae replied, unperturbed. "You started working with the Arcana Council when you were little more than an artifact hunter and Tarot card reader. You had no formal training and even less predisposition for that training."

"I was really, really good at finding stuff," I argued, peering in her direction through the glare of the candles. "That seemed to work out for me."

"It did. But then you began working more in earnest with the Magician of the Arcana Council. Do you remember when you and I first met?"

I cast my eyes skyward, staring into the darkness. "We were in Las Vegas, and...dealing with a god-containment problem. You came to help reinforce the ley lines beneath Las Vegas."

"Exactly. Here I was, one of the oldest and most well-known witches in the northern hemisphere, and I was being asked to support a young woman who barely knew what a witch was. You stared at me as if you'd never seen any of my kind before."

"You know, I'd been kind of busy." I struggled half upright now, curling my knees beneath me. I still felt a little woozy, so I wasn't much in the mood to stand up, but I felt like this was the kind of information that should at least be taken sitting up.

Danae's laugh was quietly amused. "And yet, even then I sensed your abilities as a spell caster, as a sorceress in your own right. I was happy to support you in your efforts. I also noted that the Magician already loved you more than he loved his own life."

I rolled my eyes, though the effect was lost in the gloom. "He needed more cannon fodder to target his own spells, if I'm recalling correctly."

"He needed you, perhaps more than I truly realized. His need for you is even greater now. You are arguably one of the world's most quickly evolving magic wielders. Some would say you could easily become a consecrated witch, should you wish."

"I'm no witch," I said, frowning down at the pentagram. "And I'm not big on spells. What I do is…" I shrugged. "Simply what I do."

"You're correct. But as one of the strongest sorceresses in the world at this moment, you could reasonably be a target for the energy of Myanya. Do you understand the danger of this?"

"Wait, what?" I shook my head. "Danae, you've got this completely backward. I was there in Vlad the Impaler's cave of doom when he summoned Myanya. I was also there at the tail end of the Jones brothers nearly getting their ankles ground up like hamburger. In both cases, I was on the outside of the pentagram, not the inside. I would have noticed if the reverse had been true."

"And in both cases, you made yourself known to the scarred warrior's spirit. That means she can identify you."

"Well, that's super unfortunate since I'm the one who's supposed to be identifying her." I rubbed my head. "How does this figure into you pulling me out of Armaeus's little torture pageant?"

"By allowing me into your inner sanctum, you accepted my care and concern for you. I heard your pain and trauma, and I moved to end it."

"Uh-huh. Once you made a little voodoo doll of me, right? And, what, you invited Kreios over to help you set up your candles?"

The silence between us suddenly grew heavy in the room, and I peered around, trying to fix both of them with my glare. I couldn't do it.

"Are you guys hooking up?" I asked, trying not to choke on a laugh. "If so, I am *really* sorry for harshing your mellow."

"My dear Sara Wilde, your imagination has always been one of your best features," Kreios practically purred, but I noticed he didn't confirm or deny. "I was consulting with the Mistress of Swords because her challenge is one that intrigues me. It's not every day that we have the rage-filled warrior prophecy enacted in our world."

"Well, maybe not every day, but at least every twenty-eight years, right? For you guys, what, that's basically about as often as you go in to get your oil changed?"

"The prophecy was broken in 1962, and it was not detected in 1990, though it's possible that it was fulfilled but the legacy of the scarred warrior never acted upon," Danae said. "That brings us to today."

"Back up, Sparky." I waved her off. "What do you mean, never acted upon? What's the point of going through all that pain if you're not going to reap the rewards?" There was something else pinging in the back of my mind too, something Armaeus had mentioned. What was it?

"The spirit of Myanya is not for the faint of heart," Danae said, cutting through my thoughts. "And though she chooses her vessels as carefully as she can, she has experienced more than a few times the results of overmatching the physical and emotional strength of the vessel in which she places her faith. In 1962, her attempts to overpower her chosen warrior and draw her deep into the veil of submission failed."

The dots connected abruptly. "Armaeus said that too. The vessel witch she chose rejected her?"

"That seems to be the case. It was not well publicized, of course, but what I've uncovered is that a young woman in Moscow successfully fended off Myanya's attempt to make her the vessel witch to bring the prophecy to life. Then, in 1990, Myanya either did not make the attempt, or she did and the result was the death or mental destruction of the vessel witch she chose."

"Death or mental destruction? You guys seriously don't know which way it went? How bad is your record keeping, anyway? Because it seems like this is kind of an important prophecy to keep track of."

"As you might say, we've been a little bit busy," Danae said. "The prophecy of Myanya seems quite important now, but there were many who felt it was permanently laid to rest with the resistance of Iskra Mikhailova in 1962, since Myanya didn't fully inhabit her vessel but was rejected outright."

"Iskra? That's the witch who resisted the crazy?"

"In a manner of speaking, yes." Danae paused. "Are you feeling yourself again? We can remove you from the pentagram if so. You've received the full blessing."

I let that little nugget of nuttery slide right by me, but I was more than ready to exit the pentagram of doom. I stood, only a little wobbly, and crossed over the chalk markings. I could feel the pressure try to slow me down, and then Kreios was there, his strong hands grasping my forearms, pulling me through.

I blinked in the suddenly bright light.

"That's...kind of a lot of juju for you all to be throwing at me, no offense," I groused, looking around. I recognized where we were now — the inner sanctum of Kreios's office at the Flamingo. Not the interior oasis he favored so much, but a room resplendent with old-world art, thick wooden furniture, and deep plush carpet. And, of course, Kreios himself.

The Devil of the Arcana Council assumed many forms, but his most usual glamour was the one he was effecting now — his hair long and loose, tawny against his tanned skin, his lean, elegant form draped in a white linen shirt and loose, ragged-hem trousers. His feet were shod with sandals that looked more at home on the beach than in a casino in Las Vegas, but the look always managed to work for him. And for once, his jade-green eyes weren't fixed on me, assessing me with his coolly seductive gaze, but on the carpet.

Carpet that was now stained a deep black from scorch marks in the shape of a pentagram.

"Sorry about that," I said.

"Life is little more than an illusion," Kreios countered, but he didn't remove the evidence of the pentagram. If anything, he continued to study it with deep interest. "I remain curious for Mistress Danae to explain how it evolved from the design we initially created, however."

He pointed to the pentagram, and I saw what he meant. Two crescent moons that interlocked with each other, one open to the east, the other open to the south. "I assume that symbol is important?" he continued.

Danae nodded, but she didn't look happy. "It's the symbol of Myanya," she said. "During the very first incarnation of her prophecy." She looked at me. "But there's no reason for it to be appended here. Her energy was not drawn upon for this effort. To my knowledge, there is nothing in what you were doing to trigger her awareness."

"Nothing in what I was doing, perhaps," I said. "But you pulled me out of Armaeus's library. Could something there be relevant to her?"

"It shouldn't be. The only reason for those conjoined crescent moons to be drawn is if Armaeus or yourself were already locked in combat with Myanya. And neither of you were."

"Well, I wasn't," I corrected. "I have no idea what the heck Armaeus was up against. It didn't feel like the incarnation of divine feminine rage, though. I mean, there was plenty of rage, but I got the sense it was pretty gender neutral."

"It wouldn't have been Myanya unless Armaeus was directly seeking to draw her out," Danae said. "That's not it."

She paused, then fished about at her waist, and I realized she was wearing a thick leather belt hung with bags, along with a pentacle and a cup, that I could see. The tools of her trade, at least some of them. A moment later, she drew out a slender silver pendant on a chain and handed it to me. "I would be blessed if you would wear this, Justice Wilde. It's meant to go under your clothes, next to your skin."

I squinted at it as I took it, noting her formal use of my name. The pendant was an ankh, hung from a chain long enough for it to hit my belly button. "What's it do?"

"Nothing," she said, waving her hand. "A talisman for safety, nothing more."

I glanced at Kreios, and he gave me a barely perceptible nod, so I shrugged. Danae visibly relaxed as I slipped the long, thin chain over my neck, tucking the necklace beneath my shirt. Danae was right, I barely felt it, and she *had* just pulled my feet from the fire. I could wear her friendship bracelet for a while.

"Is there anything else he told you about Myanya?" Danae asked as I turned back to her. "Where to find her, or what he'd learned?"

"Not really," I said. "He was intent on me taking Nikki and going to Moscow to interview Iskra, and he said that trip was something he couldn't take with me. At the time, I thought he was simply playing coy, but now I think his reticence had more to do with the fact that he was getting the snot beaten out of him than any issue with his passport.

"Iskra." Danae nodded. "She was questioned heavily at the time of her trial, but it's possible there is information she will share differently now, with the benefit of so many years to consider what transpired at St. Basil's."

I perked up at that. "Armaeus mentioned that too. Aren't there rules about that?"

"The Eastern Orthodox church is an entity unto itself, and far more careful with the pagan wellspring from which it grew than its Western European counterparts," Danae said. "Nevertheless, Iskra did what she could to protect herself from Myanya's energy. She feared that she would be targeted. Her energy was very strong, very pure. She had to dig deep within herself to be able to find the strength to resist the primal rage of the scarred warrior witch." Danae sighed. "And she was not left without her own scars, to be sure. Afterwards, the Muscovite coven faltered in strength significantly, which was quite a blow. It had been a power seat for magic up to that time. The energy of Myanya was held to blame."

"So what you're saying is, Myanya's not very popular."

Danae curled her lip. "On the contrary. Every season has its dark side when the old ways seem far more successful than the new. Wherever that nostalgia for the power of the ancients lies, that's where Myanya will target her next vessel witch."

"Well then, hopefully Iskra can shed some light on what to do once we find Myanya. And Danae?" I waited until she met my eyes, and gave her a smile. "Thanks. I'm not sure what I was up against in Armaeus's library, but I appreciate you having my back."

"You're welcome," she sighed. "I only wish I'd been there earlier."

"Why?"

"Mistress Danae worries." Kreios turned us both easily toward the door he opened to the main part of the Flamingo Casino. He was a big fan of the truth, and given the smile on his face, he was deeply relishing the truth he was about to share with me, despite the stricken look on Danae's face. "She believes that what you experienced in Armaeus's library damaged you, but I disagree. There is nothing you encountered while working with the Magician that you can't handle, now and evermore. By his careful design."

That sounded like a trap about to spring, barely hidden in the high grass of deliberately complex language. I narrowed my eyes at Kreios, but he merely gestured forward. "After you, Sara Wilde."

CHAPTER THIRTEEN

Y"ou're kidding me. This is where Myanya attempted to get her grind on in 1962?"

We stood in the middle of Red Square, looking toward the iconic St. Basil's cathedral, its lofty towers topped with huge onion-shaped turrets even more breathtaking in person than they'd been in all the tourist guides and online travelogues I'd been able to read before Nikki and I had made our hasty trip to the Kremlin. That monstrosity of a government building sat behind us and to the right, looming like a malevolent god, and it was all I could do not to look over my shoulder to make sure it hadn't advanced upon us while I wasn't looking.

We'd left Danae and Kreios in Vegas. Kreios to keep an eye on Armaeus, and Danae to track reports of Myanya's global appearances, in hopes of narrowing down the possibilities of where she and her vessel witch were camping out. Meanwhile, Nikki and I needed to figure out what to do with Myanya when we caught her.

I focused on St. Basil's. The church—while undeniably beautiful—was simply that, a church. A very Catholic, orthodox church that was a rabbit warren of tiny chambers and intricate passageways on the inside, the only real space to breathe evident when you looked up. We'd been booked on an official tour on this chilly morning, but nothing about this place felt like the setting for a witch to have a throwdown with an ancient spirit facing the fated cycle of possession, oppression, then redemption. Especially a witch who beat the odds and the spirit and lived to tell the tale.

"This is where Armaeus said Iskra Mikhailova would meet us," I said, though I didn't want to think too much about the Magician and his reasons for sending me off so abruptly...let alone the whole romper room setup in his library. Had I missed any sign in his penthouse office of something deeper going on? He'd been acting weird—the whole Council had been acting weird, but was it really my job to keep up with their internecine politics? I had a job to do here. I was *busy*.

Still, I couldn't help extend a thin thread of connection all the way to the other side of the world, where I suspected Armaeus was still holed up in his fortress. I wanted to feel him, sense him. Know he was there.

I got nothing back.

"If so, she'd better get a move on," Nikki grumbled. "I didn't douse this coat in borax for no reason." She fluffed her coat, which didn't need the help—a voluminous bright white faux-fur tent that ended well north of her knees, the better for her to show off her tights-clad gams that were also encased in fur-topped knee-high boots, complete with thick, chunky platform heels and faux-fur tassels. She also had a bright red faux-fur hand warmer and a matching cap that settled on her ice-blonde updo as if defying the wind to knock it askew. The wind, wisely, didn't take that challenge.

I drove my hands deeper into my wool-lined leather duster, my outerwear of choice for the brisk Russian morning. We'd made the journey to Moscow with my evolving skill of teleporting. While I was still unfortunately singed by each new experience — which explained Nikki's garment treatments — I had to admit I appreciated the advantages of avoiding commercial air travel.

First, there was the benefit of instant gratification. You needed a flight to Moscow? You simply braced yourself and went. Particularly when traveling to places like Moscow, there was an added benefit of no customs lines. I was becoming more and more of a fan.

In fact, there was no official record of us even being in Moscow, now that I thought of it. I frowned. How many people in the world had this ability, besides myself and Armaeus? Because the temptation to use such a skill for personal gain could very well prove impossible to ignore. As one of the more avaricious artifact hunters back in my day, I felt a familiar itch along my spine…

"Justice Wilde!" The voice was thickly accented, but the words were in English, and Nikki and I both turned to see a young woman bustling through the square, her stylish wool coat swinging along her calves above sleek leather boots. She was wearing a cap similar to Nikki's, though also in wool, and her face was bright, blue eyed, and — undeniably young. This wasn't Iskra Mikhailova. She could have been Iskra's granddaughter, if Iskra had ever had children. Which, after her date with Myanya, she hadn't.

"Welcome, welcome," the woman said, turning immediately. "I'm Svetlana Mater. Thank you for meeting me here. Dr. Mikhailova is not so happy with the cold in our beautiful city anymore, but she wanted you to go through the church before you met her. The church, it is everything to her and her story. Especially if the prophecy…" She shook her head, pursing her lips. "Well. There will be time for that. You have seen the cathedral?"

"Only the outside," I hedged. "But we could take the tour. We're signed up."

"Ah! You have not done so already. I was hoping that was the case. I will show you a bit of a secret, if you would allow me." She flashed us both a winning smile and started moving briskly across the square towards the church. "I have credentials for us all, given Dr. Mikhailova's position with St. Basil's."

"Which is what, exactly?" I asked. "I thought she worked with the university."

"She did, for many years. But what most do not know is that, though St. Basil's no longer had any religious function at the time of her trial, Dr. Mikhailova secretly converted to Russian Orthodoxy Catholicism immediately after her tribulation and became a nun. She remained in service to the Father for eight years before exiting again, and has made volunteering at the cathedral her life's work thereafter."

We'd entered the cathedral's main doors by now, bypassing the ticket booth with a flash of our credentials, and Svetlana pitched her voice higher, talking about the nine chapels housed within the building as she ushered us past two other groups. "The original church was commissioned by Ivan the Terrible to honor his victory over Mongol forces in 1552, and in the very beginning, it was as white as snow, the domes painted gold. But very little is known about how the church evolved over time. Some believe the structure was intended to mimic the churches of Jerusalem. Some say the idea of building eight churches around a ninth chapel in the center was intended to evoke the symbol of the eight-pointed star. Regardless, the result has the effect of being buried under several layers of mysticism, cloaked and framed in it, if you will. It's a labyrinth in all directions but up, which is very much intended."

"Up," Nikki echoed, peering skyward. "Not so useful if you don't have wings."

"And yet we are all angels sent here to learn, are we not?" Svetlana said cryptically. "So in the end, an exit up is all we truly need."

She let us chew on that as we meandered through several more corridors, taking in the crowded red-hued splendor of two of the chapels. Finally, when we were alone in a narrow hallway lined floor to ceiling with heavily framed paintings, she turned and gave us a smile. "You are not allowed to touch anything or take any flash photography, you understand? It is vitally important."

I frowned at her. That sort of warning was typically given at the start of any proper tour. "Of course—"

I lurched back as Svetlana's hand swept forward, cracking against the wall. Instantly, the panel clicked and swung inward, and she urged us forward rapidly. "It becomes harder and harder to open this door, but there is no way for us to get in to fix the hinges now that Dr. Mikhailova is no longer on the restoration committee. So we do not use it so much, but you had to see what is above to understand what is below."

"I—sure." I had no idea what Svetlana was talking about, but I was willing to go along with it if it got us to Iskra more quickly.

We descended into a stairway that had none of its own lighting. Svetlana used her phone as a makeshift lantern to guide the way. The stairway curved down thirteen steps, clearly cut inside a column of stone given its tight spiral, as if it were some sort of refurbished well. After a short landing, it continued down another thirteen steps. "You won't have to exit this way, of course," Svetlana murmured. "But you understand the sense of this space now, I think."

"When was this built?"

"We believe this underground chamber was created at the same time as the primary cathedral, the mechanism to its entry cleverly concealed. Ivan the Terrible had no real need to hide here from his enemies, but he was nothing if not a practical ruler. The rumors that circulate regarding the blinding of the original builder to keep him from ever building a similar church stem in part from the creation of this underground escape route. While it is a historical fact that no such blinding occurred, the threat was leveled not to keep the builder from erecting a more beautiful church later on, but from revealing the location of this hideaway. It proved an effective deterrent."

"But if Ivan didn't really need it, what was it used for?" Nikki asked. "Because it's definitely been used."

I squinted in the confined space as Svetlana flipped switches, flooding the subterranean space with light. This chamber resembled a drawing room from a bygone era—large wingback chairs, shelves lined with books, couches draped with heavy blankets. I glanced around, trying to get a sense of how the place was heated and lit, if, in fact, it was intended to remain hidden. "The custodians have to be aware of this place."

"The custodians, no. Certain agents in the government, of course. But the information about what lies beneath St. Basil's is a question of national security, and it always has been. As a result, very few people know the truth. Dr. Mikhailova was part of the Muscovite coven, which was active at the time St. Basil's was built and provided workers for the project. The information about not only the location of this shelter but also the secret passages that link to it is a coven secret." She smiled. "And now your secret."

A dry, rattling laugh sounded from deep in the room, and the voice that followed it was as soft and murmuring as the air around us. "There are no secrets that can be held forever from Justice."

I turned to see one of the piles of blankets shift. As Svetlana hurried to the center of the room, a petite woman with white hair stood, wobbling only slightly. Out of habit, my third eye flicked open, and both women lit up like Christmas trees. Not every witch was a high-powered Connected, or even Connected at all, but both Iskra and her young assistant qualified. Interesting.

"Justice Wilde." Iskra inclined her head.

I roused myself to action, moving across the thick woven rug to grasp her hand. She held mine with both of hers, and her eyes narrowed as she dragged her thumb across the barely healed wound in my palm.

"Nul Magis," she murmured. "Wielded by a very strong magician—and now residing in you. It won't help you with Myanya."

It was all I could do not to pull my hand back sharply, embarrassed, but Iskra had called it. The holdover toxin had taken up permanent residence in the palm of my hand, and I hadn't had time to see about removing it.

That said, I wasn't in the mood to have any of my secondary skills second-guessed.

"I wasn't planning on using it for Myanya," I informed her, gently removing my hand from her questing grasp. She turned and reached for Nikki's hand, then paused, but was a second too late. Though any high-level Connected could block Nikki's ability to read memories if they were expecting it, if Nikki caught them off guard, it was all over. Nikki pumped the old woman's hand with enthusiasm, her jaw working as she quickly and efficiently read Iskra's memories. Her brows shot high as she turned to me, but Iskra started speaking.

"You have come for knowledge on how to beat the spirit of Myanya, to keep it from flowering to its full force, but I say to you, you're already too late. Myanya is a hungry spirit who must see the fulfillment of the cycle. She has no other choice."

"Well, about that," I said, as Svetlana clucked and fussed at Iskra's side, eventually getting the old woman to take her seat again. "Why is she back? She apparently skipped one generation. Why not two?"

Iskra grunted. "Skipped? No. She didn't skip a generation. She changed tactics. The witch she chose was already one in an established coven, already promised to a male not of her choosing. The girl's subjugation was preordained, and there was nothing she could do to stop it. Regrettably, she did not survive the ordeal of Myanya's challenge. The coven was powerful enough to cover up the evidence of what happened and let it be believed that no attempt had been made."

I stared at her, two things bothering me about this recitation. One, that it appeared to be common knowledge to Iskra, and two, that it belied what the Jones brothers had claimed. "The coven can hide all trace of Myanya from their peers? Even from the men who reportedly get some sort of supernatural call to action when Myanya rises?"

"They can and they must. It is only when the prophecy is fully executed that the coven that takes on this great power is able to leverage it for their own benefit. Far more often, the initiate witch dies during her trial and tribulation, or comes back so scarred and weak from the ordeal that she is of no use as a figurehead to her coven. This prophecy was conceived in a far more brutal time. Over the centuries, the covens have not kept up with their training as rigorously as they should. As a result, we've grown weaker, particularly in the face of such primal power."

"What about you?" Nikki asked. "You not only were chosen by Myanya, you rejected her. And you lived to tell the tale."

"Not without great personal loss," Iskra whispered, her voice cracking. "I believe Svetlana told you of my time in the convent after the trial. That was in payment to a group of exiled nuns, whose prayer on my behalf dramatically altered the outcome of my challenge. I entered their order as a novice and remained in service for eight years instead of the usual five. When I left, they allowed me to maintain access to these sacred rooms. I had long since recovered from the physical trauma of my trial, but it took me those eight years to expunge the mental trauma. The spirit of Myanya does not give up her chosen easily, and I will feel her power evermore."

"You *still* feel her," Nikki groaned empathetically, ever the cop and psychic who had connected with far too many victims of especially heinous crimes.

Iskra nodded and her gaze shifted to me. "Which is why I can feel her now, and her building fury at being denied her rightful vessel."

I straightened. "You know who she's targeting?"

The old woman grimaced. "Yes, to my everlasting dismay. She's targeting the last remaining member of my family."

CHAPTER FOURTEEN

W hat?" I blurted. "The doomed witch was a member of your family?"

Nikki sighed beside me. "Hell hath no fury like a prophecy spurned."

Iskra didn't respond, which was okay because I was still ramping up into full freakout.

"Whoa, whoa, whoa, whoa," I said, holding up my hands. "You're telling me Myanya has made this a family issue? That ever since 1962, she's been targeting your descendants—so that means not only now, but in 1990, too? I thought you couldn't have kids after what she did to you."

"I couldn't," Iskra said, her words matter-of-fact. "But I could before."

Before, I thought. Of course. And then: *oh no.*

Iskra nodded, watching me. "To protect myself from a future determined by those other than myself, I defiantly delivered a child when I was eighteen years old, a child I gratefully gave to a family who could love and support my baby in a way that I could not, given the path I was on."

"You chose to have a child? Doesn't that..." I made a vague swirling motion with my hands at the approximate level of my uterus, the sum total of my knowledge of how coven magic worked. "Mess with your power, or something?"

"It absolutely did, which was exactly the point." At my startled look, Iskra chuckled. "This generation, they think reproductive rights are a modern issue. And not all covens are the same, of course. Some have been formed on the basis of equality between the two sexes, with very little regard for how one's access to magic is affected by your awakening sexuality. But the coven that harbored me had different rules. Virginity allowed the initiate witch access to her untapped potential. A sexually awakened witch had a different, though in many ways lesser, access. Finally, a witch who has delivered a child had her access split. I not only delivered a child, I sent her to a secular home. It was my full intention that she never learn who and what she was, at least not by teaching pressed upon her by a coven. It was my intention that she grow up free."

Nikki made a face. "And if she had questions?"

"I made provisions for that as well, but she never tripped any of those triggers. Understand, though, at the time, my priority was my own body, my own abilities. For me, in my coven and with my abilities, I had a very clear choice. I could take ownership of my body and my life, lose my virginity and thus sully my power on my own terms by giving birth to a child who would split but never augment my abilities…or I could be set up as a pawn for those in power. Mind you, I wasn't even thinking of the prophecy of Myanya at this time. I was worried about far more mundane concerns." She smiled, the lines in her face crinkling as her eyes danced. "And of course, I was in love, as far as anyone knew."

"Of course." Nikki snorted. I could only stare at Iskra. Perhaps this was the gift that old age gave—perspective on troubles that must have seemed insurmountable at the time.

"So, wait," I said, my head beginning to hurt. "You weren't in love?"

Iskra cast her clear blue gaze at me, her smile turning ineffably sad. "Of course, Justice Wilde, but not as much with the young man in question as I was with bringing life into the world on my own terms. I thought this child would be safe, far away from the path of a witch. I thought she would be blessed and consecrated, grow tall and strong and happy, unencumbered by the expectations of a community she did not choose. I purposely did not keep track of her progress with her adoptive family, and then, only a few short years later, I encountered Myanya. In the years that followed, I redoubled the protections around my daughter, seeking to ensure her safety, but ultimately, it was not enough. By the twenty-eighth year after my assault, I knew only that my daughter was happy, healthy, and most definitely not an initiate."

"Someone lied to you," I guessed. "Your coven?"

She sighed, glancing away. "I believed what I wanted to believe."

She wouldn't be the first parent to do so, but Iskra was no ordinary parent. "How did she become a witch if you sent her into a secular family?"

"Because there is nurture, and there is nature. The path we choose for another is not always the path they seek for themselves. My daughter had no knowledge of me, no idea of the trials I endured. I never wanted her to see me, what I had become."

The woman before me was beautiful, wrapped in a radiance I didn't need my third eye to appreciate.

Distractedly, I realized my third eye had dropped shut again. I flicked it open, then realized why I'd kept it closed. It was weirdly bright in this basement room, no doubt the result of a long history of Connected influence, whether the church was officially sacred ground or otherwise.

But Iskra was still talking, and my attention refocused on her. "In retrospect, my decision to leave my daughter to her own life was a mistake. But I had no way of knowing at the time that my attempt to protect my beautiful baby girl would in fact lead her to her own demise."

I flinched. "Wait, so she *did* die as a result of Myanya targeting her."

"She did. And because Myanya never completely left me, I saw my daughter's death. I lived it as Myanya wanted me to, as punishment for refusing her. Now, however, she calls to me again, with visions of a girl who looks like me at that age. In my nightmares, Myanya whispers I should behold my granddaughter, her newly chosen vessel. I...I don't know if my daughter had a child of her own, but it's possible." She shuddered. "It's possible."

"Oh, man," Nikki muttered, and I glanced her way, but my friend wasn't looking at me. Nikki, more than most, understood the pain of watching your children grow from afar, unable to interfere with their lives. If one of her children had endured the fate Iskra's daughter had faced...

Iskra nodded. "I have no claim on my daughter, nor any right to judge her path, nor that of my granddaughter's, if she exists. We are each on this earth to fulfill a purpose we have chosen hand in hand with the goddess, and it is not my place to direct anyone's path but my own. But the fact remains that, though I believed I was the last woman of my line remaining, I can feel that Myanya has returned. I can sense the malevolent power within her, like a quickening in the heart, an anger in the blood. Even all these years later, it calls to me. I am grateful, in the end, that my daughter did not have to endure Myanya for long. But if there is another child…" Her words drifted off.

I folded my arms, disgusted with the entire idea of three generations being haunted by the same prophecy. "But I thought the spirit of Myanya was supposed to empower women."

"Not women," Iskra scoffed, the two short words the closest she'd come yet to a snap. "It is supposed to empower the coven. The vessel of the woman in whom the prophecy is fulfilled becomes a scarred warrior along the way — and that scarring is emotional, physical, and psychological. It is the true mythology of the goddess debased and defiled, only to rise up again in righteous fury, her light so strong that it cannot be shut out. Only then can she lead her coven to victory, a dawn of a new world."

"Tell me about that victory, then. Because it'd better be pretty impressive to justify that much pain."

Iskra's lips twisted. "You forget, it's a woman bearing the pain. And such pain is a sacred grace to the eyes of many, particularly in less enlightened times. But as the woman in question, you — you do know what is in store for you. Myanya's spirit makes it very clear what she intends you to endure."

"How?" Nikki put in. "You get visions? Nightmares? And how much notice do you have?"

"In my case, I had nightmares for several weeks. Always the same, where an exalted goddess is captured and delivered to the underworld, roasted on a spit and defiled for all her believers to see, then returned to the world of day a scarred warrior—smarter, stronger, more powerful, wiser. She has been broken, but she is ineffably stronger in the broken places."

"I hate that phrase," I muttered. *Stronger in the broken places.* I'd lived it too many times.

"More to the point, she leads her coven." Iskra tapped her chest. "I tried everything to avoid taking on that mantle. I dimmed my own powers. I conceived and then gave up a beautiful child. I forswore relationships. I worked hard for my independence. I wasn't about to let an ancient prophecy seeking to kindle itself in my blood undo all my hard work."

"And you succeeded."

She shook her head. "With the perspective of age, I'm not so sure of that anymore. It was only with the grace of hidden and persecuted holy sisters of that I was able to find the strength within me to fend off Myanya's challenge. It took me eight years to recover from that challenge, and a lifetime of fear and loneliness followed. So who truly won in that equation?"

We sat for a long moment in silence, then Svetlana appeared again at the door. To be honest, I hadn't noticed her stepping away. "Dr. Mikhailova, it's safe for you to leave."

"Safe?" I stood with Nikki and once more attempted to see around the room with my third eye, instinctively flinching away when the brightness bore down on me. "Why wouldn't it be safe?"

"There are many types of rage in the world," Iskra said, struggling to stand again. She picked up an elegant walking staff and leaned on it. "Some of it you can bury, some you can't."

"Amen, sister," Nikki muttered.

Staff in hand, Iskra hobbled toward the door, her back hunched, her eyes sharp beneath her corona of white hair.

"Did Danae say anything about people wanting to take Iskra out?" Nikki asked quietly as we followed behind. Svetlana opened another panel in the antechamber beyond the sitting room that led to a dark corridor of rough stone. No artwork lined the walls here, and no carpets covered the floor. I suspected we were now moving beneath Red Square to one of the nearby residential areas—all of them some distance away. We'd be underground for a while.

"Nada." I shook my head. "By all accounts, Iskra is a revered elder of the community, adored by university students, witches, and secular residents alike. No one should be targeting her."

"It's to the right, dear," Iskra said ahead.

"No, that way was blocked, Dr. Mikhailova. A construction team cracked the support structure, not realizing…" The voices of our guides dropped into easy conversation as we wove our way to the left, but I didn't miss the tension in Nikki's body. I felt it too.

"By the pricking of my thumbs," she muttered, and I reached inside my leather duster for my card deck.

"Light?"

Dutifully, she flicked her phone light back toward me, and I pulled three cards. High Priestess, Queen of Swords, Page of Swords.

Nikki scanned them too. "You think we're going to get a message from Myanya? High Priestess has to mean Iskra, though I didn't think her powers were all that high anymore."

"They're not," I said. I shoved the cards back in my pocket and felt the ungainly ridge of another two cards poking out. I snagged them and drew them out, peering down in the reflecting light. Five of Wands and the Moon. "I don't like the feeling of this."

"So the High Priestess is Iskra, and the Queen of Swords has gotta be our lost queen. Page of Swords, that's a message, and then we've got the card of confrontation as well as the card of hidden knowledge. You think we're walking into a fight?" Nikki asked when I showed her the cards.

"I think we're not being told the whole story here. I think we may be walking into an explanation we're not expecting. Maybe Iskra's been lying to us, maybe not. Either way, we could be about to face something that she's orchestrated, a betrayal." I grimaced. "That doesn't feel right, though."

"Oh, well, this does take me back," Iskra said from farther ahead. "I thought these old passages had been blocked long ago."

"They had, Dr. Mikhailova. But the construction…"

"Yes, yes, of course. It's just—well, I never thought I'd see the day when I'd willingly walk back in here. I'd never even imagined it would be safe."

"It's the safest way, Dr. Mikhailova. We're all here for you."

As Nikki and I caught up, we saw Svetlana draw back an enormous dead bolt from a metal door hinged into the stone. It swung silently into the room, and Iskra turned back to us as she entered the room behind Svetlana. "You'll forgive me if we don't tarry, but this room—it had meaning to me a long time ago."

"And it will have meaning to you again."

The voice sounded loud and strident in the small space. Nikki and I nearly crashed into an Iskra who had gone stock-still with shock. I quickly saw why. There were easily twenty hooded and cowled figures spread around a pentagram etched into the floor, and in the center of that pentagram was a white and twisting column of flame, almost—but not quite—taking on the form of a woman.

"Or, we could be walking into a fight," Nikki said, as I opened my hands wide, blue flame kindling in my palms.

The fire in the pentagram exploded.

CHAPTER FIFTEEN

It only took a heartbeat for the vortex of flame in the pentagram to fill the entire enclosed space, and the cowled figures who were standing guard at its tips strained back. They were holding the line, but they clearly had not been prepared for that level of intensity.

"What are you doing?" demanded Iskra. She stood rooted to the spot, Nikki and I flanking her. "You cannot seriously believe you can summon Myanya to this space and live, Svetlana. We are not prepared!"

"You *are* prepared." Svetlana was now facing the doctor from several feet away, though still on this side of the pentagram. She'd shucked her coat, and for the first time, I saw that she wore a chain of silver around her waist, hung with icons. Had that been why I couldn't use my third eye effectively in St. Basil's or even in the chamber immediately below the church?

Well, it was doing its job now. The witches were doing their level best to throw up a temporary wall to keep Myanya contained, which gave me a breath to study the twisting fire in the center of the pentagram. As it had been in the cave in Budapest, it was vaguely feminine in shape, but there were absolutely no markers as to facial features, height, or weight — everything was grotesquely elongated and flaring with heat, down to her fiery mane.

"I command you," a voice howled from inside the pentagram, and everyone in the room seemed jolted with electricity—except for Nikki and me. Even Iskra jerked as if she'd been electrocuted, and I drew closer to her.

"Hang in there," I said tightly, not knowing where to throw my magic. "We've got you."

"It's her," she said, her voice frozen. "It's my daughter."

"Whoa, whoa, whoa," Nikki said from the other side. "Not your daughter. Your daughter's dead. You checked that. I don't know what kind of illusion you're being fed, sweetheart, but it's not your daughter."

Iskra nodded, but I could tell she didn't believe Nikki. Or she didn't want to believe. I moved in tight beside her, but I sensed the force field around her. Iskra—or someone else—was keeping us from reaching the older witch. Meanwhile, the wall of witches opened up between Iskra and the roiling ball of fire inside the pentagram.

Iskra took a step forward.

"No," I gritted out, shooting one of the balls of flame I'd been forming toward the ceiling. It exploded against an electrical field, betraying the secrets of the coven. They weren't relying on magic alone to draw in Myanya. There was some sort of radio frequency that was beaming up and away from this cavern beneath the Red Square, apparently broadcasting on Air Crazy Witch. All they'd needed was the appropriate programming to hook their audience, and Iskra was it.

Iskra, who even now was taking another step closer to the pentagram.

I tried again. "Think about this—you know what they're trying to do."

"Do you know, Justice Wilde? Truly? Because the Justices of the past have not." This mocking accusation came from Svetlana, who was now protected by three witches of her own, which was the only reason I didn't smack her into the ground with my next ball of blue flame. "Because for all your knowledge of the practices of our world, I don't think you do. When Iskra successfully fought off the glory of the prophecy of Myanya, she didn't merely change the course of her own life direction and the course of her daughter's. She changed the course of our entire coven. By selfishly not sacrificing herself for the greater good, despite knowing that she'd long been marked for such a privilege, she kept our covenant from achieving its highest level of glory. Glory that had been promised to us through the ages, if only we were prepared when the time came. That time came, and Iskra swept it from us."

"Yeah? I don't see any of you asshats stepping forward to take the mantle of Myanya on now. If you feel so strongly about it, throw another hat in the ring."

"Myanya has already chosen her queen," Svetlana retorted. "It is she who comes to us now. The only witch in our coven who can bend her to her will is Iskra."

I stared back at her with my own mocking look. Apparently, Iskra hadn't shared with her the visions of watching her own heirs die.

"Really," I said. "A seventy-six-year-old college professor is the best you got to offer the lost queen. I'm surprised she's giving you the time of day." As I spoke, I moved forward. I didn't know what would happen if I ended up inside Myanya's pentagram, but the fact that I'd been pulled into Danae's with little or no ill effect made me curious. If I stood inside the flames with

Myanya's mental outreach creature, could I track her back to her own lair? Would I be able to figure out where the lost queen resided?

"Ariel," Iskra murmured, and I flashed my gaze to her. Her face was completely rapt, but that was the first I'd heard that name. Still, Disney Princess alert. It didn't take a genius to figure out that Ariel was the name Iskra — a brazen eighteen-year-old determined to make a different life for herself and her child — had given to her baby girl.

"She's dead, honey," Nikki tried again. "You did your best, but she's passed on."

"She's not dead!" There was an air of desperation in Svetlana's voice, and as if in response, the roiling flame in the center of the pentagram twisted and sputtered, gaining in volume. "She seeks you, Iskra. She pleads for you. If you enter the pentagram and convince her to kneel — she will not suffer. She will not be broken. She will be made whole. The shattering of her mind will be erased, and you will both live in glory, claiming the power of Myanya for our coven the way it should have been all those long years ago."

"That is utter bullshit," I spat, but the combined power of the witches deflected my anger back to me. It wasn't that they were stronger than me, I recognized instantly. It was that they were differently stronger, and I didn't know enough about their culture, their source of magic, to effectively work my way around it. I could — I would, I knew it in my heart. But I didn't think that was going to happen in time for me to help Iskra.

"All you have to do is reach out for her," Svetlana kept wheedling. "Let her touch you, hear you, know that you are waiting and ready to bring her into the coven, as the controller of the vessel witch. She will listen to you. She wants nothing more than to feel your touch and know that she is home."

No, no, no. This wasn't at all how Danae said the prophecy was supposed to go. Myanya wasn't interested in cruising in and setting up house with a controlling witch who wasn't a consort at all, but a mother. She needed her host to suffer, to bleed — and she needed a ruling force who was a witch on wheels to make that suffering happen. I might not like it, but I wasn't the one who'd come up with the prophecy. I didn't get a vote.

From the looks of things, however, Iskra was drinking the Kool-Aid. She took three long strides forward, her face now glowing in the reflected fire from the pentagram bonfire. "Ariel," she whispered, and my heart about broke for her. She lifted her hands, reaching out. "My beautiful Ariel."

"*No.*" Nikki's roar sounded above the inferno inside the pentagram, and, abandoning all hope of a magical intervention, she lowered her shoulder and body-tackled the three witches nearest Svetlana. The blonde witch screamed, and a rush of energy shot around the room in all directions — clearly, Svetlana was the most powerful witch in the room, not Iskra. The circle of witches around the pentagram faltered and nearly fell apart, even as Iskra stepped foot across the thick charcoaled line.

The wall of magic snapped shut behind her, but not before I barreled forward too, pushing in beside Iskra. I'd been riding elevators from way back. I knew this trick.

Inside the pentagram, it was — hot. Like pits of hell, surface of the sun, Vegas in mid-July hot, my skin immediately attempting to melt off my bones and the air in my throat turning to pure sulfur before I even took my first full breath.

"Iskra!" I screamed, or tried to scream, turning toward her. I could make out her face, her eyes, her lined visage somehow unaffected by the whirling torrent of pain—and I saw what I needed to.

She'd been wrong after all. Whoever she was staring at, dead in the face, it wasn't her daughter Ariel.

"You dare!" A voice as old as time lashed out, and twin rushes of fire caught up the small woman in its embrace, circling around her face, her torso, her legs and squeezing tight. Iskra glowed mirror bright for one long, breathtaking moment, then her body began to sputter and crackle, a battery shorting out. I reached her in another step and plunged my hands through the fire that enveloped her, and for just a moment, the two of us became one being, one witch…

One target.

"You dare!" the fire spirit howled again, and I whirled around, clutching Iskra tightly as I stared into the face of the vessel witch who currently harbored the spirit of Myanya.

Definitely a woman, medium build, medium height, a little taller than I was with long, dark hair, but the face on the woman was every face. It wasn't that it was nondistinct. It was literally every face that had ever served Myanya's prophecy, I suspected, most of them beautiful, most of them young, but some defying what I knew of the prophecy. Those faces were as old and wizened as Iskra's, their eyes shining bright from a sea of wrinkled skin. The woman stood in an open space but—not an outdoor space, I decided, some room that had large windows with a bright blue sky outside, indistinguishable from a million other bright blue vistas in the world. There may have been…palm trees? But I wasn't sure. Myanya was dressed in a long, black robe, its cowl shrouding her face, and as she narrowed her focus on me, her eyes went milk white.

"You dare!" she screeched again, and I tried to figure out the tonality of her cry. It wasn't high-pitched like a young girl's, or scratchy and frail like Iskra's. That only narrowed my quarry down to about a fifty-year spread. Not helpful.

The vessel witch refocused on the old woman in my arms, and a new spear of energy flew from her, piercing my hold and burying itself in Iskra's heart. I didn't even feel it pass through me, and I scowled as I focused on it quickly. With a surge of energy, I cracked its hold on the failing doctor, and the spear shattered and fell away. The vessel witch jerked back, her eyes wild with fury.

"Iskra wants no part of your prophecy," I shouted. "She was trapped into this. She's not your consort."

"She will pay for what she did," howled the spirit of Myanya, and it was all I could do not to roll my eyes.

"You killed her *daughter*," I snapped back. "I think she's paid enough."

And, just that quickly, the fire winked out.

I stood in the center of the pentagram, holding the slumped body of Iskra in my arms, and turned suddenly to find Nikki gripping Svetlana in a headlock.

"Did you—" I asked even as she barked the same question.

"Let go of me!"

The trouble past, Nikki let Svetlana break free, but the witch merely turned, then turned again.

"There is no power here," she wailed, her eyes going wide. "We—we've been stripped of all our power!"

I immediately produced a ball of blue flame, illuminating the room around us. "I'm still good."

"You!" Svetlana turned on me and held up her hands, though there was none of the force field I'd felt before. Either way, I wasn't in the mood to deal.

"We must try again," Svetlana said, her entire body trembling with the effort. "The ancient texts were clear. The path is plain. We only need our chance at the spirit of Myanya again for us to succeed. We will succeed!"

She sounded eerily like the Jones brothers, I realized. As I focused on her, I saw the long line of silver gleam at her temple, and a surge of violent vindication coursed through me. "Oh, you'll succeed, all right. Nikki?"

Without batting an eye at the order in my voice, Nikki strode toward me, leaning in as if to take Iskra from me. When she did, her eyes widened to the size of saucers, right before the edge of her blonde hair caught fire—

And Nikki, Iskra and I rematerialized a half breath later inside the coffee shop where we'd breakfasted that morning.

"Couldn't you at least poof us someplace tropical next time?" Nikki grumbled, pushing a few tables away from a bench as she slowly and carefully laid Iskra down. The other three people in the coffee shop, who clearly realized that we hadn't been there a second earlier, sat staring at us, their hands still on their mugs. They weren't leaving, though. Because: coffee.

"We've got you, we've got you," I murmured to Iskra as the woman started convulsing, more relieved than I thought possible as I flicked my third eye into action, surveying the damage. I'd more than halfway thought Iskra was already dead. I could fix broken. I couldn't fix dead.

"Here you go." Taking a deep breath, I laid my hand on her shoulder, willing myself to see her body not as flesh and blood and bone, but as a maze of circuitry, some of it still crackling bright, some of it dead, lifeless. The spear of Myanya that'd pierced her heart hadn't done the damage I'd thought it had, but the energy around her throat chakra was feeble at best, and her sacral center was nothing but ash.

Only...it'd been that way for a long time.

"Oh, Iskra," I murmured, moving my hand to a point right above her abdomen, the seat of her personal power. "What did Myanya do to you?"

"My daughter, my poor daughter," Iskra sobbed. Beside me, I could feel Nikki's strength, her solidity supporting my energy as I worked on restoring connections that had been dead for more than fifty years. There was nothing I could say to Iskra that would make her feel any better, but she would, at least in some small part, be healed.

"Hey," Nikki said, and I blinked back into partial awareness as she pointed to the TV screen. It was silent, but a scroll of English and Russian subtitles ran beneath it, letting those about to caffeinate have something to watch while they waited in line. It was a CNN Entertainment report, but the blonde talking head was grim, her mouth turning down as she mouthed words in sync to the subtitles. Some celebrity dead, it looked like. There seemed to be a lot of that going around.

"You know the guy? Or girl? Or whoever it is?" I asked distractedly. Beneath my hands, I could feel Iskra's sobs even out, her breathing regulate. She would sleep, I thought. Longer and more deeply than she probably had since Myanya had exploded her personal power center, she would sleep.

"I do not," Nikki said, regarding the TV thoughtfully. "But I will say this. That's the third luminary in Hollywood to get her star knocked out of orbit in the past week. There're simply way too many dead bodies showing up. One dead guy who was caught up in the #MeToo movement for all the wrong reasons, this woman who apparently stranded her assistant at a seedy bar while she went and partied and the woman was attacked, and a third that was a near miss—a rapper and his entourage who all should've died in the mother of all car wrecks. I don't know which one of them was the asshat getting targeted, but I've got my suspicions."

"That's...odd," I said. I had reached more deeply into Iskra now, probing at the shattered circuits around her throat. How long had it been since she'd last spoken her truth? Too long, far too long. She'd carried the curse of Myanya with her for decades, the pain overwhelming her.

"It's more than odd. It's a freaking epidemic of dead or nearly dead dickheads in a very narrow geographic space."

Suddenly, it all came together for me. My eyes widened as I stared at Nikki. "You think she's in LA? But Myanya is a spectral entity when she's in the pentagram, not a person. Presumably, the LA victims are human and were killed by a human."

Nikki nodded. "Thought about that. What if the vessel witch isn't simply sitting around painting her nails while she waits for her consorts to text their digits? What if she's using her Myanya energy to settle some scores?"

"Or...since the bodies are showing up now but none of them are fresh kills, she could have been trying to get Myanya's attention. The spirit needed to choose a vessel. Maybe this was one witch who wanted to be chosen."

"That too."

I thought of the vision I had of the vessel witch, where she stood in front of a window, framed by bright blue sky. I thought of the palm trees I'd barely glimpsed. "It's possible…" I allowed. "More than possible. It's also possible that Svetlana knows something about where the vessel witch was coming from."

"I wondered about that too."

Iskra shifted beneath us, and I nodded to Nikki. "You got her?"

"I got her," Nikki said. "You go get Svetlana."

Chapter Sixteen

I t took Gamon only a half hour to get Svetlana to give up everything she ever had the misfortune of knowing about the location of the vessel witch, and even then, we didn't have a name, only the confirmation of what we already suspected.

Where else would a prophecy look to make one unknown, hardworking witch a superstar but Los Angeles, California?

While Danae got to work securing our introduction in to the LA coven, Nikki and I needed to track down another person of interest, the rapper who'd nearly died within the last week, whom we suspected had been targeted by the vessel witch. There was no guarantee that Richard Zachariah knew how close he'd come to a date with Myanya's darker side, but if he could help us identify his attacker in any way, it was worth having a chat with him.

The LA Ink Emporium Tattoo Convention had drawn a record crowd this year, with more than two hundred tattoo artists lined up in booths throughout the convention center perched just a few miles away from open ocean. It drew an eclectic crowd, featuring some of the hottest artists in the world, and drawing everyone from the virginally skinned to those covered in ink from head to toe. There was a straight-up tattoo contest, a pin-up contest, and a Miss Ink contest, with the winner getting a tattoo from the hottest designer at the convention.

Death.

Nikki and I loitered three aisles over from where the artist most people knew as Blue was bent over a first-timer whom she'd apparently picked out of the crowd, a middle-aged woman with light brown hair and a long, lithe figure. The woman, who'd clearly never gotten a tattoo in her life, was blushing bright red as one of the oldest members of the Arcana Council pressed a needle gun into her arm.

Death cut a decidedly recognizable image as well. Slender and muscular, her hair bleached white and spiked on one side of her head, shaved on the other, today she was wearing her usual working outfit of ripped jeans, shit-kicker boots, and a muscle shirt that bared her cut biceps. One arm was untouched by ink, the other was completely covered in a sleeve of intertwining tattoos. At this very convention, there was an entire coffee table book dedicated to the artwork on Death's arm, captured with surreptitious video, found footage, and a few rare up-close and personal photos. The book was being sold by a third party, with the most popular rumor implying that the original chronicler was spending an extended stay in rehab after finally publishing the book. Needless to say, Death had offered no comments on the work, and most were afraid to ask her about it.

"You know, I think that's gotta hurt," Nikki observed. We'd been in LA only about three hours, and she had elected to go full Marilyn for our first day, from her platinum-blonde wig to her beauty mark to her trademark white dress and platinum pumps. She wasn't the only Marilyn in the crowd, but she was by far the best.

"Has to be a reason Death picked her," I said. "And the location—on her wrist. It's not like she's not going to be able to see it every time she looks down, unless she covers it up with jewelry."

"Yeah, I'm not thinking you're going to cover up Death's work," Nikki said. She looked up at the display on the ceiling, tracking the silent auction for exclusive art from "Blue." It was already up to $100,000, and it was the first day of the convention. "That'd better be some impressive art."

"You almost hope you don't end up winning it," I agreed. This close to Death, my own ink I'd received at her hands always stung, and today was no different. I absently rubbed the spot on my right arm where she'd inked an intertwined path that at the time had been a roadmap back from a very dark place, and later had been altered to allow me yet another escape. A separate patch of real estate on my left arm was given over to a tattoo that I'd gotten to ensure I could always find my way to Nikki. Because…Nikki.

"There's our boy," Nikki said, interrupting my thoughts. She nodded to the collection of men in suits at the other end of the line of artists. One of them, clearly the central star around which the others rotated, removed his jacket, revealing a tight leather vest beneath. Visible on every inch of skin around the leather was a plethora of tattoos.

Nikki filled in the details. "RZ to his rap fans, Richard Zachariah to his cult followers, and dickhead to you and me, this guy is some serious bad news to anyone paying attention. He uses a combination of synth pop and designer drugs to convey his message of domination and oppression, and he actually has churches dedicated to his name. All of it unofficial, and he makes a big deal about not taking donations from his followers except in the form of anyone who wants to come listen to his shows or buy his music."

"And this is the guy who survived Myanya's hit?" I asked, seriously impressed. "How'd he manage that?"

"Safety in numbers is all I can tell," Nikki said. "When he travels, it's always in sets of three—three different caravans of three vehicles each, no way to tell who's in what until the very beginning or end of the journey. The accident, which is how it's officially being described, was a semi barreling into one of the caravans at a crossroads, and though one of the vehicles was banged up pretty well, it wasn't the one he was in. That was three vehicles back, same make and model. So Myanya was close, and the pileup that ensued still sent everyone to the hospital. But that was a few days ago, and they clearly weren't banged up enough to keep them away from inkmageddon here."

"Good to know." I eyed RZ's entourage as they shooed off a line of potential clients and took over one of the inkslingers' stations, a curvy blonde whose billboard announced her as Taz. "How do we get close to him?"

"We don't," Nikki said, fluffing her Marilyn hair. "Apparently, he's a wannabe male witch, and I mean that in the truest negative sense of the word. Knows nothing about true magic, but once you get close, you'll notice that he's inked himself with a lot of necromancy symbols, and he's got a real hard-on for Satan and all his minions. He's also a voracious womanizer and believes that women were made to be the vessels for his seed. That kind of guy."

"I begin to understand why Myanya isn't a fan." I narrowed my eyes at Nikki. "You think he'll look at me as a potential threat?"

"Hopefully not. Because I think that, despite his asshattery, he does have Connected ability. And if that's the case, he might actually know something about the Myanya prophecy. If he does, and if he reached out to her, then that can only help us."

"That doesn't track, though," I said. "If he reached out, he'd be dead. Not just run-off-the-road dead, but *dead* dead."

"All the more reason we need to get close to him. And for that we need some bait."

"Bait," I said, smiling. One of my newer abilities was that of summoning members of the Council while I was under extreme duress, but I hadn't tried it when I wasn't in the midst of a dire emergency. Now seemed a good time to try. I knew what Nikki wanted, who she wanted. In fact, I could see him clearly, completely, perfectly formed as if he was actually…here.

The energy in the room practically buzzed with excitement as beside me, Nikki grinned. "I was so hoping you would go that route."

At the end of the long corridor, striding toward us with a broad grin, walked Aleksander Kreios, the Devil of the Arcana Council. Today he looked slightly less Mediterranean and more Hollywood chic, with his hair dark and slicked back from his beautiful face, his long, lanky body encased in an elegantly cut suit that hugged his body in all the right places. His white shirt was open at the neck, displaying the slightest brush of hair along with a heavy gold chain, and I'd bet serious money there was a ram's horn pendant hanging from that chain.

As he walked, he created his own wake of murmuring people, the clamor eventually reaching

RZ's entourage. They turned and looked, then one of them leaned over to where RZ was chatting up his tattoo artist. The rapper stood up abruptly and snapped something, right at the moment when Kreios walked by their booth, Kreios lazily turning his head to meet the rapper's stare.

I saw Kreios's face change the same time RZ saw it. Not simply an expression change either, but a full-on, man-in-a-devil mask, glistening red skin, horns close to his head, DayGlo-red eyes, and a long forked tongue that flicked out to whisk over Kreios's lips as he grinned at the rapper.

RZ shouted and fell back, and in that same instant, Kreios was back to looking all playboy cool, sweeping past the rapper's churning entourage and walking up to me. "My dear Sara Wilde, you really should summon me more often. I find it so...invigorating," he said, holding up my hand and kissing my knuckles. I felt my entire body warming, but not with sexual response so much as the reaction to the incredible level of power that was rolling off the demigod.

"Well, you do seem invigorated," I murmured.

"I'll say," Nikki cracked. "Get me a fan."

"And Nikki Dawes." Apparently not needing anywhere near the same restraint with Nikki, Kreios turned to her and enveloped her Marilyn magnificence in a full-on, back-arching swoon kiss, his hand sliding along her back and down her thigh to hike her leg high up against his own. I was standing right there, and knew it was for show, and my eyes still halfway popped out of my head.

"He's watching," I said happily.

"So don't care," Nikki sighed, still in Kreios's arms. He chuckled, then gracefully returned her to her upright and locked position.

"It is always a pleasure working with you both. I think I may need to apply for an official position in your office. You'll find I have excellent filing skil—"

"Yes. Absolutely. You're hired," Nikki interjected, and I straightened as RZ approached us, his long, swaggering gait telegraphing his nerves. "And I'm outtie. Nothing like a big strong girl to make the hands of dudes like that sweat."

To cover her departure, Kreios reached down and gathered me in another embrace, looking deeply into my eyes.

Very...very deeply.

"Is there something wrong with my retinas?" I asked, sensing RZ's approach, though I was totally fine with Kreios's inspection. He did this far better than Armaeus did, I decided. I only felt a little like a bug when Kreios stared at me.

"You've changed," he purred. "In quite the most delicious of ways. I suspect this is what is driving Danae's concerns and pushing Armaeus to such levels of self-torture. I daresay he hasn't fully recognized how much you have been altered by your ascension to—"

"Excuse me."

I was so entranced by Kreios's analysis of me that I legitimately jumped at the sound of RZ's smooth-as-buttercream voice, and I turned in Kreios's arms to stare at him. To my surprise, RZ was watching me back, his mouth curving into a smile that had predator written all over it. It was only Kreios's sudden tightening of his arms around me that made me keep my flutter on.

"Oh!" That seemed to be the right word to utter breathlessly around RZ, never mind that it was mostly due to Kreios crushing my lungs. A second later, the Devil released me, allowing me to stand on my own two feet. A real gentleman, Kreios.

"I couldn't help but notice you as you walked by," RZ said, his attention once more on Kreios. "Which I'm sure was your intention. It seems we have quite a lot in common."

His gaze once more slid to me, and I didn't have to fake my startled blink. Was RZ trying to put the moves on me?

"And I knew you had excellent taste," Kreios said, drawing RZ's attention back to him. "But I sense more than simply a kindred spirit." He sniffed the air, the move so surprising, I had to forcibly restrain myself from a grimace. "You have been indulging in the darkest of magics, Richard Zachariah, meddling with coven business."

"My business, you mean." RZ's lips stretched over his teeth, and he practically preened beneath the Devil's approving stare. "There is a prophecy about to be fulfilled. I reached out and touched its essence two weeks ago. But it was not ripe enough — it was too bold, too flashy. It needed to be wearied by the touch of other magic. Soon, though." He turned to me, his eyes alight. "Soon I will have the power of all the covens flowing through me. For the prophecy will be fulfilled here."

I straightened. This was what I wanted to know. "Here, here?" I asked. "In LA?"

"Yes, my little witch," he said, his smile turning into a full-on leer. "But don't you fret. You are not the vessel of power for that spell, but your time with Richard Zachariah will come. And you will glory in the wonder of it, I promise you that."

I stared at him, Kreios's hand on my shoulder quickly dousing the balls of flame that were bubbling up from my hands.

"Um...thank you," I said, as humbly as I could without throwing up. "I, ah, look forward to that."

"Not nearly as much as I do." RZ straightened, and he fixed on Kreios again. "But allow me to let you in on a little secret."

"Ohhh, secrets," Kreios said indulgently. "They are absolutely my most favorite thing."

RZ nodded. "The coven of LA is completely upside-down with confusion and chaos over the prophecy that will be fulfilled with my assistance. They don't much care for me."

"No," I protested, credibly aghast.

"It's true."

Because I couldn't stand it anymore, I widened my eyes and asked breathlessly, "But aren't you scared? I mean, you're the star who was in that terrible accident the other day, aren't you? You could have been killed!"

"I could have, little one, but I wasn't." RZ preened. "It was the barest taste of Myanya's power in its first flowering, which I lapped up with delight and cunning. An attempt to dissuade me that amounted to little more than a tease. And I am far better at such seduction than the vessel who sought to tempt me."

"Gosh, who could possibly try that? Do you know her name?" I sensed Kreios going for my rib cage again and shifted out of the way. I needed this information, dammit.

But RZ wouldn't bite. At least not on that question. "I don't need to know who—the who is irrelevant when I will mold her with my hands into something far more than she could ever hope to be herself. She is fated to be mine, my slave and my consort, into whom I will pour the seed of my dominant strength."

"Ah." I was truly at a loss over this. Flames erupted again over my fingertips as Kreios moved smoothly into the conversational gap.

"And when will this transformation take place?" he purred, his interest fetching a broad smile from RZ.

"Soon," the aspiring necromancer promised. "The prophecy has not fully ripened yet, but we are on the very cusp of it. I will glory in the devotion of the flesh and the submission of the soul when the time is perfectly right."

CHAPTER SEVENTEEN

I t was another fifteen minutes of me struggling not to set RZ on fire before he and Kreios ambled off down the corridor, two old chums discussing the art of dead-guy magic. Ordinarily, I would have paid good money to continue to listen to the Devil squeeze the rapper for information, but I didn't think I had it in me to keep my cool or my hands to myself. RZ had seriously started to shuck my corn.

"Got your six," Nikki said behind me. I turned, and she brushed hair away from my face, her long fingers grazing my cheek.

"You had your mental gates clamped down so hard, I couldn't read you, and that's saying something," she said.

"You have no idea," I said, drawing in an unsteady breath. "But the salient points are these: He, like everyone else we've encountered, thinks he's God's gift to Myanya or, more specifically, the vessel she's inhabiting. He's convinced that vessel is here in LA. He is further convinced he can overpower any display of strength that Myanya puts out because he's encountered her once, lapping up a taste of her power as she was in her first flowering, as he described it. There's something to that, I think."

Nikki wrinkled her nose. "You mean beyond me needing to shower with bleach?"

"Beyond that. I got the sense that it wasn't RZ demanding Myanya through a magic pentagram, but encountering her in some other situation. In person. We should look up any sort of costume ball or other major event that's taken place recently, someplace where he could encounter Myanya's proxy without knowing her identity and nobody would think that's weird."

Nikki snorted. "That's half the bars in LA."

"And he was all over the LA coven being upset about him about to rule them, so clearly, he believes the witch is part of that organization."

"Danae has already cleared our introduction there, though she's insisting we have to dress for the part."

"Like that's ever a problem with you."

"*Both* of us, dollface, and by dress, she means we need to have a man on our arm. Or a woman. The witches of LA show their power not only in the kind of power they wield, but who they have in attendance. I offered to be your date, but she said no, that we needed to both ante up, and the easiest way for me to do that was with an appropriate dose of man candy. I voted for Kreios, so you can't have him, but she thinks Armaeus would come out of his pointy-tipped penthouse for a visit to Lara Drake, the high priestess of the LA coven. They've never met."

"Oh?" I thought of Armaeus hanging from the Olympic rings, streaming with sweat and blood. "Any chance Drake is our vessel?"

"It's always possible, but unlikely, according to Danae," Nikki said. "Lara Drake is no blushing violet, and though Myanya does occasionally go for older witches, her norm is the ingénue. Plus, Drake's about sixty years old and on her third husband. I think if anyone like RZ came calling to crush her under his heel, she'd roast his face off."

"Fair enough."

"And that's not your only issue," Nikki said. She pointed to where Death was working. "According to Danae, you need to access your inner power a little more completely, and for that, you've apparently gotta go talk to Death. Your reactions in the Moscow coven were quick, but not quick enough, she's decided, now that you're this close to Myanya."

"And how exactly would Danae—" I stopped and put my hand to the necklace around my neck, jerking it off. The chain snapped easily, and I handed it to Nikki. "No. This has to stop. I can heal myself spontaneously, but Danae can't—especially if I don't know she's been hurt while she's peeking over my shoulder. I don't need her watching over me just because I'm working inside the covens."

Nikki took the ankh, but frowned at me. "Well, actually, you kind of do," she said. "You don't know witch magic."

"I *didn't* know witch magic," I corrected her. "As of this week, I've been on the inside of more pentagrams than most witches in the western hemisphere have in their entire lives. I don't want to drag Danae into danger unexpectedly, and I might if she's watching me that closely."

"Okay, then keep this. Just not around your neck, maybe," Nikki said, unstringing the ankh and handing it back to me. "Because I've also got no clue about witch magic, and I would feel much better knowing that you have someone in your corner who does." She scowled, rubbing her chin. "We probably should have looked at ascending Danae to the Council, not merely to the House of Swords."

I shook my head. "I think Ma-Singh would have something to say if I started making the House of Swords a feeder system for the Council."

"Oh, I don't know. I think the big lug likes to keep tabs on what's going on with them. Having you in place qualifies as an exceptional coup among all the generals. He's working it."

By this time, we'd made our way over to where Death was set up. The middle-aged woman was gone, and though an entire wall of people were standing around, staring at Death in utter adoration, there was nobody sitting in her chair.

She looked up when I approached and gestured to the seat. "About time," she said.

"Um, you wanted to see me?"

"What was your first clue?" She waved again to her inking chair. "Sit."

"Really?" I said, eyeing the crowd. "You don't think we couldn't find a private room, maybe have dinner first?"

"What's your issue? Relax. They don't know it's you." I stepped up on the dais, and could feel the net of magic close around me.

"Who do they think I am?"

"Young tough, green hair, full leathers, nose ring. Rumor has it it's my kid, though half the crowd disputes that."

She gestured lazily, and I glanced out at the crowd. Sure enough, there were several small knots of people in heated dispute, most of them pointing at the dais.

"This won't take long, anyway." Death picked up a tattoo gun that wasn't connected to an ink stream hose, and I raised my eyebrows.

"Isn't ink part of the point?" I asked, shrugging off my jacket, smirking at my own words. I was a black belt in defensive punning, particularly when I was nervous. I was also wearing a black T-shirt underneath my jacket, to match my black jeans and heavy boots, pretty much the standard attire for the ink show, unless you were Nikki Dawes. I took a seat in Death's souped-up dentist's chair.

"It is usually. Not for you. Left arm."

I sighed and stuck out my left arm, angling it wider as Death targeted a point just inside my bicep. "So what is it I'm getting permanently inscribed on my body this time?"

"A short cut. Try to remember to breathe."

She put the needle to my arm, and pain immediately shot through me in all directions, radiating out from the point where the needle pierced my skin, sending shock waves throughout my nervous system. Every one of my chakras roared to life, even the one that hung out about sixteen inches above my head. I tried not to howl with pain, but it was a close thing.

"Can they see this?" I gasped, staring at the crowd, who looked at me with complete unconcern. "Because if I'm your kid, somebody should be arresting you for child abuse."

"You're such a baby," Death muttered. "No kid of mine would sit there whining like a ten-year-old with a skinned knee. You need to suck it up."

"And you need to—ouch!" My eyes almost crossed as she changed the direction of the needle, tracking a pattern up the curve of my muscle. I dared a look at my actual skin, but I couldn't see any stream of ink. Especially since all the skin around the point of the needle appeared to be smoking. "Is that seriously the way this is supposed to be done?"

"What you fail to realize, despite constant reinforcements from the universe around you, is that you are not an ordinary person, Sara Wilde," Death replied, eminently unperturbed by my yips of genuine pain. "You allow yourself to access your deeper magic in fits and starts, and while that has served you well up to this point, there's going to come a time where you will need to access a steady stream of power, a power you can't simply cut off because you get scared."

"I don't get scared," I protested, lifting my right arm to swipe away the sweat that was gathering on my forehead. "I just don't think I need to go all Jean Grey, Eater of Worlds, every time I run into some trouble. I want to control the flow of magic through me, not let it take me over."

"And that's where you make your mistake," Death said. "You're not Jean Grey. She's a comic book character, the creation of some illustrator's fevered mind. You're the creation of your own mind, while your body was forged in an unholy alliance between a goddess and a demigod member of the Arcana Council." As if to punctuate her words, she punctured me a little more forcibly, making me jump in my chair. "Don't think I haven't noticed that you have not returned to Sensei Chichiro since you ascended to your role as Justice."

"I've been a little busy," I retorted. The sensei had been recommended to me to help me control my rapidly increasing abilities. And she had helped, truly. But she had a similar form of tough love as Death did, and there were limits to how much I hated myself.

"I know, which is why I am taking pity on you and cheating a little bit." Death forced the needle into my skin at yet a new angle, the fresh wave of pain so intense, I almost passed out. "Now, when you feel the

173

urge to stifle the flow of magic, I want you to focus on the design I am etching into your skin."

"I can't even see the design you're etching into my skin."

"You will shortly. It's the Eye of Horus, but invisible as such to anyone other than you. And, arguably, to the Magician, since he has a similar tattoo etched into him."

I frowned. I happened to have an exceptional memory of every inch of the Magician's skin, and I did not remember seeing such a tattoo. In fact, to my knowledge, Armaeus had absolutely no tattoos anywhere on his body. "Why would he hide such a thing from me?"

Death didn't need me to explain what I meant. "It's not intentional. The ink the Magician received was in the first hundred years of his ascendency to power. He did not have any true spell-casting abilities when he first ascended, and he quickly recognized this as a weakness he could not afford to let stand."

I nodded, grateful for the distraction as well as the moment's breath Death gave me while she laid down one gun and picked up another. "He mentioned that," I said. "How exactly is it that he ascended to his role of Magician without having ever cast a single spell?"

"Because when the need is great, the Council acts with the greatest level of efficiency. Spell casting is something that can be taught, the same as you being given tools to access your powers despite your concerted efforts to avoid formal training. But it is the magic within that cannot be discounted. There are members of the Council who should be in maximum security prisons, but instead of paying for their crimes, they've been exalted."

"You got that right," I said, thinking of Viktor Dal, the Emperor, whose pre-Council activities included an unfortunate collusion with Nazi Germany — and even of Gamon, whose life before her tenure as Judgment was not exactly something that anyone would put on a résumé for anything other than a wet work specialist.

"Stop focusing on the impropriety of it and analyze the need," Death said. "And I told you, breathe."

"I'm breathing," I gasped as Death bent over me again, this new needle smaller and more delicate than the first, but I didn't think that was going to have anything but a negative impact on the level of pain it exacted from me.

I was right.

"What in the *hell*," I screeched, practically jerking out of my chair while Death somehow managed to follow me for a half second more before she pulled the needle free.

"You're lucky I was expecting that reaction."

"You're lucky I didn't just vomit on you," I shot back, reluctantly straightening in my chair before I held my arm out again. "Will you please finish this up sometime before my hair turns white?"

She chuckled and bent over me again. "The Magician began trying to convince you to ascend the moment he met you. You didn't realize it at first, but that doesn't change the truth. He knows you are fated to bring great change to the Council, but you have to be the one in control of that change. You can't wait for his permission, or the Devil's, or mine. You can't wait until the mortals you encounter are ready for you to do what you must. You carry the mantle of your friendships like a protective cloak, but ultimately, they are not your shield. You are both shield and sword. The sooner you realize that, the better you'll be prepared for what will come."

She straightened and stood away from me, and I scowled at her. "Yeah? And what's going to come?"

"So many possibilities for you, Justice Wilde. Insanity. Death. Domination. Love. Creation. Destruction. But all of it relies on you, if you will only reach deep within and give rise to your power when the situation demands. Now you are ready to do so."

I looked down at my arm, and the implacable Eye of Horus stared back, the thick line of the Egyptian symbol etched in deep, glistening purple. An unreasoning apprehension slithered through me. What had I allowed to be done to me?

"So, uh, that's it?" I asked as Death set down her ink gun, and held up my left arm toward her, fanning dry the glistening symbol. "No instruction manual on how to use this tat, no video tutorial? You're just going to leave me all by my lonesome—me, myself, and eye?"

She glanced back, grimacing. "You have more access to resources now, not less, Sara. You'll understand how to use the access point I've provided you when the time comes. There's no need for you to retreat into humor merely because you're frightened."

"Eye, eye, Captain."

"Don't make me regret my actions today."

"Never," I said, scooting off the chair. "In fact, we took a vote as to whether or not you were our favorite Council member. Guess what?"

"Don't."

"Yup. The eyes have it."

An expression of genuine irritation crossed Death's face, and satisfaction rolled through me, which was a nice change from the waves of pain that were still cresting and crashing across my nervous system. She continued. "Once you're finished, you'll do well to remember that you can choose how you manifest your power and where to place your energy, but ultimately, no one can help you more than you can help yourself."

"Right." I frowned down at my bicep. "I guess it's you and me against the world, buddy," I said. "Keep an eye out for me, will you?"

Death sighed heavily, then turned away. "I knew this was a mistake."

CHAPTER EIGHTEEN

Nikki and I checked into separate suites at the Beverly Hills Hotel. Because if you were going to be charged with cleaning up the crazy of the world, you deserved your own suite. Besides that, my room had an executive meeting area that allowed us to set up a temporary war room on all things witchery. I'd even invited a few guests to join us.

We were sitting in that room now, fully stocked with coffee, bourbon, and donuts, staring at an enormous whiteboard that I'd ordered rolled in for the meeting. I was becoming quite fond of whiteboards. I had a feeling they were going to start multiplying like tribbles in my world. In fact, when I did finally return to Sensei Chichiro to start improving my powers of manifestation, I was pretty sure I was going to start with office supplies.

Nikki had helpfully written "Murder Board" at the top of this whiteboard, to make it official, and we'd posted pictures of all the victims starting from the midpoint down. Above the midpoint were our list of LA witches voted most likely to make someone bleed.

There...were a lot of them.

"How is it that the LA coven has so many assholes?" Nikki grumbled.

"It comes with the territory." Kreios leaned back in one of the oversized captain's chairs that passed for conference room seating, still in his LA suit but looking perfectly comfortable. "The coven was first established well before the coming of money and film to the area, and the witches owned the land. Whoever owned the land owned the power, and no one ever accused a witch of not being a good business person."

Danae snorted. "I'd make that accusation. LA isn't symbolic of most cities, let alone most covens. There are a lot of people out there who don't wear Gucci to do their gardening, nor would they ever want to. The way of the witch is not intended to be a path solely for profit."

"Fair enough." Kreios nodded, glancing her way. I watched him watch Danae, the gleam of interest in his gaze unmistakable. Now she was the one being stared at like a bug, but Danae didn't seem fazed.

"What we have here is approximately a half-dozen candidates, all female, all highly placed in the coven — including the presiding priestess, Lara Drake, who we originally ruled out because of age, but now..." Danae gestured at the board and shook her head.

"It's not her," I said definitively. I stared at the victims' pictures, then the coven members, trying to imagine any of the other women as likely targets for Myanya and her prophecy. "Lara's sixty years old, and the energy I picked up in the Moscow pentagram was decidedly young."

"Could be a smoke screen to throw you off."

"It could, but I don't think so. When I say young, I mean largely untested, unformed." I pointed at the picture of Lara — her bright, discerning eyes, her hard jaw, her determined smile. "This woman hasn't merely been around the block, she probably built it. I'm not saying she isn't involved in the Myanya prophecy, but I don't think she's our vessel."

"That's an interesting idea," Nikki said, moving toward the board now, her eyes narrowing. She'd changed out of her Marilyn Monroe costume for a classic Lauren Bacall silhouette, her tawny hair styled into a perfectly coiffed wave over her shoulders, and her body clad in long, flowing trousers and a high-necked blouse with voluminous sleeves and narrow cuffs. "What if all the coven management is in on the gig? They know the prophecy is coming, they want the power for their own coven, they put forward their strongest candidate, and everybody breaks out the bubbly when Myanya goes with their girl. It's like the NFL draft without all the drug testing."

"Except she's resisting," I said. Danae and Kreios turned their attention to me, and Nikki nodded as I continued. "The Myanya vessel's got one job. It's a shit job, but it's one job: to knuckle under the oppression of the boy most likely, suffer at his hand, and emerge the scarred warrior. That's not what's happening here. What's happening is a vessel witch getting steadily stronger by besting the male witches foolish enough to try to be her consort. Before any of that happened, though, my theory is one aspiring vessel witch decided to catch Myanya's eye by taking out random asshats she decided aren't fit to live. Richard Zachariah. Judith Granger. William Macpherson. And..." I picked up another sheet I'd had printed off on a hunch...a hunch that might still play out. "Herm Lannister, a guy who was known as a super sleaze in the sci-fi fantasy world...but a highly successful super sleaze. About a month ago, he told off a group of young women at a con who'd shown up to protest him, and got a standing O from his fanboy coalition."

"Nice," Nikki put in.

"Exactly. He was found dead of a self-administered drug overdose about a week ago, no foul play indicated, but given his history, I'm including him here. All these folks' bodies are now turning up, with the exception of Richard Zachariah, and he got lucky. And all of them, presumably, had drawn the ire of the witch Myanya is targeting."

Nikki snorted and tapped a folder in front of her. "Her choice in bad guys isn't all that bad, actually. The lists of grievances against these folks are long." She tapped a folder in front of her. "Most of them unproven but widely rumored, especially here in LA."

"But despite what she may believe, her audition for vessel witch doesn't give her clearance to be judge, jury, and executioner," I countered. "And none of these victims are connected in any meaningful way to the coven, except for RZ and his delusions of becoming the next Great American Necromancer. He's the only one who straddles the worlds of entertainment and witchcraft, and we can't link him definitively to anyone inside the coven. The rest...don't make sense."

I pointed to the still shot of the smug-looking Judith Granger. "Yes, I get it. She pressured a lot of starlets to accept the cult of silence, and the #MeToo outcry didn't manage to unearth her, so maybe she deserved some pain—but she's dead now. Ditto William MacPherson. Skeevy? Definitely. Worthy of criminal prosecution, oh yeah. But dead? No. Same with Herm Lannister. He used his cred as a comic book adapter to do some intensely objectionable things in the writing community, to the point that Comic-Con nearly had a revolt on its hands during his last scheduled appearance, for all that the fanboys were screaming for him. But none of that was ever brought to trial, so how did the vessel witch know about it?"

"She's got to be plugged into the creative community," Nikki said thoughtfully.

"Agreed. But so far as we can tell, none of the LA witches had major roles in Hollywood productions that any of these people touched."

"Doesn't mean they weren't bit players," Nikki offered. "That's half of Hollywood."

"And it doesn't mean they weren't moved by the plights of those less fortunate," Danae agreed. "It could be simple vigilantism."

I considered that. It felt right, probably the most right of anything so far. "Okay, but that doesn't serve the coven, does it?"

Danae shook her head. "Not in the slightest. Murder is trouble in any situation, but to a coven, it can be deadly. Not only does it put the coven at risk of being discovered, its members outed, it goes against certain, well, covenants."

Nikki cackled to the right, but my gaze was back on the board. "So if I'm Lara Drake, I'm pissed."

"You're definitely concerned," Danae agreed. "And for more than the PR issue. A witch willing to go against the most basic of self-preservation doctrines is likely one looking to make a power play. Remember, the witch who is the vessel for Myanya will eventually parlay her subjugation into eventual control of the coven. If the current high priestess isn't on board with that transition, that could be a dangerous game."

"A very dangerous game." I studied the three women whose pictures we'd placed beneath Lara Drake's. Tammy Butler, Gail Fredericks, Monica Jones.

All of them in their twenties and thirties, all of them Hollywood perfect.

Too Hollywood perfect. Almost as beautiful as Danae, now that I thought of it.

"Do big-shot covens not accept ordinary-looking witches?"

"They do," Danae said. "But in this city more than most, beauty is power. That extends to the LA coven as well."

"Maybe," I muttered. But something about that truism nagged at me. There were other paths to power, trickier and darker paths than beauty. What path had Myanya's vessel taken?

"Okay, another angle. What have we found out about the past activity of these witches—charities, politics, internet, any of it?" I asked.

"We've got nothing so far," Nikki reported. "I'm not saying these women are clean, but they're careful."

"They have to be," Danae put in. "As I said, Lara isn't someone to be trifled with. As much as she would want the coven to benefit from the prophecy, she's not about to have a murder charge hung on her. There are too many people in high places who already are gunning for the coven."

That was news. I turned to her. "What do you mean? Who've they pissed off?"

"Lara is politically active enough to protect her interests as a landowner, and she still owns a great deal of the land in and around the city. She sold some, bought some back, then realized she'd make a lot more money renting than selling. So that's part of it. She also can raise rents or terminate contracts at will, which gives her more power than many are comfortable with. Aside from that, she was an outspoken proponent of many of the movements for women's, writers', artists', and actors' rights over the years, and because of her position, people have to be polite to her."

"But all that's narrowed in on her, and she's not our guy," I said. I glanced again to the board, eyeing the women of the LA coven. "Any of these witches coupled up with power players in the city?"

"Off and on over the years, but there are no current alliances in play," Nikki said. "Gail Fredericks is the last to have an alliance of any interest, and that's her now ex-husband, who was also romantically linked with victim number two, Judith Granger, though before Gail and he were wed. I've done some digging on that, but Gail has an alibi for the time of Granger's death and by all accounts, there was no ill will between her and the victim."

"Still, bears a conversation," I said.

"That it does. If you have time to investigate." I didn't miss the change of pronouns, and I turned to Danae with raised brows.

"You're not coming with?"

"I shouldn't even be in the city," she said with a dark chuckle. "Lara is not a fan of mine, as I'm one of the few witches in the northern hemisphere richer than she is."

This wasn't exactly news to me—I knew Danae was loaded—but still good information.

Danae continued. "Add to that the issue with the Myanya prophecy, and it makes for some tricky business. Technically speaking, if the LA coven is elevated by a successfully fulfilled prophecy, Lara or this new witch could make a run at my base of power. My attention has been split with my recent adoption of the role of Mistress of Swords, and there are some who distrust an alliance of any stripe with the Council."

I pursed my lips. "Then you're in danger being here. That was never my intention."

"It's a danger I happily sought out. And unlike you, I don't shrink from the assistance of others. A perceived alliance with the Council puts me in a power position, regardless of any distrust I may sow," Danae said, her smile icy. "You may not wish to use the leverage your position allows you, Sara, but I'm not quite so delicate."

"Fair enough." The Eye of Horus tattoo on my arm flared with heat, and I rubbed it absently.

"Bottom line, if I'm perceived as trying to interfere in the rightful business of the LA coven, especially if they are on the cusp for challenging my authority, it would undermine the eventuality of me stomping Lara on the neck when she does attempt to usurp my rule."

"Burn," Nikki offered from the corner.

Danae nodded. "I look forward to her attempt, because such challenges are watched keenly by the other covens. New York and New Orleans have been eyeing the brass ring as well, and there's always Sedona to contend with."

That surprised me. "Sedona? That's the first I've heard of them. Why weren't they listed among the possibilities of attracting Myanya's prophecies?"

"Because their witches are...particularly not receptive to subjugation of any kind, no matter what the cause. But don't let the pink jeeps and vortex tours mislead you," Danae said. "There's powerful magic in those canyons, and there always has been. And that's merely in the US. There are several midlist covens who wouldn't be likely to be targeted by Myanya, but who remain eager to get into the dance, and a host of cities in other countries who would like to expand. As I think you found in Moscow."

"Yeah, well," I said, thinking of Svetlana's expression as I introduced her to Gamon. "Moscow's gonna be a little busy for a while."

"Something else to consider," Kreios said into the ensuing silence. "What will you do when you find the witch that Myanya has chosen as her vessel? Whether it's one of these women or someone else? Would you challenge the spirit of Myanya for control?"

I made a face. "I may not like the prophecy—and I don't—but that's not the immediate problem here. The immediate problem is that a witch is using the prophecy as an excuse to ice her enemies."

"Who all seem to richly deserve it," Kreios said, amiably enough.

"That's completely not the point," I shot back. "A few days ago, we had four witches or their associates who came in as cases for Justice. Mrs. French has reported a dozen more since. And that's only the ones who petitioned for retribution. How many others have been trying to win the Myanya lottery and ending up with more than they bargained for?"

"They know the risk," Kreios demurred.

"See, I don't think they do." I looked at Danae, and she shrugged.

"The prophecy has been playing out once a generation as long as records have been kept. It's well known among true believers."

"The prophecy, yes, but the part about the witch taking it into her own hands and using it as a dark-magic super soaker? How often has that happened?"

A heavy silence followed my question. "I didn't think so. It hasn't happened because through time immemorial, the subjugated witch has allowed herself to be subjugated first, then ask questions later. So there hasn't been any precedent for this. Not even Iskra—and I'm sure Iskra's not the first witch to balk at being ground under someone else's heel—not even she sought to *annihilate* the male witch who stood waiting to subjugate her, before he did anything wrong. All her focus was on rejecting Myanya."

I shook my head, looking at the board again. "I don't get the impression that whoever the vessel is this time around is resisting Myanya so much as she's using her."

"Successfully," Nikki agreed.

"Which makes her arguably more powerful than any of the witches who have come before." Now Danae was looking at the board as well, her eyes narrowing. "I hadn't considered it in that light."

I glanced at her, then went still. The smallest streak of silver had now appeared at Danae's temple, a streak that hadn't been there before. Was I now able to see *potential* danger in a Connected before they ever did anything wrong, like some sort of *Minority Report* precog, minus the lottery balls? Was this a bonus of my new Eye of Horus add-on?

The very thought made my head hurt. I knew Death should've given me a manual.

We argued for another hour, back and forth, but until we met with the witches in person, there was nothing more we could do. Kreios assured Nikki he'd be her plus one for introduction to the LA coven, and Danae announced she was heading to the local House of Swords enclave, where she was assembling the highest-level members of her coven to monitor the ley lines of the city.

Part of me knew that wouldn't be all she was monitoring, but eventually, everyone left, and I was once more alone in the room.

"You've been listening to all this, haven't you?" I asked aloud. No response from Armaeus, and I scowled, turning to the window. "I know you're there, I can feel you. And I need a date, Armaeus. I need cred. You provide both."

Still no response. Annoyed, I padded over to the liquor cabinet. No pay-by-the-shot mini fridge here; it was a fully stocked setup. I poured myself a glass of Glenmorangie, eyeing the amber liquid as it sloshed in the glass.

I wasn't a fan of Armaeus ignoring me, or maybe monitoring me on remote to stream when he got around to it. I was even less a fan of going to tomorrow's party alone, particularly when plus-ones were a status symbol.

My arm flared again with heat, and I scowled down at it, flexing my bicep. The Eye of Horus stared back.

"You know, you would be a lot more useful if you were the mouth of Horus and could simply tell me what to do."

The smallest current of energy seemed to ripple across Death's design, and my brows perked. I had successfully summoned Kreios, after all. Summoning Armaeus was worth a shot.

"Well, now that you put it that way…."

I set down the scotch and focused all my attention on Death's newly inscribed design…and on a particularly stubborn Magician, more than two hundred miles and a Fortress of Solitude away.

I just wasn't expecting all the blood.

CHAPTER NINETEEN

A rmaeus!"
I reared back from the body that came crashing at me, arms flailing, mouth open in a rictus of one part horror, two parts misery, and five or six parts sheer unmitigated agony. I wasn't fast enough, of course, and a second later, the long, powerful, naked, and irretrievably gory body of the Magician flattened me to the floor, splaying my arms and legs wide. Before I even hit the Turkish rug, I'd created an intense blue force field of magic around us. A breath after my head smacked the thick piled carpet, I pushed Armaeus's body off me and scrambled out from beneath him, rolling my makeshift electric blue energy gurney out of the conference room and into my suite's enormous bedchamber. Eyeing his body, I wasn't sure if a shower would help or if he was too perforated for it. Talk about *A River Runs Through It*.

"Miss Wilde. This is…not really the time for humor."

"Yeah?" I used my outside voice, because my inside voice was too busy screaming as my magic guided him to the bed. "Well, it's also not the time for you showing up like Swiss cheese. Tell me what to fix first."

He did a full-body flinch as I shifted the magical field around him, so I kept it in place, sort of a flexible superglue. Whatever worked in a pinch.

Then I laid my hands on him...

And it was all I could do not to rear back.

I'd seen the Magician injured before, I'd seen portions of his body gone dark, his electrical circuits ravaged by magical attacks. But this—I'd never seen anything like this before.

"What the hell are you *doing* to yourself, Armaeus?"

"It is part of the evolutionary process," Armaeus groaned, but apparently, he wasn't so far evolved that he minded my cooling hands on his body. And cooling was the operative term here, as every single one of his magical circuits glowed with the white-hot intensity of a supernovaing star.

"You've overloaded all your circuits," I hissed, feeling the energy radiate off him.

"It is the power of the gods," he said simply. "Available and accessible to any who would take part in it."

"Yeah, well, heroin is available and accessible too. Doesn't mean it's a good idea to shoot up," I growled, trying to cajole his nerve endings back to a nonnuclear status. "You may be immortal, Armaeus, but you're still sort of human. Your body wasn't meant to handle this level of radiation. As evidenced by the fact that your bones are weeping marrow."

"Must—gain strength," Armaeus muttered, but his voice sounded a little stronger now, so I pressed closer with my cooling hands, grimacing as I encountered the first superheated circuit. With all my focus, I grabbed it, and remarkably didn't howl with agony. Much.

"Gain strength for what?" I gasped, though at this point, I didn't so much care about his answer. I moved slowly through his body, hand over fist, dousing the internal flames he had set within himself on purpose. In my wake, what looked at first like crackling ashes remained, but—as I continued working, I could see that it was more complicated than that. New filaments were twining through the wreckage of Armaeus's neural networks, filaments I couldn't readily identify as the typical magical currents. It was like all the slender branches that had once stretched through Armaeus's body had been replaced by rolls of spiderwebs—an interconnected mass of compounding energy. Still frail and weak, but definitely, distinctly different.

"What did you do this for?" I practically moaned, and Armaeus's laughter was low, rumbling, and heartfelt.

"Would you believe I did it for you?"

I lifted my head to look at him, and the expression on his face tightened. With a wince, he lifted a hand and brushed it across my cheek. His attempt to remove something from my face failed miserably as I felt the slide of gore across my skin.

"I…" He looked down at his hand as if he was seeing his own body for the first time. "I didn't feel most of this."

"Well, you maybe didn't, but what's left of your body sure did. This isn't what they mean by a crash diet." I ignored his grunts of pain as I returned to my work, cooling down one bundle of nerves after another, watching with a mixture of dismay and curiosity as the spinning whirr of new connectors moved into place behind me, glowing bright pink from the charred remains of what came before. Intuitively, I knew that what I was seeing wasn't technically possible, that Armaeus wasn't some kind of hollowed-out shell, a receptacle for magic that could be filled up with new transistors and chips and circuitry. He was flesh and blood and sinew and bone and human.

At least he had been. Once.

"How is this even possible?"

I didn't realize I'd asked the question out loud until Armaeus shifted beneath me, opening one eyelid with a decidedly icky clicking noise. Eyelids shouldn't click, I knew from personal experience. "What are you asking about specifically?"

I frowned at him, but it was a fair question. Part of me wanted to know the *how* of what had happened to Armaeus's body. How his magical networks could be so completely replaced, albeit with severe damage to what remained of his corporeal form. But an even greater part of me wanted to know *why* he'd done it.

And that part won out.

"You've lived for nine hundred years, and I don't know everything you've done to evolve over that time. But it seems like this is a somewhat extreme evolution, if that's what you want to call it. When I saw you last, you were in a fair amount of pain, all of which seemed self-inflicted. And I'm willing to bet that nobody was holding your feet to the fire to replace your normal circuitry with a bunch of pink flamingos. Why did you do it?" I bit my lip, half knowing, half dreading the answer. "Was it something I did?"

I knew the truth of my guess in the silence that followed, and I bent again to what I could do now instead, which was healing Armaeus's body. As always, with my assistance, his own natural healing abilities gained strength rapidly, and while I focused on the interior issues, the exterior shored up as well. In only a few minutes, Armaeus's skin was no longer riddled with oozing gashes and blackened rents, but was pure, untouched. Pristine.

The interior circuitry was taking a fair amount longer to resolve, but even it eventually shook off the trauma of what had been written upon it and surged with new, pinkish purple light.

I sat back on the bed, my gaze sweeping Armaeus's body as our hands found each other's, and held. Somewhere along the line, his clothes had fallen off him or been burned away. Now he lay half-covered in the sheets, looking at me from hooded, intense eyes.

"Your assessment?" he asked, and I shrugged, more upset than I wanted to be.

"You're back in one piece, which is saying something. But you look like you've been filled with alien DNA."

"Is that a problem?"

"Well, there are things we need to do," I said, my tone deliberately flippant to mask my churning hysteria. "We have a party to get to tomorrow, which I know you're aware of, and I don't know if you'll be my plus-one or plus-fourteen. You've got that kind of energy bouncing around inside you."

"You seek to impress the LA coven." Armaeus was now breathing more or less steadily, but he didn't let me go. "You want me on your arm to do so, but you give yourself far less credit than you should."

"I don't need you to look pretty, Armaeus, I need you as a shield." Not exactly true—I did need him to look pretty. But he could do that without even trying, now that he'd been all Humpty-Dumptied back together again. It was the shield part of the equation I still needed to work out.

The Magician's brows lifted and his eyes drifted shut, presumably to do some interior scope work of his own. When I would have moved away, however, he shifted his hand to curve his elegant fingers around mine. Without knowing quite why, I covered our joined hands with my other hand, willing him to feel me next to him, no matter how deeply he went inside his own body.

A minute passed by, then several more, then eventually, Armaeus exhaled. He squeezed my hand, and I thought: maybe that was why he'd reached for me. He needed to remember the touch of a human, the touch of his own race. Or at least what I hoped was still his race.

Armaeus chuckled low and deep in his throat, though his eyes remained closed. "Are you really that worried?"

I looked at him tangled in the sheets and my lips twisted. I thought of Myanya and the power and promise that she carried in her terrible gift of a prophecy. How different was what she was offering to her chosen witch from what Armaeus was doing to himself? Other than the whole choice part, anyway?

"Yes, I'm that worried," I said. Without thinking, I leaned forward and laid my head on Armaeus's chest, mainly to hear his heart beating. Because he did still have a heart, right? I didn't miss that on my cruise through his nervous system?

I'd barely skimmed his chest when Armaeus's chuckle rolled over me and his hands circled my shoulders, hauling me higher on his body, then turning me until I faced him. My legs parted, and I straddled his torso, bracing my hands on his chest. I inched my left hand across his pec, and he closed his hand over it, bringing my fingers to his lips.

"I'm not sure I've ever seen you actually worried, Miss Wilde," Armaeus said, and the insinuation in his voice made me snap my gaze to his. His eyes were dark, swirling with power, but I didn't know how much that had to do with his near-magic experience or the simple fact that he was alone, naked, with a woman in bed.

"I feel overdressed," I murmured, and as easily as I could manifest an elevator full of stilettos, I'd manifested my own clothes off my body and onto the floor. Another handy skill I had heretofore underappreciated.

"Your abilities never do fail to disappoint."

"Mm." I leaned down until my face was a bare inch above his, some part of me shocked at how natural it felt to share an intimate moment with Armaeus. More natural than it really should, given what I'd witnessed going on inside his body. "I should know better than to trust you, shouldn't I?"

"You should definitely know better than that," he agreed with a soft smile. "I will attempt to bend you to my will without blinking if I think it is for the greater good, and even more quickly if I believe it is for your good. You, of course, have the ability to stop me at every turn. You always have." He shifted beneath me. "And now that you have the Eye of Horus upon you, your connection to your own abilities is increased tenfold."

"So you knew about that?"

"Of course."

"Great. Anything I should be aware of?" Though I wanted to know the answer, I mostly wanted Armaeus to keep talking as I reveled in the heat of his body, the touch of his skin against mine. There was the magical healing that a being as powerful as the Magician could enact with a thought…but there was a different kind of healing too. The healing of simple touch between two people, a connection as old as time itself. The combination of the two in this moment threatened to overload my senses, but only in the best possible way.

"About the mark? No. Nothing of any import, anyway," he said. "But there is something you should know, something I feel you may not understand."

"Okay…" I pursed my lips. That didn't sound like a good opening.

I was wrong.

"I love you," Armaeus said, his gaze once more meeting mine. "I love you so much that I will move heaven and earth to be with you, to support you in any way that I can. But if it were to ever come down to the world going up in flames because of something you did or something you were becoming…"

"I know, I know," I sighed. "You would sacrifice me for the greater good."

"No, my dear Miss Wilde," he said, his eyes a fathomless black. "I would sacrifice myself for the greater good. That is the change you are detecting, that you cannot quite understand. You should understand it. It's the truth of the matter."

I stared at him, not even blinking, my heart suddenly too full in my chest as the power of his statement, his meaning rolled through me. *You can't!* I cried inside, desperation and terror echoing down the long corridors of my mind. *You can't, you can't.* Tears welled up unbidden, and when Armaeus's soft, beautiful mouth quirked into a gentle smile, they slid down my cheeks.

With that, he moved, quickly and easily, rolling me over onto the bed as he covered me with his own long, sleekly muscled form. I drew in a shaky breath as he slid himself along me, every inch of him hard and sure against the give my body allowed. My legs fell open easily, and as he moved to take the opening I'd given him, his gaze caught mine again. "You are more powerful than you realize. You would do well to remember that."

"Is that—oh," I shuddered as Armaeus slid into me, and the field of magic around us didn't just vibrate, it practically exploded into myriad colors and lights, the pressure from both within and without almost too much to process. I studied him in the midst of all that drenching energy, understanding suddenly lighting through me.

"That's why you've leveled up," I whispered as he started to move. I didn't want to think anymore, I didn't want to do anything but feel, but that didn't change the reality of what I'd just learned. Armaeus was literally pushing himself to the limit to ensure that he was my equal—to protect me? To protect himself?

Or merely to make himself a big enough prize to offer in my stead should the absolute worst come to pass?

I didn't know, and I no longer cared. Not when he was with me and only the two of us mattered, lost for this precious moment in a world beyond space and time.

I drew him down into my embrace, and we surrendered to each other.

CHAPTER TWENTY

Having recently sat in on a meeting of a senate of magicians in Venice, Italy, I wasn't at all sure what to expect from a meeting of a coven of witches in the heart of LA. But it definitely wasn't an exclusive set of booths at the nightclub Lure, with a line out the door that we bypassed without even raising an eyebrow, a $1,500 bottle service, and music loud enough to drown out all thought, let alone all conversation. "You're kidding me, right?"

"There's no need for you to shout, Miss Wilde," Armaeus thought in my head.

I flashed him a worried look. Despite waking up in his arms that morning, I'd grown increasingly uneasy as the day had progressed. I'd healed the man, and he was...certifiably functional. But there was a weight to his energy that simply had not been there before, and I wasn't quite sure what to do with that weight. Also, it appeared that no matter how much I'd leveled up, he still could block any intrusion into his thoughts, and his stonewalling of my attempts to read his mind hadn't lightened my mood. And now this—his clear self-assurance in the face of this wall of music and noise and light. The chaos made me want to curl up into a ball. Armaeus, however, seemed to be in his element.

Which surprised me. Nightclubs like Lure were supposed to be Kreios's element, and in fact, the Devil of the Arcana Council was currently holding court with several men and women near one of the opulent bars, a glittering Nikki on his arm. But Armaeus seemed much more inclined to be muttering imprecations over some foul-smelling cauldron deep in his twisty lair than hanging out in a trendy nightclub.

But he wasn't putting on a show. He practically vibrated with the energy of the place, clearly drawing satisfaction from it, even pleasure, which made me feel…at a loss. What else didn't I know about him?

Probably too much. I was determined to find out exactly what—later. Later, I promised myself, I'd have all the time in the world. Now, however, I needed to hear myself think. I wanted to have an in-person touchpoint with the leader of the coven, plus the three witches most likely from our murder board. Once I met them face-to-face, I hoped to weed the three down to two…maybe even one. They were undoubtedly too skilled to show their cards—or that they were marked for Justice—now that they knew I was looking for them, but there were other tells.

I hoped.

I refocused on Armaeus. *Believe it or not, you're not the person I actually need to speak to here. That means I'm going to have to use my outside voice.*

"And do you really believe that the witches of LA haven't found a way around a pesky issue like sound? Because, as I believe I mentioned, the members of this coven have several unique talents that have evolved specifically to meet the unique requirements of their environments."

Yeah, you mentioned. They're like geckos.

"In a manner of speaking, yes." Armaeus waved his hand, and the scream of music faded to a barely audible backdrop. It was suddenly as if we were walking through glassed tunnels underneath the ocean, while a hurricane raged all above. We could see everything happening all around us, but we were separate and protected from all of it.

"You did this?" I asked, this time speaking out loud. I immediately had to ratchet my voice down to an acceptable level. "Or did one of them cast some sort of spell?"

He smiled, and I was reminded again why so many of the women and men in the room instinctively gravitated toward him. There was something about the Magician, even before he'd given himself a power upgrade, that always proved irresistible to normal humans. Now, with whatever it was he'd done to himself, they oriented themselves toward him like he was their true north.

"Your suspicions of me are unfounded, Miss Wilde. The spell that was cast to allow for polite conversation is not of my doing, but it is accessible to any who know it. You could access it as well."

I lifted my brows. "This is another nudge for me to get formal training, isn't it? Because you're not super subtle, if you're wondering."

He chuckled. "Training would be wise. But here, you've only to demand it be done, Miss Wilde. That's all you've ever had to do."

A second later, the cacophony of sound dropped around us with the force of a sonic boom, and I went rigid with shock.

"Oh!" I exclaimed, pushing back at the noise mentally, lifting it up—

And there it was. A thin skein of electricity, rolled up tight like yarn, with the end hanging loose. I pulled on it, then pulled harder, and suddenly, the yarn sprang free, not as a single thread but an entire cloak, blanketing the space around us.

Silence reigned again.

"Well, that was cool," I allowed. "I thought witches used spells."

"Witches use nature, and bend nature to their needs, as do any of the Connected," Armaeus corrected me. "While it's true that only a master magician should have been able to access that spell, you've proven my newest hypothesis quite effectively. You are not classically trained, you're not trained at all, in fact, and yet when it comes to accessing the wavelength of power that is open to a trained witch—you can co-opt it, neatly and effectively. That bears some study."

"Plan on it." I smiled at him. "After we're done here."

"Agreed."

We'd approached a small enclave of deep, curved, upholstered seating, the roar of music still quieter here, allowing for the conversation of those seated around the cluster of small round tables. One of the women looked up, then smiled expansively as she stood. I recognized her immediately as Lara Drake.

"The Arcana Council," she said, her voice rich with approval. "Welcome to Los Angeles."

"I've stayed away too long," Armaeus said graciously, and I didn't miss the undercurrent that passed between him and the woman I'd only seen stuck to a board up to this point. I sort of preferred her that way now that I could see her in person and witnessed the way her gaze traveled over Armaeus like a hacker's spider on the dark web.

Lara Drake turned to me, her manner still smooth, and my eyes narrowed as I felt the sudden and insistent touch of her Connected abilities against my mental barriers. Did she not know who I was?

"Justice Wilde," she said, the epitome of grace. "Allow me to be the first to welcome you here. We are honored by your presence."

"High Priestess Drake," I said, through ever so slightly clenched teeth.

The pressure from the leader of the LA coven didn't ease up as she uttered a light and tinkling laugh. "No need for formal titles with me. Call me Lara. You will find the coven in Los Angeles to be one of the most progressive in all the northern hemisphere. I understand you've had the opportunity to meet High Priestess Danae?"

Throughout this entire recitation, the witch's pressure did not ease. If anything, it increased in its intensity. As if she was so confident in the distraction of her words that she didn't even bother to monitor my reaction.

I shrugged mentally. Two could play at that game, but I wasn't necessarily sure that a display of power was my best gambit here. Not when I was the one who needed the information. No matter how irritated I was at the lack of respect from the high priestess of the LA coven, I continued to suffer the witch's pressure on my mind and gave her a winning smile.

"Of course. I've had the pleasure of working with Danae a number of times, starting in Las Vegas."

Lara's attention flicked by to Armaeus, ever so slightly frostier. "There really was no need for that, as the LA coven was so much closer to Las Vegas than the Chicago coven."

If Armaeus picked up on her censure, he didn't betray it. His answer was as smooth as hundred-year-old scotch. "My specific requirement at the time dealt with ley lines. I'm sure you'll agree that Danae's expertise in that area is undeniable."

"Oh, I suppose," Lara said, "though it's not as if she invented the discipline of managing such energy sources. We also have a great deal of experience in ley lines, as well you know."

"Of course," Armaeus murmured. I watched Lara more closely, flicking open my third eye to improve the view. Her energy was a study in contrasts. When she focused on the magician, she was all feminine guile, sultry and alluring and powerful. On the outer edge of her focus, she was acutely aware of the conversations and positioning of all the other witches in the coven, at least the ones currently present at Lure. She did manage to maintain a tendril of attention toward me, poking and prodding at my mental barriers, but even as I watched her, her interest in that was waning.

Suddenly, a flare of energy bloomed at my solar plexus, coils of interest snaking toward me. I blocked them without hesitation, and I didn't miss the flash of frustration across Lara's face or the narrowing of her eyes on Armaeus.

This provided me with a wealth of information. First, Lara had totally drunk the Kool-Aid that Armaeus was the most powerful member of the Arcana Council, bar none. She was so convinced of that fact, she wasn't giving me the time of day. She completely did not believe that I was the one blocking her efforts to crawl through my brainpan. I tried not to take that personally, since I fully planned on using her prejudice against her, but it did piss me off.

Armaeus, for his part, merely gave Lara a rich and indulgent smile. He could clearly read my thoughts.

"But now we are here, and I'm sure you know why," he murmured, turning subtly toward me. I was the star of this show, after all. It was time for me to shine.

Lara dutifully pivoted my way. "I can't imagine why Justice would take such an interest in the private business of a coven—any coven, but especially one as old and revered as ours."

Irritation cycled through me, and I regarded her a little more shrewdly. Was she *trying* to annoy me, or was she merely exceptionally good at it? I decided to play it cool.

"I'm hoping that I won't be interested in your private business for very long," I said smoothly. "But perhaps some education is in order. I don't randomly show up on people's doorsteps without a summons to do so. In the case of your coven, I've received multiple summons."

"*Multiple,*" she echoed in disbelief, drawing up straighter. "Who? Who would dare to denigrate one of my witches?"

"Given your activism, your willingness to doubt the victim rings a little false, Lara." As that gibe sank in, I kept going. "You know who we're here to see."

"Tammy Butler, Gail Fredericks, Monica Jones. All of them among the most powerful and venerated of our number," she said frostily.

"Then I'll need to talk to them."

As Lara Drake stiffened enough to give her chiropractor fits for weeks, I flicked open my third eye. And realized that, once again, the full effort of her blocking mechanisms were trained on the Magician, not on me. Annoying though it was to be treated as a lesser player, I really did need to take Armaeus out more often. Because with him by my side as a distraction I could easily delve into Lara's energy field. I couldn't read her thoughts, which was definitely a skill I needed to put on my "developmental studies" list, but I could read where she was placing her energy.

And where she was placing her energy was…interesting.

"You're afraid." I spoke the words quietly, but from the way Lara reacted, you would have thought I'd announced it on the loudspeakers between synth pop rotations. She whirled on me, her face apoplectic with rage.

"Lara," Armaeus said quietly, and her expression instantly went slack for a hairsbreadth moment. Then she recovered.

"How *dare* you?" she seethed at me, which I thought was an interesting opening, since we'd already been introduced.

"Why?" I asked in return, and she knew what I meant: why was she afraid? I wasn't going to say the words aloud again unless she pushed me to it, but I was more than willing to be pushed. "What am I not understanding?"

"There's no end to what you don't understand — either of you," she said darkly, targeting this last comment to Armaeus. "But I'll start with the basics. I know Danae is here, and I know why — it's not to track the pattern of ley lines on the western coast, no matter what she wants you to believe. The coven of Los Angeles is in the middle of a power struggle, and though we are nowhere near as strong as the coven of the Iron Sea, we are not to be discounted."

"Who's looking to overtake you?"

"Who isn't?" she retorted. "But what's important is the prophecy of Myanya didn't come to our coven by chance. She sought the best-trained and most experienced witch in the world—and one with a taste for power."

"That implies age," Armaeus said amiably enough. "The women we're targeting are all younger than thirty-five. Are they Revenants?"

"They are not," Lara shook her head, clearly disgusted. "Nor are they reincarnates, though don't think I didn't check that when I realized the energies that were building. But I categorically deny that they are killing anyone who is not a witch in order to draw Myanya to them. Any consort who attempts mastery of Myanya knows the risk as well as the reward. They get what they get."

"That's your line?" I asked. "Really? A prophesied witch turning deadly to her potential consorts—killing them before they have a chance to fulfill the prophecy—is an outcome that should've been expected after how many thousands of years?"

She slanted her eyes at me. "You believe a powerful witch should be subjugated by a male not her equal?"

"Dude, it's not my sick prophecy. I'm not saying that the male witches who have reached out to subjugate the subject of the Myanya prophecy are winners, but they are following the script. Whoever Myanya is currently targeting as her vessel has changed that script. And I think that's a little sketchy." I looked around the room. "Where are the candidates, anyway? And do they know they're under scrutiny?"

"They do." Lara gestured to the tables to our right, and I turned, only to be drilled practically into the next century with the glares aimed my way.

"Well, nothing like getting off to a good start," I muttered.

"Gail Fredericks and Monica Jones have been friends since they were new initiates. Tammy Butler is younger, greener, and with more of a chip on her shoulder, which would indicate that she's more a candidate, but she's nowhere near as strong as the others."

I surveyed the women, particularly Tammy, who seemed to have a serious case of resting witch face. "Well, wouldn't she want to level up, then?"

"She would, ordinarily. But she's a descendent of one of the richest bloodlines in the coven and has never been one for subjugation. It's far more her style to strike a deal to get all the goodies without paying any price she didn't want to pay."

I nodded. "Fair enough. Lead on."

As we reached the tables, I realized it wasn't three witches, but six. Behind each of the woman sat their lesser counterparts—assistants, I had to assume, or initiates. They all looked frightened of their mentors, which raised my hackles. What was it about some groups that instead of nurturing the next generation, they preferred to eat their young?

"Justice Wilde," Lara announced. "Please allow me to introduce—"

"She knows who we are," snapped Tammy. "Heather spilled the beans." She shot a dark look at her apprentice, who cowered back. Lara watched Tammy with cold speculation, and I, in turn, watched them both. Tammy had disrespected Lara in front of me. That wouldn't go well for the young, brash witch.

Then Tammy addressed me directly. "As we know who you are. You've been sent here to take what's rightfully ours."

I lifted my brows. "I have?"

"Tammy," clucked Gail Fredericks. Her sleek chignon of ice blonde hair complemented her patrician features beautifully. I found myself wanting to like her, which was a clear indication she was trouble. "Justice Wilde doesn't go where she's not summoned. She's not the one with the agenda."

She shifted her cool eyes to me as I caught sight of Nikki moving toward me from across the room. "But there *is* an agenda, I believe. I'm not sure if you know what you've stepped into, Justice Wilde. But it's about to get—so much worse, I fear."

I didn't have time for a snappy comeback before Nikki reached me. Her face was grim. "We've got an almost certain homicide, right in the heart of Beverly Hills." She flicked her gaze to Lara. "It's the rapper."

Lara's face was triumphant. "How tragic. But as you can see, we're all here."

"You are," Armaeus said summarily. "Though, of course, your immediate presence proves nothing. Not when you're a witch."

He reached for my hand, and we disintegrated before their startled faces.

CHAPTER TWENTY-ONE

W"ell, this isn't what I expected."

Armaeus and I crouched down in CSI gear, surveying the crime scene. The room looked like an old-world gentleman's study that had been converted to a magic romper room. The inlaid wood floors, walls painted the color of deep burgundy, and muted Renaissance master artworks in gilt frames were in stark contrast to the bloody corpse on the floor.

RZ lay on the ground, his arms and legs outstretched, what was left of his head filling in the top pinnacle of the pentagram that had been painted on the floor. Though Armaeus had more of a grasp on his glamour, I was still working through how mine worked. Accordingly, it was probably better for me to keep my head down and focused on the floor. Armaeus had explained the finer points of the requirements as we'd poofed back into existence in a place I knew I'd never been and suspected he hadn't as well.

Which begged the question — how had he gotten us here? Did the Magician not have the same constraint I did — that he needed to physically see a location before he could travel to it? I sighed. Probably.

"Who are you? I thought Joe was on call tonight."

The gruff voice brought Armaeus to his feet, but I remained on my knees, studying the body. When the two of them walked a few steps away, I flicked my third eye open.

And determined that RZ was well and truly dead.

I winced as I focused on the rapper, or what was left of him. There wasn't much. While most magical circuits did not survive the killing blow, there was generally at least a hint of the power that had been there before. I'd studied RZ when he'd been alive, I knew that he had some skills.

Those skills hadn't been merely shut off, I realized. They'd been stripped away.

"Who got to you, RZ?"

Despite my distaste for the rapper and nascent necromancer, I hadn't wanted to see him dead. At least not like this. I suspected he hadn't seen his end coming either. His end, or his executioner, or both. I leaned forward and sniffed, and smelled a mixture of frankincense and eucalyptus oil, his body still glistening from his preparations to subjugate his target.

But why tonight? RZ more than most knew the players in the LA coven, knew where they would be. His minions would have kept track of them for him, if nothing else. Why would he make his play now?

Had we been misled entirely?

"Tell me what I need to know, RZ," I muttered. RZ, unfortunately, was not very forthcoming.

"Did he die immediately? Please tell me he died immediately. Oh, my God. Oh, my God."

The voice came from somewhere above my head, and I leaned back to see a tall, slender man wringing his hands and looking positively gray. "Um, this is a crime scene," I said, trying to sound official. "I don't think you should—"

"Oh, they can't see me." The man waved me off, and I blinked at him, staring a little harder. He gazed back, looking yet more gray. My tattoo of the Eye of Horus flared on my left bicep, practically glowing through my glamour.

A tattoo I'd gotten from…

No. Just, no.

"You're not a dead guy," I said flatly. "I can't see dead people."

"Oh, for heaven's sake, you can too," the dead guy said. "I've lived in this house for two years since RZ raised me from the dead, and that was before he really knew what he was doing, God love him." He sighed as he looked at the body on the floor. "But I was halfway across the city at a spa when he decided to go full frontal today. I got back as fast as I could."

"I…" I shut my mouth, then opened it again, doing my best impression of a guppy on a pier. So many parts of what the gray man had said hurt my brain. "You live here?" I finally managed. "You know how he died? And—he really could raise the dead? That wasn't merely schtick?"

"Well, how he died is kind of obvious, don't you think?" The gray man flapped a hand at what was left of RZ's skull. "And of course he could raise the dead. Not very *well*, all the time, but—he tried. What I want to know is if he suffered. He didn't deserve that, for all his tendency to swing his dick around."

"Ahh—sure. Well…" I looked down at RZ. He looked back at me, his expression more surprised than anything else. "I really don't think he did. But wouldn't you know better?"

"No, no, it doesn't work that way." The gray man sighed irritably. "You'd think Death would at least have given you the basics if she was going to slap the Eye of Horus on you."

"I'm right there with you. So tell me how you knew RZ, then."

"Well, it was hard not to. He moved into this place three years ago, fully knowing that the prophecy was going to be fulfilled. He had an entire map upstairs dedicated to it."

"You're kidding," I said, peering up. "Does he still have it?"

"No, no. He didn't want anyone to know how much work he put into the process, preferring to make everyone believe that it was all, you know, *divine inspiration*. And it wasn't the only prophecy he was following. You know necromancers and their ridiculous ways."

"Uh, yeah. They sure are a crazy bunch."

The gray man nodded in contented agreement. "Richard more than most. He was convinced that he needed the blood of a true witch to reach his goals. He wanted the virgin that Myanya had targeted for her blood even more than he wanted to subjugate her — he thought she *might* have known that too, but then he decided she couldn't. She was only a woman desperate for his touch and all that. He was a little sexist, you ask me."

"A man who wanted to drain the blood of a virgin witch in the middle of a magical ritual to fulfill a prophecy that enabled him to subjugate said witch," I said drily. "I can't imagine where you got the idea he was sexist."

"Yes, well, I've been around awhile. I've seen a lot of that sort of thing. But he wasn't as bad as some of them who've moved through this place." The gray man glanced up. "Oh!" He shuddered, then poofed out of existence.

"Miss Wilde." I turned and squinted as Armaeus approached, the police officer apparently satisfied for the moment with our credentials. The Magician dropped to one knee, giving RZ's body only the most casual of glances. "What have you found?"

I decided against telling Armaeus about the dead guy, since the Magician hadn't told me anything about Death's little gift with purchase, and I really thought he should have. Instead, I transferred my attention to RZ.

"He's about as dead as a Connected can get," I said. "His magic wasn't neutralized. From the looks of it, it was velcroed off him. It wouldn't surprise me if whoever nailed him now has a taste for hip hop."

"As always, colorful, if not particularly useful," Armaeus said. "He made the attempt to connect with Myanya's proxy?"

"Definitely." I crouched back on my heels. Setting aside the intel I'd gotten from the gray man, there were all the classic signs of a man who'd read the fine print of the prophecy, as shared by the brothers Jones as part of their agreement to avoid Judgment's grasp for the time being. "He's wearing the symbols of a high priest, so he was definitely bringing his big guns to the party. But there's nothing on his body that explains what happens next."

"His head exploded — without signs of an entry wound."

"Yeah." I shivered. "It's all exit." I pointed to the top of the pentagram, where bits of gore and bone lay piled up as if there'd been a wall there. Several more inches along the circle, the fragments burst out in a splatter of gore outside the circle. "Circle broke there. Don't know if it was from the force of the internal blast, a weakness in his design, or sabotage. But I don't think the break in the circle had anything to do with his death."

"Agreed," Armaeus said, regarding the circle thoughtfully. "I don't believe there was anything wrong with RZ's magic. He was, perhaps more than most of her challengers, one of the best candidates to ensure that Myanya achieved her prophecy. Because of his unique vices, he also is someone she could have controlled. His failure in his attempt to trigger the prophecy is…interesting."

"Because you're thinking that she would've gone for this guy?"

"He fits all the requirements. He's strong, extremely vital, he has a background in the appropriate practices to satisfy the ancient requirements of the prophecy. He's brash enough to give it a try. And he's weak enough that the period of Myanya's subjugation would likely not have lasted all that long."

"I don't know, he seemed like kind of an asshole to me."

"An ass, yes, but once again, one who was beholden to his own vices. Sooner or later, that was going to prove his undoing."

I glanced at Armaeus, noting that his eyes had turned a curious milky black. He was invoking deep magic, but with a twist I hadn't seen before. He was viewing the future, I knew without a doubt, though how I could know such a thing was beyond me. Was this the benefit of his new DayGlo-pink circuitry?

"What are you seeing?" I asked quietly, not wanting to disrupt his flow. Would my eyes start to look like that if I focused on my magic more? I didn't think that would be an awesome look on me.

"There were many likely futures for Richard Zachariah," Armaeus said. "He could have grown in

214

power and strength in his chosen field of necromancy. He could've become a sorcerer of legitimate renown. One path had him walking in step with Kreios, sweeping his way through a world gone mad with chaos and pain."

I made a face. "That doesn't seem like a future we wanted to support."

"Not at all, but it was one that was viably open to him. What was not open to him was a sudden and violent death before he had reached the next level of his development."

I frowned at the dead body on the ground. "I think you may need to adjust your settings."

"No," Armaeus said thoughtfully. "It's not me that's turned the channels of the world to a new frequency. The witch that Myanya has chosen as her vessel has changed the game. Now, combined with Myanya's growing power, she has become chaos and rage, and can no longer be contained."

"What are you saying?" I looked at him, confused. "We've got to be able to rein her in, Armaeus. We can't just have her go all Hulk Smash on the entire witch community, not to mention random people she's decided have misbehaved and so she's going to enact her own kind of vigilante justice on them. That's not her job, it's mine."

"Agreed, and I am not saying there's nothing to be done. I'm saying that...this bears serious study." The Magician's eyes were even darker now, the milkiness completely gone, replaced with a deep black almost liquid in appearance. Staring at him was like staring into the primordial goop that had formed a world. He looked altogether distracted, like he was fading from existence in the mortal realm.

Wait a minute...

"Hey!" I leapt to my feet, making a dash toward him, but I was left grabbing open space. I pivoted around, feeling totally exposed.

"Look, can we have—" The cop who was standing at the other end of the pentagram turned and squinted at me.

"Who the hell are *you*? Can we not go one day without us running through another rotation of scene techs, for chrissakes? I can't keep track of you people as it is."

I didn't wait for him to finish his tirade. I couldn't poof as neatly as Armaeus could, but I did have a certain set of skills, and I was getting better and better at them. They merely involved slightly more fireworks.

"What in the hell!"

I caught the cop's gaze as he scrambled back and gave him a cheery wave, barely avoiding setting him on fire.

CHAPTER TWENTY-TWO

I poofed back into the same space I'd left at Lure, only there was no one at the collection of tables but Tammy's admin, bawling her eyes out. The other witches and their sidekicks had left.

"What's going on?" I demanded, and the weepy Heather looked up at me, her eyes red, her hands folding and unfolding in exactly the same manner as the gray man.

"T-they killed Tammy," she gasped, then burst into another round of sobs. Even from five paces, I could feel the power wafting off Heather like a protective net. The girl was legit scared.

"*What?*" I looked around as if there would be another body under one of the chairs, but not only were there no dead witches, the party at Lure was going full tilt. Surely they'd have taken a bio break to move the gurney out if Tammy had bought it at the club. I hadn't been gone that long!

"Dollface." Nikki pushed her way through the crowd, the relief on her face evident. "Armaeus let Kreios know where you guys went to, then he went radio silent. The police scanners have blown up with the RZ death, and the paparazzi are all over it."

"And here?" I asked, pointing at Heather.

"That." Nikki grimaced. "About two seconds after you left, Tammy started showing signs of distress. The others swept her up and bundled her off to the bathroom, ordering the admins to stay behind in case you came back. They got her about halfway, and it was clear she wasn't just suffering from a spiked mojito. Kreios got them out of the club and into the limos without anyone batting an eye, then everyone was ordered to hit Witch HQ. Tammy died before they reached it."

"They killed her," Heather cried.

Nikki shrugged. "The only people in the limo with her were Gail, Monica, and the driver, who reported that Tammy was screaming in pain, grabbing her stomach tight, looking very credibly sick. When she died, it was...messy."

I winced. I'd seen how RZ's life had ended. "Well, she was one of our top suspects, so that whittles down the list a bit.

"They *killed* her," Heather moaned again, hugging herself.

"The admins headed out, but Heather here stayed put, insisting that you would return and that she wanted to talk to you when you did. The cops are now crawling all over the limo, but they won't hit Lara and the witches until tomorrow. The crime scene, such as it is, is already contaminated as shit, since the witches of Eastwick were in no mood to remain covered in gore. They bailed almost immediately."

I nodded. "You said Kreios arranged transportation?"

Nikki nodded, clearly appreciating my leap of logic. If Kreios had set up the transpo, there would be video and audio of the drive. We'd see most of what we needed in that. "The Council was happy to help the coven in their time of need, though no one could have predicted the cleanup required."

"You have to stop them," sniffled Heather.

I motioned Nikki to move off for a moment, then sat down next to the weeping admin. She was only an initiate, but she was a high-level Connected in her own right. With her so obviously on her guard, Nikki wouldn't be able to get anything out of her memories, and I couldn't read minds. That left me with old-fashioned interrogation.

"What do you think happened to Tammy, specifically?" I asked her, as gently as I could.

Heather's face seemed to crumple, and I thought she was going to burst into another round of tears. Then she rallied. "She wasn't the best mentor, but she did try. She wanted the coven to be strong. She was ready to sacrifice herself to be Myanya's vessel. And they knew it."

"They being Gail and Monica?"

"All of them," Heather said darkly. "Gail and Monica have been allies for decades, and they knew this was coming as well, but they were too far into their own self-importance to make such a sacrifice, even temporarily. That said, they didn't want someone else to steal the glory. You can see the problem."

I couldn't, really, but I attempted to restate. "They wanted Tammy to be the fall girl, but they were worried that after the prophecy was fulfilled, she would emerge stronger than either of them."

"Tammy was already stronger than Monica, but she didn't have faith in her abilities. She wanted to be a celebrity, wanted to be respected. And she was so beautiful, mixing and mingling with them, so full of power and hope. She'd let me come to all the parties and now…and now she's—" Heather put her fist to her mouth briefly, then resolutely dropped it again. "She didn't deserve what they did to her. She didn't want to take power from anyone. She wanted it all for the coven—everything in her life for the coven. They didn't have to—"

This time, Heather did burst into tears, and I let her cry for a bit, handing her some of the linen napkins that had been teased into tiny swan shapes on the table. She dissolved for another minute or so, then looked up. Her makeup was barely streaked, and I was reminded again of how young she felt to me. She'd been well paired with Tammy, by far the youngest of the trifecta of witches caught up in the prophecy.

"How did they do it?"

"A spell," Heather said, sounding utterly defeated. "It's against coven rules to attack each other, but Tammy seemed to be the only one concerned with coven protocol. When I saw her—the last I saw of her—she had a strange cast to her skin. It didn't surprise me that she wasn't feeling well, but I watched her stumble and them both swoop in and—I knew. The poison or bad food or whatever she consumed was enough to weaken her. They did the rest."

"Why didn't you move in to protect her?"

"Me?" Heather looked at me in disbelief. "I'm not all that good at magic, if you want me to be honest. Tammy was patient, but I…I don't know what I'm going to do now." She balled up the napkin in her hand, dropping her eyes to it. "They'll reassign me to a new mentor. That's going to be a joy."

"We'll figure that out," I said, standing. I didn't know if covens ever traded their initiates, but Danae might know a better place for this girl. "What about the other two initiates? Were they aware of the plot against Tammy?"

"*Them.*" Heather shook her head and stood as well, shooting me a grateful smile. "You know, I shouldn't say anything bad about them. They're nice, or they try to be. It's not easy to make friends when you halfway think you should be competing with each other, but they're fun to talk to. They really like their mentors too, so I try to give them the benefit of the doubt but—I know they were worried about Tammy. That she might be the one, and what that would mean."

"Worried in what way?"

Heather sniffed. "Well, she was…different, you know. She didn't take shit from anyone, no matter how important they were. She wanted to be an actress, a celebrity, as much as a witch, and did everything on her terms. She even told off Herm Lannister so hard at Comic-Con, he blackballed her."

"Really. You know Herm Lannister is dead, right?"

"I…*no.*" Heather's lower lip started to tremble.

"Yes."

"What's happening?" she mewled, crumpling all over again.

We moved through the club, Nikki on our heels, but there were no other witches remaining at Lure. The drive to Witch HQ was subdued. The farther we got out of LA, the posher and more high-rolling the estates. When we finally turned off the main thoroughfare, we were near Santa Monica, and I began to catch sight of the ocean.

"Pretty swank," I murmured, and that stirred Heather to attention.

"It's one of the most exclusive neighborhoods in Los Angeles," she said, her focus finally off her hands and onto the countryside as long, well-lit lanes streamed off into the darkness of treed estates behind massive gates. "I don't know all the details, but the LA coven has a lot of money and even more land. They've been sitting on most of it, and whoever rules as the head of the coven gets the house for the duration of her tenure. When she's replaced, she's set up in another palace up the coast. There's, like, a half dozen of them, some of them sitting empty, so there's never any question of there being enough space."

"So no real incentive to stay head witch," Nikki put in. "Seems to me retirement on the coast of the Pacific Ocean in your very own castle would be a pretty graceful way to step out of the limelight."

"It would, but that didn't mean it's something anyone wants," Heather said, her voice rueful. "You get a lot of power as the head of a coven, and this is Los Angeles, after all. If you're not the top dog, you're pretty easily forgotten. Once you've been around the city long enough, it becomes a burning obsession to stay relevant. Witches aren't that different from movie stars in that respect. At least not here."

"Fair enough." We turned off the road and glided through an enormous white gate carved out of what looked like marble. Instead of proceeding to a mausoleum, however, we coasted along a lane bordered by manicured fruit trees until the lights of the main house emerged as we crested a low rise. Lara Drake's mansion spread out in front of us, and I whistled.

"Whoa," Nikki agreed, leaning forward. "This is where you throw witch parties?"

"Only for the most important celebrations." Heather laughed. "I've only been here a handful of times. Most of the time, we gather in a central assembly house a few miles away. Still very beautiful, but—not quite as grand."

"It'd be hard to find someplace as grand as this," I said.

The house looked like something a Rockefeller had built or at least stayed in, a sprawling three-story building with a large entrance atop a sweeping staircase. Additional staircases led to side entrances in the two-story flanking wings, and every room in the place was lit up. Even the curved driveway that nudged up to the central entrance arched gracefully, giving the place the feel of a palace.

"I do not even want to know how many millions of dollars this cost," Nikki muttered, and Heather sighed with appreciation as well.

"It's been in the coven for so long, and was built by the coven, that I'm sure there's no official appraisal on the books. The coven has a way of avoiding the kind of taxation questions the way a lot of billionaires do. And then there's the rumor mill that helps things along too. It doesn't take much to convince the superstitious to leave alone women suspected to be witches—at least when those women are already in power." Her voice shaded a little darker. "It takes quite a lot to get to that position of power, unfortunately."

"Preach," Nikki said.

The car stopped, and we exited, only to be escorted up the stairs by three silent footmen. They weren't wearing powdered wigs and we weren't wearing ball gowns, but I still got the eerie impression that we were stepping into a strange and distant place. Only a few weeks ago, I'd attended straight-up costume parties in ancient homes, but Lara's bungalow put them all to shame. It was both thoroughly modern and thoroughly steeped in history at the same time, leaving you with the sense of being stranded in a parallel reality.

I was sure this was an illusion Lara was deliberately trying to foster, but that didn't make it any less successful.

We reached the grand foyer. It was lit up like a runway, and it was clear that an assembly of some kind was going on in the room to the right.

"That's where we have the high celebrations," Heather confirmed as the footmen bowed away from us at the door. "I've never explored beyond this floor and—oh—"

Heather's voice broke off abruptly, her eyes going wide. I turned to see what she was looking at. And I totally got why she was staring.

"Miss Wilde," Armaeus said from the doorway, Lara on his arm. The high priestess of the LA coven looked ready to faint. "I'm so glad you're here."

I blinked, then blinked again, my feet moving forward of their own volition while my heart seemed frozen in place.

"Sweet Mother Mary on a Vibrator," Nikki breathed beside me. "What's gotten into him? And where can I get me some?"

I understood exactly what she was saying. Standing before us was the Magician, a being I'd known going on two years now, a being who'd shared my bed. Recently, in fact. Yet the man standing in front of me was like nothing I had ever seen before. Armaeus seemed practically on fire with sexual energy, far more like Kreios than the Magician. His deep black hair was swept back from his high cheekbones, his smile easy and expansive. His suit was impeccably tailored, open at the neck, with gleams of platinum silver at his cuffs. The outfit alone was enough to turn heads, but it wasn't the clothes that made the man in this case. It was the magic.

"Oh," Heather sighed again, and I smiled, looking at her. She was saucer-eyed with appreciation for the Magician's magician-ness, and once again, I didn't blame her.

"I can introduce you?"

"Please," she said and she seemed to shiver a little before she turned to me, her eyes starry with awe. "I—I mean I have seen him before. He was talking to Mrs. Drake earlier. But I didn't notice… I mean he seems so—different here."

Nikki snorted. "He's definitely working it. We can only hope he's doing it on purpose. Otherwise, God help us all."

By now, we'd reached Armaeus, and I greeted an exceptionally distracted Lara, then turned to Heather. Before I could speak, however, Armaeus moved forward and held out his hands. The young woman could do nothing but lift hers to his, her entire body jolting when the Magician squeezed her fingers.

"It's been my pleasure to meet all the witches of the LA coven, but I don't believe I have ever had the pleasure," Armaeus murmured in his richly rolling lilt.

"Heather is only an initiate," Lara said, and I didn't miss the edge to her voice, or the sudden dimming of Heather's star. Armaeus, however, didn't diminish his focus on the young woman.

"Then you have a lifetime of extraordinary discoveries before you." He gave her hands another squeeze. Heather brightened again, and I turned to Lara before she could get off another zinger.

"Can you tell me what you know? What's happened?" I asked, and she flashed an irritated look at Armaeus before she returned her focus to me, then seemed to re-center herself. I didn't know why the Magician was pouring on the charm, but as Lara and I entered the assembly room, I could see she wasn't the only one who'd been affected by it. The other two initiates were staring at Armaeus with open adoration, and so were half the more established witches, male and female alike.

"Heather, you'll wait here until the other initiates come for you," Lara said haughtily. "Then the three of you should head home."

"But—"

"I'll wait with you," Armaeus, said, which did an excellent job of convincing Heather to accept Lara's decree. He curled her arm into his, and moved down the hallway as she stared at him, completely transported.

"And I've got a date with the security guys the Council has rustled up to lock down the house. We'll make sure no one gets in or out—at least by ordinary means—without us knowing it." Nikki winked at me. "The rest is up to you."

"Very well," Lara said, then glanced my way. "Justice Wilde, please come with me. I can tell you everything I know. But the only thing I'm sure of is that our coven is under attack."

CHAPTER TWENTY-THREE

L ara quickly crossed through the knots of whispering coven members, and though she was moving with speed, our route was not the most straightforward to the open door at the far end of the room. Instead, she made sure that everyone saw her walking with me. By the time we entered the antechamber that appeared to serve as her office, we were drawing almost as many stares as Armaeus.

"Finally," Lara said, crossing to the bar. The high priestess of the LA coven poured herself a glass of wine, then turned back to me. She didn't offer me a drink, but I tried not to judge her for that. Much.

"What do you know?" I asked again.

She waved her glass, glaring at me. "You think I'm overstating our problem. I assure you I'm not. As Justice of the Arcana Council, it's your obligation to intervene."

That wasn't exactly the way my job worked, but I was willing to work with it. "Did you know Tammy had been targeted? Richard Zachariah?"

"I told you, Richard Zachariah was a pestilence and a sham," she sniffed. "His death is nothing but a boon to any serious practitioners of the craft.

"I examined him, Lara. He was no sham. He had real magic within him." *Had* being the operative term, but Lara was still hand-waving me off.

"You saw what he worked hard to show the world, whenever he wanted to gain credibility," she said. "Whatever lingering spell was still in effect to give him the illusion of true power, I do not begrudge him. But he sought to advance without proper training, creating a cult of personality around himself that was an affront. No coven would have him."

"That didn't stop him from trying to co-opt the prophecy of Myanya," I pointed out.

She sniffed again. "Well, now that horrible chapter is put to rest."

My brows shot up as she took a long swig of wine. "It is?"

"Of course," Lara said. "With the death of Tammy Butler, our coven will return to its natural state. I had hoped that we would advance sharply with the fulfillment of the Myanya prophecy, but in the end, it remains too much for any one woman to bear. I shouldn't be surprised. Since Iskra Mikhailova rejected the prophecy in 1962, the magic has never recovered. And, too, we are in much changed times. Perhaps there is no place for such ancient magic anymore."

"You think Tammy's death will end Myanya's claim? Won't she simply jump to the next witch up?"

"This isn't a sporting team, Justice Wilde," Lara said thinly. "The prophecy takes time to establish itself in a witch, to grow. Tammy Butler was not my top candidate, frankly, but she was certainly a candidate, one you had also targeted. With her abrupt demise, there is no possibility that Myanya continues."

"But the two witches that were our other suspects were sitting right next to Tammy in the car when she died," I said. "How hard would it be for energy like that to simply transfer?"

"I have questioned both witches quite carefully," Lara replied dismissively. "They're still in trauma, understandably. The Magician was kind enough to show me the footage from the debacle in the limousine. I can show you as well, if you would like."

"I would like that." I watched as she moved to her desk. She picked up an elegant remote, and a second later, a screen whirred down from the ceiling. With a single click of the remote, an image flickered to life on the screen.

It was the interior of a well-appointed limousine, the video having been shot in bright color. The three witches were clearly visible, with Tammy partially stretched out on the backseat, the other two witches seated along two banquettes that lined the sides of the car. Both Gail and Monica appeared credibly upset, but the real star of the production was Tammy. She clutched her stomach, her face positively green, her lips peeled back. Light flecks of yellow bile stained her lips, and she moaned in genuine distress.

A second later, the scene abruptly changed. Tammy screamed and her head jerked back as a foreign substance coated the camera lens, obscuring the other two women, who lurched back as if they'd been scalded, their mouths open in terror. After that, the car swerved abruptly, clearly being pulled over to the side. The women scrambled for the doors, falling out into the darkness beyond. Meanwhile, the body of Tammy Butler remained completely motionless. I couldn't see her head anymore, but given the angle of the camera, her hands and feet were flung wide, frozen in an exaggerated pentagram position. Just like RZ.

"Who did this?" I breathed, speaking more to the screen than Lara. Unfortunately, Lara was more than happy to answer.

"None of *us*, I can assure you," she said tartly. "One of the oldest and most sacred charges for any of our witches is that the coven reigns supreme. No one makes an attack on one of our own witches. To do so would unravel the very fabric of our organization, and we are nothing if we cannot maintain our core of strength. There is no other alternative than that we are being attacked from the outside. Someone is using our focus on the Myanya prophecy to strike when we are at our weakest."

I blew out a long breath, still studying the video. At this point, the driver of the limo had poked her head into the back of the vehicle and recoiled, but had left the body where it lay. "Well, that's certainly a possibility," I said. "But it's only one of several."

After all, Heather had been certain of Gail and Monica's guilt. The girl might be an initiate, but she wasn't stupid.

Lara didn't respond right away, but that was okay. I could let her stew for a second as I tried to make sense of what I was seeing. "Could you run that feed again for me?"

Lara gasped, and I rolled my eyes. "Look, it's a reasonable request," I said, swinging toward her —

Then I bolted forward. I caught Lara as she slumped to the floor, the glass hitting the carpet and spilling red wine all over the creamy pattern. I didn't wait, but immediately flicked my third eye open, fixing on Lara's skittering circuits.

If my third eye had sported an eyebrow, it would have shot straight up. Because in this case, there was absolutely no magical attack occurring at all. Lara's body was compromised, quite heavily so, from a shot of pure poison. There was no question in my mind that said poison had come from the glass of wine she'd just inhaled. Poison, however, was usually an organic compound, and any organic matter was made up of energy. Energy was my game.

I sent a burst of healing power through Lara's inert body, stripping away the strength of the poison and reinvigorating the muscles and nerves it sought to deaden. It was an extremely fast-acting poison, but I reached Lara's heart a moment before it did, and her brain was never seriously in danger. In another moment, Lara coughed, and I rolled her over to her side, pulling her hair out of the way as she further damaged her expensive carpet. I was pretty sure that no amount of magic would render that carpet redeemable at this point, but such was the danger of running a coven. Cleaning bills were the least of your problems.

"I'll go get—"

"No!" To my surprise, Lara staggered to her knees, waving at me frantically. "Don't tell anyone of this. No one must know."

I stared at her for a second, my lips curling in a derision I didn't try to hide. "Look, I get that you don't want people to know you have a weakness, and I even get that you don't want people to know you could've just been killed. But the fact remains, you could've just been killed. You've got a big problem on your hands, and unless you're not telling me something, it's almost certainly coming from somebody in the next room. Exactly how many enemies do you have?"

"More than I like to think about." Lara scowled, then took a deep breath. "The doors were open when I left to greet you. Anyone could have come in then—or this wine could have been poisoned weeks ago."

"True."

"But you misunderstand me," Lara continued. "I don't want you to tell everyone I've just been attacked. I want you to tell everyone I've just been killed. The attacks—they're still coming. I want to see who reveals themselves as being behind this little coup."

She waved at the mess on the floor, then at the bar, then herself. "Please—a towel, napkin. Anything."

"Right." I hurried to the bar and ran water over a towel, then brought it back to her, brushing her hands away as I wiped her face. "So you want me to convince the others you're dead. Keep you hidden away."

"I'll need to stay hidden away," she agreed. "Until we know the truth. But there are witches here who've known me a very long time. I'll need your help in convincing them I'm dead. Starting now."

I wasn't entirely convinced this was a good idea, but I nodded, reaching for and creating the same bubble of silence that I'd accessed in Lure. Anything within the bubble still was kicking along, but those outside the bubble...

She lifted her brows. "You're in here with me too. Your Magician will notice immediately."

"He's good at faking it, and we need his reaction to convince the peanut gallery out—"

At that exact moment, the door to Lara's study blew open, the heavy panels rotating completely on their hinges before smacking into the walls. Armaeus filled the doorway, his eyes wide. "Miss *Wilde*."

"Help me!" I managed with a credible amount of sincerity as Lara slumped in my arm. "Close the doors!"

That last was purely for show, but Armaeus complied anyway, slamming the doors shut with a wave of his hands. He advanced into the room more cautiously now, his gaze going from Lara's grinning face to mine, then to the mess of wine and vomit on the floor. If anyone had seen that, it was only going to improve our story.

"What...is going on?" He reached out and tested the force field I had built, and it was his turn to smile thoughtfully. "You do learn quickly, Miss Wilde."

"Someone just laced Lara's wine with a straight shot of poison. I thought it was—" I frowned, looking at the spot where the guard had stood, but didn't much feel like biting into that cupcake of crazy right now. "Someone in the next room. Either way, it's probably someone close."

"It could be anyone," Lara groaned. "We held a ceremony here two nights ago, on the full moon. The entire coven was in attendance. Slipping into my office with a hypodermic filled with poison would have been child's play for half of them. It was merely a matter of waiting for me to drink it."

"Right," I said. "Especially with that in mind, Lara's convinced me that she's better off dead."

The tide of conversation was rising in the room outside, and Lara nodded. "If I'm dead, there must be a successor to lead the coven. Ordinarily, that successor is chosen in a naming ceremony within these very walls, one that can be called by even the newest of our number—which is why I don't often hold celebrations here, nor have witches for centuries, other than the ones in which we are very strong."

"The death of Tammy Butler," Armaeus said. "The gathering here."

"It can't be a coincidence. If I'd been thinking clearly, I would have seen it, but I felt absolutely no threat," Lara insisted. "It was only natural for me to gather my strongest witches close to reassure them. That level of reassurance is best achieved here, not in the

Assembly House, especially after the ceremony earlier this week. We wouldn't have another reason to meet here for weeks. I also believed—would still like to believe—the threat comes from outside the coven, not inside it. But now…"

"Yeah, probably not. Nevertheless." I withdrew my arms from her, and she sat up, smoothing her hair. "We can't keep you here."

"I can transport her," Armaeus said. "She'll be safe. You'll need to stay here, however, Miss Wilde. Nikki's still on the grounds, and I'll alert her to keep the perimeter closed. But if there's going to be some sort of claim to power, your magic is most closely attuned to the coven's."

"Well, you seemed to be dialing yours in quite nicely too," I teased, and Lara watched us with patent curiosity, her gaze shifting like a rabid tennis fan's as each of us spoke.

"I was working on my own theory, as it happens." Armaeus smiled as he spoke the words, the curious pink-gold light flaring in the depths of his black gaze. Something was ratcheting up his alien DNA, without question. "The witches of the LA coven, like many organizations worldwide, know the Arcana Council only tangentially. That's been by design, of course. There's been no advantage to advertise our strength, especially when we weren't as strong as we now are. As a result, a certain measure of mystery has grown up around the Council. Mystery can be useful. Ignorance is not. And a lack of respect least of all."

The dots connected in my mind. "They know you're the Magician, and they know—knew—remembered—or thought they once heard something about your magic being born of Enochian sex magick. You were playing them."

"Not exactly playing them." His lips curled into a sultry smile. "My strength is born of sexual mastery, yes. However, it's a very, very old variant of the practice, one that predates what is now known as modern sex magick by several thousand years. None of that is as relevant as me giving the impression of power to a group that was...perhaps unaware of or, more troubling, unimpressed with that power."

"Uh-huh. For any particular reason? Or did you simply want to get your rocks off while you passed the time waiting for something more interesting to happen?"

Armaeus laughed, and the sound ricocheted around the room, the effect on both Lara and myself immediate and visceral.

"Please tell me that wasn't felt by anyone outside the force field," I muttered, glad I was leaning against Lara's desk. Lara looked equally happy she was already on the floor.

"It wasn't," Armaeus said, eminently pleased at the impact he was having on us, and no doubt riding the same high of sexual response from the witches in the room beyond. "And primarily, it was an academic exercise. What I found, however, is that half the witches in the room were trying desperately to be noticed for their abilities, half of them were trying desperately to advance their abilities, and a very small subset — whom I could not identify — were trying desperately to *mask* their abilities. I was very close to identifying who when...your energy shifted.

"Interesting," I said, stepping away as Armaeus stooped to pick up Lara in his arms. "Well — take her and...I'll see if I can pick up where you left off."

"Agreed." The Magician nodded to me, his voice dropping to a distinctively low Austrian bass, channeling Arnold Schwarzenegger in *Terminator*. "I'll be—"

"Stop," I growled warningly as Armaeus disappeared, the hint of his laughter lingering on the unnaturally still air.

I stood there for a moment longer, considering all my options, barely hearing the whisper of gears. The sound was so faint, I almost dismissed it—

Then the floor dropped out beneath me.

Chapter Twenty-Four

I crashed to the floor after a drop of only about ten feet, rolling away from the opening as it slammed shut above me. "What the hell is this?"

An irritated voice floated out of the darkness. "It's not like you shouldn't have expected booby traps. It's an old house. Filled with deceivers. Traps are what they do."

I turned sharply, then turned again, trying to see in the darkness. I lifted my hand, and the typical blue glow of my magic barely created a puff of smoke.

"That won't work either," sighed the voice. "I swear, you people should do your research. You really think Lara is that smart? She's not. She merely inherited smart systems. Anything below the level of the main house is deeply and heavily warded against any magic of any type. Even that belonging to the Justice of the Arcana Council."

"Who are you?" I demanded. But I had a bad feeling I already knew. The silence that followed my question wasn't encouraging. "You're a dead person, aren't you? This little trap is where people are sent to die."

"Technically there *is* an exit," the voice defended itself. "I simply was already compromised when Miranda dumped me here."

"Miranda?"

"Miranda Green, 1942's version of Lara Drake, only nowhere near as pleasant. She'd discovered these subterranean corridors early in her reign and used to lock servants down with two days' worth of food and a flashlight, because the rumor was there was a way out to an exit corridor. Only a few made it out, though, and they were stone-cold insane by the time they managed it. Once she went through an entire season of staff members, she decided it was a good enough place to dump people she wanted to be forgotten. I was one of those people. My name is Oliver Malloy. It's a pleasure to meet you."

"Can I see you?"

"Sort of." A shift in the darkness, and a pale shaft of light eased out from behind the rock. It was barely enough illumination to discern features, but the figure was a short, slender man in a loose-fitting suit. He was crushing a fedora in his hands, and he seemed the soul of innocence.

"Why did she send you down here?" I asked, genuinely surprised. "And for that matter, why was I? Lara was already gone. Who had the controls?"

The apparition merely stared at me.

"You can't handle more than one question at a time, can you?"

"It's a question of civility, really," Oliver sniffed defensively. "You can't expect me to keep up with a train of thought that is constantly jumping the rails. No one knows the value of slowing down."

"What is this place, anyway? Some kind of basement?"

I looked around the room, my eyes slowly adjusting to the limited light of Oliver's glow. I'd expected it to be a cave system, but it didn't smell like a cave. It smelled like concrete, mildew, and rat dung.

Oliver remained quiet, and I backtracked, refocusing on him. "Do you know what this place is?"

"Certainly, though I haven't been out of this room, unfortunately. I cracked my head almost immediately. Always was a little too clumsy for my own good." He sighed as I waved my hand at him. "Civility, civility. No one has time for a proper story. But it was an underground system of rooms needed for the original structure on this property, before the witches bought it. A sanatorium. When patients died, they needed a way to transport their bodies out to sea without anyone seeing them, and then there were some examination rooms down here too. For the noisier residents."

I stared at him, horrified. "You're kidding me."

"Not at all. When the land was acquired in the late 1800s, the passages were filled in, or so it was said. But there were still the rumors of witches disappearing during high celebrations, or trespassers dispatched and no one ever knew the wiser."

"And you?"

He smiled sadly. "I had the misfortune of being a witch in love with Miranda Green, at a time when it proved not to be convenient for her anymore. She dropped me down here to tuck me out of sight when her primary lover showed up unexpectedly, and—like I said. I'm a bit klutzy."

"She killed you?"

"In her defense, she didn't mean to. And it wasn't like I could lobby a protest. I was dead."

"Did she know that you became a ghost?" I rubbed my bicep where the Eye of Horus itched with a flaring heat. I wasn't really sure how many dead people I could take in a single day. Especially not dead people at a sanatorium. Those had to be extra dead.

"I'm not a ghost. I can leave at any time."

Oliver's response brought me back to the more pressing issue: getting out. "You can? Then why are you here?"

He shook his head, and I flung out my hands in exasperation. "Come on! That technically wasn't two questions. Why are you here if you aren't actually a ghost? Why would you—" I cut myself off before I could double down on the question.

Oliver continued to twist his fedora. "Because you summoned me. That's the strength of the Eye of Horus that Death provided you." He smiled a little dreamily. "Ah, Death. Had I known she existed, I would never have fallen for Miranda. She was a real dame when she came to collect me."

"I'll try to unsee that," I muttered. I thought back to the dead guy I'd met earlier. Had I actually summoned him? He'd simply seemed to be there... I frowned, vaguely remembering my spoken question. What had I asked? And what had I said to bring Oliver back from the dead?

Either way, it didn't help.

"Why'd Lara deep six me?" I asked, staring at the ceiling.

"Not Lara," Oliver countered. "I doubt Lara knows of those particular controls, even in her own office. A woman entered—oh, I'm not even sure when. Time..." he sighed, seeming to become slightly less substantial.

"Focus, Oliver. It's important."

"It's just she was so...indistinct..." he faded some more, and I gave up.

"Scratch that question. How much do you know about what's going on upstairs? I have to get to wherever their high celebration room is."

"Ah! Yes, that I know" Oliver turned his gaze upward as if he could see through brick and earth. "In my day, there were two gathering points, one that was beneath the open sky, but you wouldn't use that. It's too cold outside. The other was in the center of the building, a solarium. Quite beautiful, in fact. The rays of moonlight would shine down on the gathered coven, bathing their bodies in silvery light. There was a center area, directly under the glassed-in ceiling, that was the focal point for the celebrations. Three full circles of seating surrounded that, though the chairs were not built in, so there may only be the daises remaining. The whole area before you reached the seats was about, oh, perhaps thirty feet in diameter."

"Big space."

"Needed to be, for all the witches. And the witches were truly glorious, particularly the women." He sighed happily.

"Poetic. Do you know if that still exists?" I hadn't been anywhere in the building but the main ballroom and Lara's study.

He looked at me mournfully. "I do not."

"Then how exactly are you helping me?"

"The spirits you summon are intended to give you whatever you don't have. Sometimes it's answers, sometimes merely…" He shrugged, making his light beam dance. "Illumination."

"Well, light isn't going to be that much use if I can't take you out of this room," I muttered. "And if I can't use my magic, I can't poof…wait. Let me at least try to do that." I concentrated hard and felt my body warm up, but there was no spontaneous combusting. "How is it that magic is so dead down here? This is a serious liability."

"It's supposed to be," Oliver said. "The sanatorium wasn't meant for ordinary souls, but witches. Some very powerful, some very insane by the time they ended up here. Their combined magic made this place very special, but some grew to be too unruly. The coven got together and created a dampening spell to ensure anyone on this ground — specifically in these halls — couldn't summon their abilities. Anything given to them, tools and wands and hats — those would work. But no organic magic. It was a precaution that lives on."

"But how am I supposed to…"

And then I got it. The cards. There was a reason I never left home without them.

I reached into my pocket and pulled three cards free, sidling closer to Oliver so I could see them. Then I frowned.

"Eight of Pentacles, Five of Swords, Queen of Swords," I murmured, staring at the cards before looking around again. There were three doors out of this room, each looking much like the next. "If you're not actually tied here, do you know where they would take the bodies out?"

"No, but I know where they took mine out, if that's of any help."

"Well, it can't hurt."

"That one," he said, pointing to the far door. I considered it, then looked at the cards again. They remained useless. "Does that, uh, go to a library, by any chance? Or maybe a —" I cut myself off before I could ask the second question.

"It does not," he said. "It actually leads to a dead end, if you'll excuse the turn of phrase. I don't remember anything after that part — I was fading in and out. They had to break out the maps and retrace their steps."

I looked again at the Eight of Pentacles. It showed a man working at a table, hammering on disks. Traditionally, it was considered the card of apprenticeship and study, but I guess it could also mean someone studying a map. I headed for the far door, then at the last second, turned around. "You're not scamming me, are you, bro?"

Oliver was gone.

"You know, this is a particularly useless gift if you're going to give me ghosts who can't actually help me," I muttered to the hidden Eye of Horus. It may have rolled its eye. I couldn't tell through my shirtsleeve. Instead, I set off.

Once through the door, I tried my magic again, but there was nothing. I had no interest in feeling my way along the cold, slimy walls, but I wasn't without resources. I pulled my phone out and swiped it on. It flickered to life, but I could see the charge was already down to twenty percent. And there was no connection this deep underground. Still, it was enough to see by, and that was really my main goal.

I continued to try to figure out the cards. Eight of Pentacles — a man, apprentice working at a work desk, hammering out disks. Several of them already done and hung on the wall. An armory? A workshop?

I turned the corner and immediately felt a difference in the air. It was lighter here, cleaner, I was almost certain. This had to be the way out. But my goal wasn't to get out, it was to find wherever the witches were gathering in the rooms above me and get back to them. If I was dumped out on the grounds a quarter of a mile from the house, then even if I immediately poofed myself back inside, it might be too late.

Too late.

My brows lifted. Had my dumping here been intended not to take me out permanently, but merely temporarily? Or…no. It was far more likely that I wasn't supposed to be dumped at all. Lara could have entered her office at any time during the day. She herself said she never invited people into her inner sanctum. She was supposed to enter, pour herself her habitual glass of wine, collapse to the floor — and fall through.

And no one would find her in time. Dead or incapacitated, she would be out of the picture.

So maybe I wasn't the target after all.

But for that idea to hold, the killer couldn't have been onsite, or at least couldn't have been in a position of control onsite, near the inner sanctum. Otherwise, they would have known that Armaeus and I were with Lara at the time of her disappearance.

Who was behind this?

I peeked into the first door I saw, and winced. It was an empty room with a lone gurney pushed up against the wall. There was a drain in the center of the floor. Everything looked found-footage white in the ghostly light from my cell phone, but I didn't want to look too closely. There were three other rooms exactly like that, then a fourth, then…

I grinned, counting ahead. Eight. Could it really be that easy?

Hurrying more quickly now, I reached the eighth room past the door and peeked inside. It looked exactly like the others, but, taking a deep breath, I entered. There were no doors attached to their frames in any of these rooms along this hallway, I reminded myself, so there'd be no one coming along to lock me inside. No doubt somebody's attempt to render this place less creepy, but it only helped marginally.

I turned around, trying to find some hint as to what to do next.

There was no gurney in this room, and nothing in any of the drawers of the medical cabinets that could help. There were no windows, of course, but also no tools. No pentacles. I moved over to the corner of the room and boosted myself up onto the counter, then rested my head against the wall, thinking. There were no symbols on the floor, no symbols on the wall, no symbols on the...

I thought of the card and let my eyes trail up. The Eight of Pentacles depicted the man, his work station, and then eight pentacles extending up in a vertical line toward the ceiling. I frowned, staring at the ceiling. It...was stained, I realized. Which was super gross.

Beyond that, if it was stained, that technically meant there had to be something *above* the ceiling that could leak onto it.

Grimacing, I stood on the counter and braced myself against the wall, then reached up to the ceiling. It was made of drop panels, and the one that was looking exceedingly gross crumbled to the touch as I brushed against it. I wiggled it free and winced as more detritus came crashing down. This was definitely some sort of hole, but for what?

Then I saw it.

Covered in cobwebs and some indeterminate slime, a wooden panel rested about one foot above the drop ceiling. Holding my breath, I punched into the panel with as much magic-enhanced strength as I could muster, even halfway warded.

The wet and rotten wood didn't break, but it definitely gave. Progress.

It splintered on the third punch, and by the fifth, it cracked clean through. I barely had time to crouch out of the way as wood, dishes, and something foul and white cascaded down onto the counter, leaving me staring. Had this been some sort of dumbwaiter system? Was I beneath a kitchen?

I kicked the pile of rubble off the counter, then stepped forward, peering up with the help of my phone light. And…there it was.

A ladder extended up the wall, the metal slats worn down into soft semicircular shapes. I had no idea where it led to, but it couldn't get any more on the nose with my card than this. Those rings led upward, and upward was where I needed to go.

Of course, I immediately thought of the next card in my draw, the Five of Swords. That card depicted a young man on a field of battle, his combatants — whom he'd clearly bested — walking away from him, their attitudes one of defeat while his was one of smug superiority. Drawing the Five could mean any number of things, but its most usual underlying meaning was "be careful what you wish for." You win, only to discover that winning wasn't so much of a great idea.

Sort of like finding that your way out of a creepy sanatorium basement was up through a chute that smelled like death, body fluids, and spiders. I mean, hooray that this was undoubtedly the way out and — if the cards were to be believed — the fastest way for me to find the lost queen. But boo for all the spiderwebs.

Somewhere, deep in the house, a gong rang — loud enough for me to hear it all the way in the basement.

I held my breath and started climbing.

CHAPTER TWENTY-FIVE

As I ascended the Chute of Disgusting, my mind churned through everything I knew so far. We'd had three primary witches as potential Myanya proxies. Now we had two. We had three initiates who were in various stages of freakout. We had Lara Drake, who had lots of good reasons both to want the Myanya prophecy to succeed and to want it to fail.

Then came the victims. Four of them in LA, one of which was an aspiring consort, the others not. Several other male witches had shown up as walk-ons, but they'd done little more than feed the power of Myanya. Had that power escalation allowed the vessel witch to strike down Tammy, who was a high-level Connected in her own right? The deaths of RZ and Tammy so close to each other was more than a little concerning. The prophecy was clearly on the cusp of fulfillment.

I kept circling back to the three non-Connected victims, though. Herm Lannister, Judith Granger, William MacPherson. They were the key. Where would the three of them interact with the witch and create such an impression that she wanted their heads on a pike?

It took me three more spiderwebs and a spill of what I hoped was decades-old tomato juice to figure out the connection.

"Son of a bitch," I muttered. I hauled myself up eye level of the grate and realized it was bolted shut. But with a flick of my hand, I successfully produced a blue ball of flame and so…

Boom.

Sara Wilde was back in action.

The bolted door of the grate flew outward, and I scrambled out of the hole as another gong sounded through the house. Someone was getting summoned all right, and I had a feeling it was for the big show. I spent twenty seconds getting the worst of the grit out of my hair and off my clothes, then blew through the kitchen, flicking open my third eye. I could sense the power focusing in the center of the house, and I thought about what Oliver said. His descriptions of the solarium were so real, so visceral — and so eighty years out of date. Still, time waited for no witch hunter.

Focusing hard on the mental image he created for me, I started smoking…

And landed in a coat closet. I flailed, struggling for air, only to realize that I was being smothered by thick black cloaks. If I needed a disguise, I could grab one right here.

I considered the issue. Probably not necessary, but…you couldn't be too careful. I grabbed the nearest cloak and edged open the door, pulling back quickly as a trio of skyclad women walked by. Sighing, I dropped the cloak back to the floor. Skyclad. Hadn't thought of that. But it'd been a good idea.

Besides, I should be able to craft my own disguise, even among witches.

Electing to keep my clothes on for the moment, I waited until I couldn't hear anyone pass by, and nudged open the door. The hallway was clear, and I slipped out of the closet, trying to get my bearings.

Instantly, I realized where Oliver steered me wrong. The solarium remained in the center of the house, but it had been remodeled to take up less space, now hemmed in with an interior wall that was lined with what looked like mostly supply closets and waiting rooms. The witches of previous generations had probably gotten tired of hauling all their supplies to this room for the big show.

The most recent iteration of that show was already underway.

Taking a page out of the Magician's Book of Illusions, I blended in with the crowd that was moving into the solarium. About half the group were clothed, so that was where I focused my attention. No one noticed me. I watched as the other witches, more than a dozen of them, took their places in a circle. A silver pentagram had been carved into the floor, the deep trench lined with silver. I'd seen this party favor before. Unfortunately, there was nothing I could do but wait. I eyed the secondary triangle surrounded by a circle that was next to the elaborate pentagram. I had a feeling that was going to be where my girl would be. And when she was, I was going to take her down. I didn't care how much salt she had flying through the air.

"What the hell did you crawl through?"

I froze and pivoted slowly to the woman next to me, who was giving me the stink eye.

"How can you see me?" I asked Danae.

"I can see you because Kreios gave me the exact same spell you must have gotten from Armaeus to effect this illusion, right before he dropped me off at the front door. I swear, if we got a hold of the Council's grimoire, fur would definitely fly."

I eyed her, willing to be distracted as more perfect naked bodies filed in. Did they get these people from central casting? "Exactly how many magic lessons have you been getting from the Devil? I gotta think there's some sort of conflict of interest there."

"You'd think so," she said archly. "As it turns out, this incarnation of the devil is surprisingly more...flexible than most." She turned her attention to the group assembling. "I couldn't stay away."

"Yeah, I picked up on that." I smirked. "Whatever happened to 'what happens in a coven stays in a coven'?"

"When the Magician of the Arcana Council takes it upon himself to whisk a witch to safety from a threat internal to her coven, all bets are off. That's a measure of attention that could mean that coven is about to become a challenge to the entire hierarchy of established power."

"You're jealous," I summed up.

"I'm jealous," she agreed. "I don't want the Council's interference within my own coven, and I am not too keen on it getting overly familiar with another coven either. There's been some...unusual energy surrounding the Council's intervention here that I've been watching with some concern."

"Energy related to the Council? Or to this actual location?"

"Both. There is a primary ley line through the city, but it's been split off and redirected to this location. That's been the case for well over a hundred years, and the energy it pulls to this area has remained fairly steady during all that time. But not anymore. Now it's damned near a geyser."

"How long ago did the surge start?"

"Barely a month ago, about the same time that the first whispers of the prophecy being reborn hit the covens. It took a few weeks before the attacks on the prospective consorts happened, and in that time, a handful of non-Connected targets were struck. We didn't notice those at first either, because, well, they were bad guys, in the main. It was tough not to feel good about them getting hit, until we established that the victims and witch consorts were being hit by the same woman."

I glanced at her. "And you're thinking who I'm thinking, right?"

She shrugged. "Depends. My money's on Gail Fredericks."

"Gail?" I blinked at her, genuinely surprised. "You really think she would have allowed herself to get covered in muck and gore from head to toe, and then have to sit in her own stink while the travesty was captured on video, all to establish her alibi?"

Danae seemed to consider that. "Well, there is that…"

"And you actually think she would have the balls to take on Vlad the Impaler's descendent and leave him hoist on his own petard?"

She shrugged again. "That, I can believe. The Fredericks family is of French descent and was active in the Old World for centuries. It's not unreasonable that she bore a grudge against Vlad Dracul."

I shook my head. "I'm not buying it. The energy is too strong, too virile. The attacks too personal."

She followed my line of thinking. "Tammy Butler was the obvious candidate, but she's dead now." She frowned at me. "Isn't she?"

"Exceptionally dead," I agreed. I pointed as the triangle flared into life, a sheet of flame shooting up. "But her assistant isn't. Her assistant who served as her tagalong everywhere, even to—especially to—all of Tammy's swank, wannabe celebrity parties, where she no doubt encountered the skeevy side of LA more times than she could count? She's right here."

In the center of the triangle, cloaked all in white, stood Heather. Her long, dark hair was smoothed back in a graceful braid, her ears, neck, and wrists were devoid of ornamentation, and her face was shaded a ghostly white—not from makeup, I was pretty sure, but from the power radiating through her.

I focused on Heather with my third eye and discovered something else that caught me by surprise. Her energy patterns were familiar. I knew she'd been studying under Tammy, and Tammy had been an acolyte of Lara's. Was that what I was picking up on? Or was there simply a symmetry to the way she wove her magic that was striking a familiar chord with me?

"She's not strong enough," Danae muttered. "We checked the backgrounds of all the initiates as well as fully consecrated witches. Heather Winthrop came up with nothing."

"She was invisible," I said. "An assistant. I'm sure if you look deeper, you'll find her path intersected with a whole raft of people in positions of power. People who've now been turning up dead."

"How do you know that?"

"Because she mentioned Herm Lannister in her rant about Tammy Butler, obviously trying to sell her story, only—no one's talking about the guy except us. We'd only barely attached Lannister to Myanya—and his death was ruled an accident. But here Heather was, wanting to make sure he was part of the conversation. That didn't sit right."

"Okay, but—we're just going to sit here and let her go through this process?" Danae demanded. "You know she's our girl. You've got her right here. Why not take her out of commission and end this farce?"

"I'd do that," I said, "except she's not the only player I have a problem with. The spirit of Myanya has been targeting witches for centuries now, forcing them into a power play that hasn't had the payoff it should. I think it's time for her little reign of tyranny to be at an end."

Danae stared at me. "So you said you didn't care about the prophecy. That you merely wanted to bring a rogue, murderous witch to Judgment…but here you *are* interfering with a witch tradition. A tradition you can't possibly know or understand but you still seek to stifle."

"Not stifle," I said, my eyes on Heather. "And you're wrong. I want nothing more than to understand it. So much so, I'm willing to let Heather get her full power on before I strike."

"I'm not sure that's a good idea," Danae warned. "I've never seen this prophecy fulfilled, but there's very deep magic going on here. Some of these spells are not in any grimoire I've ever read."

"That's kind of what I'm hoping." I leaned forward as Heather lifted her arms.

A raging wind whipped up inside the pentagram, fire and smoke billowing forth but held within the confines of the star-shaped structure, but I remained focused on the young initiate. Now that I could fully see her, her attention not on keeping herself cloaked but letting her magic show itself nakedly, I realized the connection I'd noticed before—this was the granddaughter of Iskra Mikhailova, a witch who'd once again defied the odds to position herself in Myanya's sights. Though in Heather's case, she clearly wanted the honor.

"The time has come for the strong to be made weak to be made strong again, to lead the chosen coven into a generation of power unmatched across the land."

Danae muttered something under her breath, and I elbowed her quiet.

"I call upon the spirit of Myanya to fulfill the prophecy and make me whole!"

The witches around the pentagram lifted their hands high, and energy crackled above the circle even as Heather went rigid. Her body jolted once, a second time, then writhed and twisted as if she was one of those hot air promotional wind socks supported by an industrial-strength fan. She screamed as the power filled her, though I wasn't sure if that was out of true distress or merely for show. I'd bet, once we looked deeper into Heather's past, we'd find a young woman who had trained as an actress too, who wasn't merely content to hover in Tammy's shadow.

And now she was on the big stage.

"Long have I waited for a Master who will help me make the most of the powers of Myanya, only to be disappointed at every turn. Their powers have fueled me though, helped me grow, until I was the one doing the searching, *I* was the one seeking my rightful consort. But the waiting is done—now I can elevate the prophecy of Myanya to an entirely different level. One that will take us into the next level of power for witches, commanding the scourge of demons that has plagued the earth."

I rocked forward on my toes, wishing I had popcorn. I found myself not really hating Heather as much as I wanted to. She'd had a hard run of it, and beyond her unfortunate lineage, I suspected she'd been treated badly, and she was just trying to scrape together a living. It wasn't a living I could support, because there were all those dead people to account for, but it was one I could understand.

Then she wailed with a cry of utter exultation and joy.

"I have found the true path of power for myself, my coven, and Myanya...and *you* will be my consort!"

Armaeus Bertrand appeared in the center of the pentagram.

CHAPTER TWENTY-SIX

E verything exploded into chaos.

I wasn't sure exactly when I started moving, whether it was the second I saw Armaeus appear in the flames of the pentagram, his body growing bright violet with the strength of his newfound magic. It could also have been the moment that Heather turned to him, her face alight with joy and power. And possession.

Yeah. It was pretty much the possession that got me.

The closer I got to Armaeus, however, I realized that something was terribly wrong with him. He'd left me a bare hour before to deposit Lara Drake somewhere safe, but now he looked like he'd been fed through a sausage grinder. His skin was flayed open, blood seeping from a dozen different wounds, and his face looked haggard in profile.

How had he had enough time to get himself into such dire straits?

Armaeus!

The Magician looked up at the sound of my voice in his mind, wild eyes swinging toward me, and I caught the expression on his face, almost skidding to a stop to stare. Armaeus wasn't in agony, he was caught up in some sort of thrall, the pain apparently hitting some receptors that went well past mortal norms. He was in legitimately dire straits, but he was...sort of glorying in it, reveling in the process.

"What in the *hell* —" I seethed.

As if on command, a voice whispered in my mind. But it wasn't Armaeus speaking. *"There is a certain pleasure being summoned, Sara Wilde, as I know from personal experience,"* Aleksander Kreios said, his voice thick with fascination and undisputed interest. *"But I counsel you to keep going. I'll explain all of it when there's more time. For now, however, assume that the Magician, through a curious coincidence that bears further study, has found himself in exactly the right spot for the prophecy of Myanya to use his power."*

But he doesn't want to subjugate anyone. That's not his jam.

"He doesn't, which makes him exactly the right choice for this young witch — she knows she's in good hands, but at the same time, Myanya will be appeased by his strength. Only trouble is, there's a reason why you haven't heard of the male witches who have taken part in the ritual once it's completed, only the female witch who is the target of Myanya's power."

Show me. I turned my attention back to the smaller scrying circle. Heather still stood within it, swallowed whole by bright yellow-white flame.

"Certainly."

The images that Kreios swamped me with had me staggering back. Magician after male witch after warlock followed the same path to their destruction. Swayed by the promise of Myanya's power, they were seduced into demanding the witch vessel as their consort. They took that power on, most of them getting sucked into vile acts of debasement from the darker undertones of Myanya's prophecy. They were ruthless to their consorts, subjecting them to physical, mental, and emotional cruelties, and my lip curled back in revulsion as I took in the tide of their heinous acts.

Then, however, the tables turned. The witch rose anew, sometimes covered in her own blood, sometimes covered in the blood of those she'd destroyed at the behest of her consort, and the first person she killed was—the witch who'd defiled her. Then she turned her rage on select members of her coven, the body count growing higher with each pass. Finally, the remaining coven members were smote with some kind of spell that knocked them out cold. When they came to, the Myanya-afflicted witch was a hero, no one seeming to assign any of the deaths to her...but to her consort. The bodies were cleared away, and the witch was bathed in the light of success.

Until another twenty-eight years went by. No one ever revealed the true cost of the prophecy, so all that remained behind was its allure.

She's not going to kill Armaeus.

"She may not have an alternative," Kreios offered up, as if he was discussing a hotdog contest. *"If Myanya doesn't kill the consort, then the only witch left to blame for the deaths is her vessel. It wouldn't take long for the prophecy to be eradicated completely, if only to preserve the covens who had been subjected to its power. In that event, Myanya would permanently die, never to rise again."*

I stared at the flickering flame. *Did Iskra know that? Did she guess what was happening?*

The Devil didn't respond to that. The heat from Heather's fire wall blanketed me, and I extended my own force field out farther, trapping all the witches in the solarium where they stood. There would be hell to pay after this was over with, I knew already. The covens weren't going to be happy that I could keep them so easily subdued. I had a feeling there'd be a lot of folks going to remedial witch school after I was done.

But first I had to stop Myanya.

Inside the pentagram, Armaeus flung his arms wide, bursting forth with a shout of agony that sounded eerily happy. At a loss for what to do, I reached inside my jacket and pulled out three cards. Two of Wands, Temperance, Tower.

So, no matter what, it looked like things were going to go kersplodie. I could work with that. The Two of Wands wasn't impossible to figure out either in this case — though his interpretation was different from the last time I'd pulled him. Depicting a young man standing between two staffs planted in the ground, he typically implied the start of a long journey, one that was sure to lead to a positive end. It also sometimes meant that the querent had a choice to make, that one of two paths were open to them, and they mainly needed to choose. He also sometimes merely indicated "go left."

In this case, though, the card's meaning was a little clearer. Taken in the most straightforward way possible, this was a seeker standing before a makeshift gateway. All he had to do was step into that gateway, and the cycle of the reading would begin.

It was the middle part of the reading that was a little more difficult to figure out.

Temperance was one of those cards that most people like to gloss over. It could mean any number of things, espousing the virtues of patient action over wild, uncontrolled effort. It could mean the careful blending of disparate materials, to create something entirely new. And it could mean an alchemist, an angel, a mediator, or a mentor. But no matter what, the face of Temperance meant that still waters ran deep, and that the querent should proceed with caution and care.

Then again, screw that. I hated pulling Temperance.

I stubbornly reached back into the deck and pulled another card free, immediately rolling my eyes. The Six of Cups, the card of childhood nostalgia, showing a couple of children in the foreground of some cute little town, playing in a field of flowers.

Hello, Captain Useless. I should've known better than to try to recast my future mid-draw.

Reinforcing the thrall that held the LA coven in place, I pushed my way through the coven to the edge of the pentagram. Armaeus was close enough to touch, but I slanted away from him and plunged inside the tiny scrying circle holding Myanya and her appointed vessel, Heather.

They'd done an amazing redecorating job.

Instead of a triangle and circle no more than three feet in diameter, Heather was operating on an empty plane that took up the whole length of the solarium. The witches standing guard and the curious onlookers were all gone, while Armaeus stood frozen in his pentagram, his hands up as if to create magic, his face relaxed, almost serene.

For some reason, that bothered me even more than the Magician's flashes of agony that I'd glimpsed when I'd been outside Heather's scrying circle. A passionate Armaeus I knew how to handle. A stone-faced one…not so much.

"You cannot have him anymore."

I turned to see Heather regarding me with fierce determination.

Ignoring her assertion, I smirked at her and asked the question I'd been dying to voice since I'd met her. "Are you a Heather?"

She stared at me blankly, apparently unfamiliar with the movie. Kids today. Instead, she held her hands up higher as I approached, as if to ward me off. There was something definitely different about her, and with a quick peek through my third eye, I confirmed that the power of the witch initiate had amped several times over. Her body writhed with sensuality and power, filled with equal parts Heather and Myanya now.

"You can't stop me," Heather said. "The prophecy must be fulfilled. And now, finally, it can do some real good."

"That's not your call," I said, knowing where this was going.

"You're wrong," she insisted. "How many oppressors are still out there, male and female alike, pushing down those who dare try to oppose them? That was Myanya's gift to me. I can smell them, feel them, taste them. I'm driven nearly mad with my need to consume their energy and drain them of their life essence."

"Yeah? What about Tammy Butler? She wasn't trying to oppose anyone."

"She got in my way," Heather snapped. "She wasn't strong enough to take on the prophecy herself, but she was too strong not to know that something was going on. She believed it was Gail's initiate who was being groomed by Myanya, because she knew that it required a certain level of edge to attract the eye of the prophecy. And she…" Heather's voice quavered, then steadied again. "She didn't believe me. About *them*. Not once."

I didn't have to ask her what she was talking about. All those Hollywood parties, all those predators with fancy clothes and bright white teeth.

"So you did your best to keep up your innocent little girl act," I surmised. "I'm surprised Lara didn't catch on to it.

"Her," Heather scoffed. "She's no leader. She can't even control her own witches. There were several who were discussing the possibility of a coup. I think part of her welcomed the energy of Myanya to see who would be left standing when it was all done, but she assumed that it was the consort who would be causing any deaths. So she pressed the consorts of her choosing forward, challenging them to engage with Myanya's power." Heather's smile was icy. "She fed my power without even realizing it."

I lifted my brows. "All those witches were Lara's ideas? Because there were a lot of them."

"Not all of them. But enough," Heather said, her disgust plain. "She tried to manipulate the system, not understanding the true depth of the game she was playing. Everyone underestimates the power of Myanya, to their detriment."

"But not you," I said. I was moving closer to her. The power on this plane was very different, but not completely alien to me. It was as if I was pushing through the murk and the mire of a dream, and I pursed my lips, trying to hold on to a shred of memory that thought inspired. It was something…something in one of the case files? Something that Armaeus said? I couldn't recall, but it felt like it was the right thing to do to push forward—so I did.

One more step, then another. Heather allowed me to continue approaching, but while her body held firm, her face seemed to morph with each step I took. First she was a withered old crone, then a fresh-faced girl of maybe sixteen, then a young woman with a deep port wine stain that spread down one side of her face, then an older woman with eyes like a fawn's and snow-white hair. I was seeing the many faces of Myanya over the years, but to a one, they looked innocent, pristine. These were the faces of the witches before they had endured her curse.

"Show me the truth," I ordered, and Heather stiffened, finally taking a step back.

"You have no power over me," she declared, and I rolled my eyes. I'd already had enough labyrinths for one week.

"Yeah, I kinda do." I lifted my hand. It was still like trying to move through Jell-O, but my energy flared to life in the palm of my hand as I spoke directly to Myanya. "Your minion talks a good game, but she's a child, and you know it. In fact, that's the only reason you've gotten as far as you have, isn't it? Show me the truth, Myanya."

Heather's lips curled back from her teeth, but a second later, her face shifted again. The old woman was ashen, clearly dead. The fresh-faced young girl had deep bags under her eyes, her skin patchy and gray beneath. The old woman with the eyes of a fawn had been blinded; the girl with a port wine stain was now fully cowled, her gaze shifting away from me as soon as her face manifested. These women were all broken, I realized, but even that wasn't the full story.

"The truth," I whispered again, and Heather staggered back, her arms flinging wide.

The power that bloomed forth rose not only from her throat but from the throat of every woman who had come before her, and it was my turn to fall back as the full force of it blew into the space between us. There was rage, and there was horror, and there was strength—but in the end, there was something so powerful, I had to bend my will against it, forcing it to retreat.

"You cannot," I gritted out. "This is not the way."

As a new and unexpected pressure call began battering against my mind, demanding to be heard, I finally understood the meaning of the Six of Cups. Two young children in a field of flowers, playing, their world full of hope and possibility. A fairy-tale image, steeped in nostalgia, depicting not whatever was, but what one person truly wished could be, truly hoped would be, if only her actions were enough.

They weren't, all those years ago. But life's a funny place.

"You have no say in the prophecy of Myanya!" Heather cried as I fixed on the distant caller, creating her likeness in my mind's eye, using exactly the same technique I'd employed to bring Armaeus and Kreios to me. I'd never tried it with an ordinary human before. "You don't know anything about the way!"

"She doesn't, not really. But I do."

Then again, Iskra Mikhailova wasn't your ordinary human.

The slender Russian doctor appeared on the plane between existences, leaning on an elegant staff, her hair carefully swept into a chignon, her deep blue business suit professional and luxurious at once. She didn't wear her granddaughter's wild patterns, but then, she didn't have to. She conveyed her power differently, internally. Power I'd helped restore. Now all her focus was on her granddaughter.

"I tried, child," she sighed, her smile fracturing a bit as she took in Heather's disheveled appearance. "The Blessed Virgin knows I tried. But I underestimated Myanya's darker side. Hard to imagine that's possible, but it's what happened. She was not content to choose a worthy witch after I defeated her. She had to return to my family. I'd thought once was enough. The prophecy was fulfilled in your mother, and that she died after it was done was not a precedent. It was finished. I never imagined that Myanya would come back to disturb a

264

third generation...or even that there was a third generation for her to target."

Iskra sighed, gazing at her granddaughter, her eyes filled with love. I thought about how many witches Heather had killed, and how many Iskra had killed in her day. Maybe there was a good reason Myanya chose this family.

"You lie," Heather snarled. "You didn't try to save me, even when you could. You left your daughter in the hands of fools. She wasn't strong enough when I eventually came to claim her. You did not protect her from me." Heather's voice was different now, stronger and richly inflected—not Heather at all, but Myanya. I could see the fight the girl was waging to try to hold on to the spirit of Myanya, but I also thought she would fail. Did Myanya know that too?

"I sometimes wonder if you knew I would break her," Myanya continued. "Because I did break her. Soundly."

I gritted my teeth. Myanya was definitely not winning points for Miss Congeniality, but Iskra seemed unmoved.

"The human spirit is too strong to be broken by an outside force unless there is a desire to be broken," she said quietly. "You among all spirits should know that. How many women have you dragged through mud and blood before you decided they had suffered enough?"

"That is not my doing."

"And that is where you lie," Iskra countered. "I know better than most what powers you bring, and I could see the doors that opened ahead of and behind me. The witch who stood forward as my consort was a despicable fool, yet his was the only bid you entertained. You knew he would be destroyed, but you also know that he would make me suffer. You relished that."

"I would make you strong," Myanya seethed through Heather's mouth.

"You would make me bitter," Iskra shot back. "The prophecy of the scarred warrior was no longer enough for you. You weren't satisfied with merely venting the rage of our generation, you added to it, twisting it. I had to stop you. I have to stop you now."

I looked at Iskra askance, but she believed her own words. I knew better, however, and so did Myanya.

"Oh, please. I am too strong for you now. I knew that you were still out there, hiding in your protected church, and I reached out to your coven. They knew the power that could come with allowing me to complete what I tried to so many years ago. When they suggested you as my consort, not my vessel, I agreed. I wanted you to see. To know."

"To know that my granddaughter lived, I know," Iskra said tiredly. "That once more, I'd not been enough. But you won't succeed, Myanya. You won't succeed."

With a speed I would never have imagined, the old lady dashed forward, lifting her staff like a javelin as Heather's face flashed with sudden recognition beneath Myanya's mask. She might not know who her grandmother was, but she recognized the old woman rushing toward her.

In the end, though, it was Myanya who roared forth to greet Iskra. The confrontation of their magic shook the foundation of the magical plane, and Iskra vanished in a crackle of smoke.

Then, moving all in one motion, Heather whirled on Armaeus, who remained frozen in the pentagram. "I command you to claim me as my consort!" she cried.

I sighed. Not this again.

CHAPTER TWENTY-SEVEN

A rmaeus stood with his hands outstretched, his face slack and his eyes fixed on a far distant point, but that didn't stop Heather from lurching toward him. I was marginally closer, and I crossed the line of the pentagram before she did. Then a surge of power coming behind me blasted past my shoulder and hit Armaeus square in the face.

What happened next shouldn't have been so upsetting, since I'd seen a version of it before, but it was. Exactly as he had in his inner sanctum, Armaeus split into twelve separate beings, each with a particular focus. Only this time, I saw as well as heard the reality of those splits. One laughed with the sheer might of his ability, bursting with power. One extended his hands out, his fingers dripping darkness. One practically oozed sex appeal, a side of Armaeus I frankly wished was closer to me, but that was not to be. Instead, the Magician nearest to me looked like Armaeus after a long stretch of bad road. He eyed me with unrestricted malevolence, and the tiniest bit of fear curled through me. This was not a side of the Magician I'd ever seen before.

I decided to try to reason with him.

"You knew this was coming," I said, infusing my voice with admiration. It wasn't a stretch. "You knew that you'd get hit with...this."

"No," Angry Armaeus seethed back. He seemed...unreasonably upset with me. "It was one of several hundred possibilities, but not the most likely. I was dealing with alters because of you. You and what you may face."

That made me slow down, and I glanced around at the other Armaeuses. Several of them had turned toward me, and I realized belatedly that Myanya *hadn't* entered the pentagram with me. She remained outside, apparently frozen in time, waiting for Armaeus and I to do battle. Which meant...probably something not very good.

Whoops.

"So, maybe you should introduce me around," I said. I turned to the next closest Armaeus to me. He stared at me with an expression of rapt fascination on his face, looking so much like the absentminded professor, I almost chuckled.

"You have much more power than you should," he murmured, lifting his hands. "That power should be fractured and siphoned off for the good of humanity."

"Wait, what?" I lifted my own hands, a spate of blue fire sparking up. I threw the mass of it at Armaeus, tangling him up in a crackling miasma.

"What...is this?" he asked, his voice so captivated that it vibrated the air around us. "How...is this possible..." He turned away and wandered off, caught in my net of power, and I watched him go with some satisfaction. He'd stay busy awhile.

A second Armaeus rushed me then, this one barely a ghost. I caught a sense of pure, heart-wrenching agony, the sense of a love being lost that could never be found. I didn't even know what to do with that Armaeus, so I did the only thing I could. I stepped to one side and let him blow by me, straight into the wall of fire that bordered the pentagram. He disappeared in a rush of black smoke, his long, mournful wail all that remained of him. My heart lurched at the sound, and I slowed...

Then was knocked sideways to the floor.

This Armaeus spread over me in a mass of circuits, all of them glowing the violent pink of his newly hardwired alien DNA. I didn't understand enough of what that power did or was intended for to be able to stop it, so I went completely still, completely dark. I shut all my senses off and walled off my mind, freezing any contact to Armaeus out—

The pink mass disappeared. Another waft of agony suddenly all that remained of it.

I really didn't like this game, I decided.

As I struggled to my feet, another, darker alt-Arma, this one eyeing me with single-minded possession, stood grinning at me. Then he moved forward.

"The magic of Myanya is ancient, primal," he murmured, his voice rich and deep. He stalked me as I stepped back. "It calls to the basest, most elemental needs of my power. And it's telling me to take what's mine."

"Ah..." I swallowed, then tried to redirect him. "Doesn't Myanya want you to take her?"

His smile was pure carnal malice. "Oh, she does. But she can wait. She can't see what's going on in this veil, now that she has set her spell in motion. She is forcing me to prove myself to her. She'll find that she should be careful what she wishes for."

Truer words were never spoken, but then Armaeus turned, backing me into a wall of white-hot coals.

"What the hell!" I gasped.

It was another incarnation of Armaeus, only this one was spitting fire. In a flash, I was surrounded by flames, and I twisted and turned, struggling to get away. I couldn't seem to gain any purchase. Behind me, sounding truly distressed, the fiery incarnation of Armaeus howled, but he didn't loosen his hold on me. I'd never felt so much pain in my life, and I'd been dipped in the primordial goop once when Armaeus was hell-bent on leveling me up.

Once I started thinking of that goop, in fact, I couldn't stop. I felt the fire of Armaeus's attack melting through my skin, muscles, and even bone, consuming me, making me one with his agony. But my brain seized on the pit Armaeus had opened deep in his fortress, the glimpse into the dark essence of creation. Seized on it desperately as someplace — anyplace — that wasn't here.

The intensity of that place in my mind, and the fact that my cells were already mostly destabilized…and the fact that I was already on *fire*…made it relatively easy for me to lurch through space and spectral fields to reach the location inside Armaeus's home. There in the center of Prime Luxe, I stood in Armaeus's magician cave, right at the edge of the deep and miserable pit that he seemed to favor so highly when he was trying to work his magic. I wasn't alone, unfortunately. I was still wearing Armaeus like road rash.

Before he could respond, and before I could really take stock of what I was doing, I stepped off the edge of the pit and plunged straight down. The moment we hit the pool of goop, Armaeus let me go. With the buoyancy of a cork plunged deep into water, I shot straight back up again, through several feet of dark, seething magic and then blessedly clean oxygen, until I lunged to the side of the pit, grabbing its edge. Barely more than bleeding bones at this point, I hauled myself up over the edge onto the cool concrete floor of the chamber. I rolled to my side, whimpering as I struggled to find my own healing magic.

It eluded me.

For what felt like a long time, most everything eluded me except the simple act of breathing. Far below, Armaeus's screams weren't unhappy ones, a part of me was relieved to notice. I huffed a garbled groan, my thoughts focusing as intently on my internal processes as I could make them.

But the fact of the matter was, Armaeus had ripped the crap out of me. He'd well and truly set me on fire, and I found my attention fracturing as I stumbled over that fact. Wasn't he supposed to love me? Wasn't he supposed to have my back—not roast it?

"Sara."

The word was spoken softly, almost reluctantly, and I lurched in a feeble roach-like motion, gasping as I stared up. Eshe stood there, the High Priestess of the Arcana Council. I knew she bunked at Armaeus's and pretty much had the run of the place, but neither of us were the kind to paint each other's fingernails. "What?" I managed through blistered lips. "I'm kind of busy here."

"I know. You're fighting aspects of the Magician, but you're missing the purpose of that battle." She glanced over the edge of the pit, where the Magician was still howling in one part pain, two parts ecstasy. "Extra style points for that, though. If you had enough time, you probably would be able to subdue each of Armaeus's aspects." She looked back to me. "But you don't. In fact, while you're busy whittling down his power, you're essentially making him weaker. And I can't help but notice that you've left most of him behind to fend for himself as a Magician in pieces, while Myanya only needs one fragment of him to succeed."

She was right. I knew in an instant she was right, and I clicked my eyelids closed, forcing a bolt of ice-cold healing magic through me, the equivalent of ripping off the rest of my skin with duct tape. "Son of a *bitch*."

I poofed out of the room and back to Lara's home, but I stopped myself just shy of entering the pentagram of Magicians. I'd leveraged Armaeus's power to get out of that pentagram, but I didn't know if I'd have the strength to break out again, especially if he was an iterative learner. But the moment I crashed back to the floor of the solarium, I understood why Eshe had moved herself to stop buying togas on QVC long enough to warn me.

Armaeus stood in front of Myanya, kneeling.

One aspect of him, anyway. The aspect of the Magician who'd burst through the wall of fire. The aspect who'd lost the most important thing to him he could possibly imagine—the love of his life. A woman who'd lived eight centuries before I'd been born and who'd been perhaps the first and most damning sacrifice of Armaeus's long tenure as Magician. I knew the Magician's love for me had no equal, but there was more tied up in his feelings for the impulsive, free-spirited Mirabel than simple nostalgia. He had failed her when she'd needed him most. He had abandoned her, never realizing the impact of that abandonment. He had pursued his calling as Magician of the Arcana Council, and she had died in a terrible accident while he'd been gone. He'd never forgiven himself for that, and he'd carried the weight of that condemnation for nearly nine hundred years.

And now she was standing in front of him.

"Mirabel," Armaeus whispered, and my heart twisted. Myanya no longer looked anything like Heather. She was a short, curvy woman with a mass of dark curly hair, and her eyes were huge and luminous. Her bow-shaped mouth tilted in a radiant smile, and she nodded at Armaeus encouragingly as she held out her hands.

"We can be together, Armaeus. You and me, as we were meant to be all those centuries ago. You can save me."

"Save...you," Armaeus said, sounding like a man who'd been drugged. And maybe he had been.

"Arma—"

Another roar of anger erupted beside me, only it wasn't Armaeus but a phalanx of witches closing in on me, ready to keep me out of the game. I groaned as I realized my force field on the solarium had failed when I'd trotted off for points east, and I hadn't reset it. The witches were taking advantage. I was smote with one, two, then six different silver rods, the small devices clearly some kind of tool that I was not familiar with, all of them spelled to the hilt.

"That hurts!" I gritted out as another rod connected with my temple, but I spun around, ducking beneath my attacker and shoving her away. I seemed to be everywhere at once for one mind-bending moment, my magic sparking to life again and exploding in all directions. The witches went down in a flail of skyclad limbs, and I raced toward Armaeus again.

He was standing, his arms open, hands tilted toward each other. I couldn't decide if he was welcoming Myanya with open arms, preparing to fry her, or setting up for one mean bout of cat's cradle—but I couldn't take the chance.

273

I changed my trajectory and barreled straight into the modern-day incarnation of the ancient scarred warrior witch.

The first sensation I had was fire. The second was…heart-rending pain. Literally…as if my heart had been split in two.

Turning around, I tried to make sense of what I was seeing. A line of robed acolytes staggered down a narrow passageway, wailing and moaning, wringing their hands. They reached the bottom and disappeared, and I lunged after them. A second later, we all spilled out into a large chamber where a spit stood above a roaring fire.

Impaled on a pike above that fire was Myanya.

Her body was broken and bleeding, her skin waxy, and flames crackled along her feet and legs. Having caught myself on fire more times than I cared to count in the last few weeks, I could attest that this was no picnic. But even as I started forward, another priest burst out of the crowd and cried out to Myanya at the top of his lungs, clearly attempting to save her.

A spear shot out of the shadows, toppling him into the fire.

Okay, so, no saving the witch queen.

As I watched, Myanya looked up at me and smiled through cracked lips. "No one saves the witch queen," she said, and as she spoke, her mouth opened wide and I saw her body was filled with wriggling black beetles. They fell from her mouth to deep fry in the fires below, and I struggled to keep the revulsion from my face.

Myanya laughed anyway.

"All who come to look upon me shudder and shy away, but you stare openly, Sara Wilde. In all the centuries of my divine suffering, you're the one most worthy of my pain."

"Well, I'm not, actually — "

It didn't take more than a second for our positions to be reversed. One moment I was standing on the side of Camp Roastable, the next I was skewered on a pike, flames licking along my clothes and hair. Even if it was an illusion, it was a damned realistic illusion, and I screamed, grabbing the pike with both hands.

"I did *not* bag Vlad the Impaler only to end up on the end of your dumbass toothpick," I growled. I inched myself along the pike, every movement filling me with agony.

"You are strong enough, and the Magician is already your consort. You'll do." Myanya said, and she shoved me back down on the pike. I stared, numb as real blood began to pour out of me. It was the oddest sensation…like I was being emptied out, a cup of wine drained to a dangerously low level. "You will be ground under the heel of *my* rage, not the Magician's. And you will be so much more powerful for it." She laughed as I struggled on the pike. "Save your strength. Armaeus will soon be called upon to fulfill his duties as consort as well, when I'm done with you. Having seen some of his aspects, you'll need all the strength you can muster. Fortunately, my spirit will be filling you by then, so what you cannot bear, I'll gladly endure."

My back flared with sudden, unexpected heat, wholly different from the warmth of the crackling fire beneath me, and I thought of the furious Magician who'd grappled me, pouring himself over and into me, drugging me with the same malevolent primal force that filled him up. I still had the lacerations from those wounds striping my back, and now they sizzled and popped with so much anger, I almost didn't mind the pike damned near bisecting me. But as I swung my gaze to the grinning Myanya, I saw her differently.

I saw her through Armaeus's eyes.

While I could view psychic souls with my third eye as crackling lines of Connected energy, this was different. Armaeus not only read people's essential nature, he categorized their strengths and weaknesses like a 1980s Dungeon Master fresh off a Gary Gygax singalong. And Myanya was rolling a twenty in strength, twenty in charisma, and twenty in intelligence, but her wisdom had tanked out. Girl didn't believe in learning from her mistakes. Maybe she couldn't. Maybe that was simply how the prophecy worked.

I wasn't sure how that could help me, then my back flared up again like I was getting flat-ironed by Hephaestus. Finally, I got it.

Myanya couldn't bear to lose.

The maelstrom of her immortal agony took on meaning only if she was able to revisit it upon an unfortunate soul and watch that individual suffer as she suffered, be redeemed as she was redeemed, and go on to power as she went on to power. Even if that transformation from victim to victor lasted only for one brief shining moment, that was all she needed to justify all her actions.

Iskra had taken that satisfaction away from her, and she'd never recovered. Her hunt for new blood wasn't merely for new blood; therefore, it was to reset the playing field and launch an entirely new generation of power.

"Not gonna happen," I gritted out.

I stopped trying to pull myself off the pike, and instead wrapped my hand around it, focusing Armaeus's incendiary glare on the pike. With the borrowed intensity of his remembered magic, the pike disappeared in my grip, a burst of healing magic pounding back through me as my body sought to put itself back together again.

I dropped straight into the fire, but surrounded as I was in Armaeus's power — with my own surging to the fore — I barely felt it. Instead, I staggered out like a true believer at a Tony Robbins firewalk and flung my hands forward. This time, it wasn't a blue orb that trapped Myanya — it was the silver cuffs of Justice.

"You dare!" howled Myanya, her roar cut off as I set us both...yep...on fire.

Because why stop now?

CHAPTER TWENTY-EIGHT

Myanya and I exploded into the brick-and-steel entryway of the fortress Gamon called home. As Judgment of the Arcana Council, Gamon's job was to take the Connected criminals I delivered to her and, well, pass judgment on them. She was exceptional at it.

She also wasn't here.

"You dare!" Myanya roared again, and I scrambled around to face the scarred witch, bemused by the fact that her bracelets had snapped off her wrists. Further, she no longer resided in Heather's body. She straightened to her full height, and I looked up, then up still farther. Myanya...was tall.

She was also masked. A Phantom of the Opera-style white mask covered half her face, baring her eyes that glared like twin supernovas and part of one cheek. As I watched, she turned slowly to take in her surroundings, which were still quite noticeably devoid of people. Several giant screens lined the circular room, all of them also helpfully blank. It was as if I'd popped in on Gamon on New Year's Eve, never imagining she'd actually be off, actually celebrating the holiday. Because...Gamon.

I straightened as well, but the effect wasn't nearly as impressive when I did it.

"You shouldn't have the power to bring me here," Myanya rumbled, her voice low and resonant. "You aren't strong enough for that. You've never been strong enough."

What was with people and the lack of respect? It was no more than what I'd accused myself of, more times than I could count, but now, hearing it from Myanya, I flat-out rejected the idea. "Try again, sweetheart."

"You brought me here, didn't you?" Myanya taunted. "You give another the right to pass Judgment upon me when you have the ability to make a choice as well."

"I don't think you're going to want to go with my choice for you."

"All the more reason for you to be the one to put the brand upon me, then, not Judgment. You seem to forget that she has also not been one to suffer fools gladly. How many has she killed because they threatened her? How many has she destroyed because if she did not, they would grind her beneath their boots, make her their slave?"

I narrowed my eyes as we circled. My Justice tools lost their mojo when I was in Judgment's fortress, allowing Gamon full rein, but that didn't mean my powers diminished. If I wanted to end Myanya, I could.

Should I? I wanted to end the cycle of her destructive prophecy, for sure, but something about the figure in front of me stayed my hand another moment.

Myanya laughed, ratcheting up my irritation. "Your silence is most damning of all, Justice. You don't dispense justice. You're little more than a protector of the weak and the foolish who can't protect themselves."

That pricked a nerve, as I knew was Myanya's intention, but I couldn't stop my immediate, almost visceral response. "Somebody needs to protect them."

"Truly? Or does someone need to give them the tools they need to protect themselves? *That's* what my prophecy provides those who are willing to work for it."

"Your prophecy takes a gifted soul and attempts to drag her into the dirt. The survivor of your spirit isn't herself, only better…she's you. Your incarnation, your self once more made flesh. That's not empowerment, Myanya, that's simply a more socially acceptable form of slavery."

"You're wrong. Over the centuries, the witches who have taken on the challenge of my spirit have gone on to lead their covens to mastery. That is not me. That is them."

"Uh-huh. And what about those women who end up with their minds broken and their hearts crushed? Whose success or failure is it then? Yours, for choosing poorly? Or theirs, for not being able to withstand the horrors that you visit upon them?"

"They have to prove their strength before they can wield the power that I would give them," Myanya scoffed. "I cannot always be expected to choose correctly."

"I'm getting the feeling you don't choose correctly all that often," I said. "I read the complaints brought to the attention of Justice. They go back hundreds of years."

"How many complaints? A handful, out of all the covens I have aided over the course of millennia?" She sniffed. "The strength of the witches has waned over the years, even as the abilities of other Connecteds have thrived. The witches have turned away from their true calling. But now there is no turning away. Now they must reach out and embrace the possibilities that the new horde of demons who overrun this world presents."

"They can do that without your help," I said. "In fact, seems to me you've done more harm than good. Some of the male witches that you have removed from the equation could have done real work in the pursuit of managing the demon horde. Now they're dead, or so damaged their magic may never be the same. How does that help the covens?"

"There are many paths to success, I promise you," Myanya said darkly. "That you are too weak to see that doesn't surprise me."

"You know, I'm getting a little tired of you throwing shade."

"And I'm getting tired of baiting you into a true battle, Justice Wilde. I assure you, your predecessor was much quicker to be engaged."

A flare of anger and belated concern for a woman nearly two hundred years dead ripped through me. "What do you know about Justice Strand?"

"I know that she had more guile in her little finger than you do in your entire body," Myanya shot back. "You may outstrip her in power, but she was resilient. Resourceful. She did what she had to do to survive for as long as she could. I almost hated making her way darker, but then, that is *my* calling. The way of strength is not for the fainthearted."

"I studied Nietzsche too," I snapped. "He had better quotes."

"You mock what you don't understand."

"And you're beginning to irritate me." I lifted my hands, the blue power now shot through with the violent pink of Armaeus's borrowed strength. "You want to make it until Judgment finally shows up, you should probably stop trying to deliberately pull my chain."

"Then perhaps I should be more direct."

Myanya turned to me and pulled her hand across her face, stripping off her mask. Her face was horrifically burned beneath it, the skin blanched and puckered.

I stared at her, unflinching. "You're a witch, Myanya. And if you don't remember, you've already thrown me onto a pike that stuck out of my rib cage, so a scary face isn't all that effective on me. Surely you can frighten me with a worse illusion than that—or heal yourself if what I'm seeing is real."

"I could," she growled, the word sounding garbled now. "But if I were to heal myself, I would forget. And I cannot ever forget." She smiled, an unsettling look with half her mouth eaten away, but as I lifted my gaze to hers, I flinched.

"You want to know one of the reasons Abigail Strand faltered? Look close, Justice Wilde. Look close and understand."

This time, however, Myanya showed me nothing further of the horrors she'd experienced. She showed me the horrors of her own soul. She was a human, or she'd started that way, a witch with ordinary abilities, advancing along the sacred path as an initiate, then a full-fledged member of her coven. But she lived in a time when ignorance outweighed discernment, a balance we still had not mastered thousands of years later. And she was killed.

I blinked.

She was…killed.

Suddenly, my mind leapt to Vlad the Impaler's descendent, with his threats of dark arts, the twins, Mordechai and Malachi, with their gleeful interpretations of the dire grimoire, and finally, Richard Zachariah, a full-on Hollywood necromancer, the perfect plastic practitioner for the shock-talk era.

"You're not a bodiless spirit. You're the spirit of a dead woman," I breathed, feeling the tattoo on my arm flare to life. "You should have hooked up with the necromancer."

"I've always chosen a necromancer," Myanya snarled back at me. "No coven would accept me in my true form, except those who knew too well the ways to control me. I couldn't have that."

"That explains why you didn't hit Danae's coven, no matter how strong they are."

"The deathwalkers," Myanya said, curling her lip. "They think they know so much. They know nothing, not about demons and not about the dead. I have more experience with the horde than they ever will. The path to the demons' destruction is not one paved with control and temperance, but with might and blood. Demons don't understand anything else. And now there are so many more of them, and their power could be turned along with that of the dead, with the right combination of strength. Strength not only to endure the worst, but to reach the greatest heights."

"It was you," I realized aloud. "You were the one who reached out to the necromancers, not the LA coven, and not Lara Drake. They created the pentagram, they filled it with salt, they did everything you asked of them...but you were the one doing the asking. It wasn't a mystical revelation or some treatise on a tattered grimoire page. It was you. You sought them out. And then you trapped and killed them. Up to and including Richard Zachariah."

"They weren't supposed to die. No one is ever supposed to die—not even me. Yet I always, *always* do!"

Myanya cried out this last, her voice ringing with a misery so profound, it rooted me in place. As I watched, she swayed, then fell to her knees, utterly exhausted.

I held my ground. "Ah...they weren't? Weren't you trying to kill them?"

"Of course," she said, her shoulders slumping now. "I had to put them to the test, bathe them in fire and blood. I had to see if their minds had a deep enough capacity for darkness. None of them did. The darkest beings upon this planet, other than the demons themselves, have always been held within the Arcana Council. Only they would not meddle in the affairs of witches. It was a time-honored tradition. Not the males, anyway." She looked at me with sunken eyes. "The females were more easily tempted."

"Justice Strand."

Her lips twisted. "Justice Strand. And others too, long since dead. If I had anything to do with that, I can hardly be blamed. It is the obligation of the Council to recruit members of sufficient strength. It is my obligation to seek out that strength. I found it too. In Armaeus. He was...so much more than I expected."

"Yeah, he gets that a lot."

"But even he deferred in the end to another. To you." She gazed at me with her flat black eyes, the sunken side of her face seeming to leach farther across the unblemished skin as I watched. "He showed me that I had been wrong about you, even when you kept trying to prove me right."

She smiled at my silence. "You know what I'm talking about. You could have killed me when I threatened your lover. You could have killed me when I threatened poor, innocent Iskra. She's dead now, you know. Burned to ash in the fire of her own granddaughter's magic."

I grimaced. I'd feared the worst, but I wasn't going to give Myanya the benefit of more of a reaction. I also couldn't believe her. Iskra had surprised people before.

"I can feel the dead as they gather close. You can too, with Death's mark upon you. I never tried to run afoul of Death, of course. I was already dead, and she knew it. There is no more patient predator on this earth than Death."

That didn't surprise me. "What will you do now? You're here to be judged. Gamon is waiting for you."

"Oh, Gamon will not get her chance. And perhaps just as well. She would take my side."

I opened my mouth, then shut it again. Myanya was probably right.

"That much I knew. And you knew it as well. You made that clear when you brought me here in chains, with so much fury burning through you that the doors were sealed from anyone's entry beyond."

They were? I looked at the distant doors, which always had been open. They didn't look sealed closed, though. They looked like doors. Shut doors, but doors.

Before me, Myanya seemed to crumple farther into herself. "Before you judge me too hastily, though, Justice Wilde, understand that I came to none of this through my own power. The horrors you saw in your vision were truly those visited upon me. But not, as you think, because I was a witch. I was something far different from that."

I began to speak, but Myanya continued, riding the cresting wave of her memories. "The pain I suffered, the endless death, the desperate surge to life—all real. All deliberate. The necromancer who made me into what I am died a terrible death, but I could never undo the endless mortification of my flesh, nor the need for me to be reborn. Only you can do that."

My head was beginning to hurt. "Myanya, I'm going to summon Gamon. She's going to—"

"No," she said again. "Gamon cannot judge me. Your time has come, as my time has come."

She clutched her throat with a pale and withered hand, silvering in the half-light, and I suddenly felt like crying. Myanya was slowly disappearing before my eyes, and for all her crimes, I couldn't deny the deep and unrelenting sorrow I felt at seeing her go.

I pushed out mentally, just in case Myanya was right and I'd been the one holding Gamon out. The doors opened with a subtle rush of air, and a moment later, a woman clad head to toe in black military gear strode toward us, her boots clicking in a harsh staccato against the stone floor.

Myanya watched her approach. "You could have delivered her to her end with a moment's thought. Her sins are many."

"She stood for me when I needed standing for. That mattered more." I knelt now. Myanya seemed to be folding in on herself, concentrating her form into that of a small, slender girl. It was unnerving, and I didn't understand what I was seeing. "If you're pulling some trick…"

"No—trick," Myanya sighed. It was a sigh of resignation, but also relief. "The tools are in the hands of the artist, and they must be shaped into the proper form. But more than that, they must be used. The time has passed for me to use them. They are yours to wield. As for me, at last, a new day can dawn."

She sighed again, more deeply this time, and seemed to drop farther into herself, a huddled mass of robes. I watched her, dismayed, and Gamon stayed quiet for a long moment, both of us staring down at the disintegration of pure power into…something else.

Finally, Gamon spoke. "You know who that is, right? I didn't until you brought her here, but once you did, there was no hiding the truth. I assume you know."

"Yeah," I said, my mouth tight. "Myanya."

Gamon gave me a startled look. "Not exactly. A closer translation of her name is Inanna."

"Close enough." I crouched and moved my hand through the smoking pile of robes. There was nothing left of the dead witch but a flattened metal star, not shaped like a pentagram, but more a ball of flame, its rays streaming to the side as if it was being hurled through the skies. I picked it up gingerly, cradling it in my hands. Sorrow pulsed from it, the last remnants of a dying energy force. "She lived a long time. I can see how her name got changed over the years.

"I don't think you get it," Gamon said as I stood. She pointed at the star. "That's a gift from an ancient Sumerian goddess, Sara, the gift of herself. She's surrendering her light to you."

I winced. "You really don't need to make me feel any worse than I already do."

"No, you idiot," Gamon said. "You're still not getting it."

"Okay, I'm not getting it. Just—give me a minute."

I held my hands close to my body. Myanya's star—that was who she would always be to me—lay in my palms, glimmering. But even with my third eye, I could detect no trapped life force in it. Myanya wasn't trying to break free anymore. She had become the final incarnation of herself.

Gamon's voice, several shades softer now, sounded beside me. "Why are you so sad?"

I waved the star at her. "Because even though she was a really bad person—and she was—she's now a lump of metal, Gamon. Forgive me for caring about that."

"A lump of…no, Sara. No. That's not what she is at all."

Without giving me time to respond, Gamon wheeled me around to the entryway to her domain. Beneath lay nothing but stars and clouds.

"Throw it." Gamon instructed. I looked at her in horror.

"What?" Instinctively, I curled the fingers of my right hand around the star, holding it away from Gamon. "What are you talking about?"

"Oh, for gods' sakes—" Moving more quickly than I'd ever seen her, Gamon reached out and yanked my arm abruptly, so hard the star fell from my fingers.

I let it go, my heart lurching, and I cried out as it dropped like a stone for a long, sickening moment. But the moment the beautiful soaring star left my hand, I knew that Gamon had been right. I had to let Myanya go—once and for all.

"This is so *Titanic*," I said as we looked over the side of the precipice.

"I hate you," Gamon muttered.

And then we were flung back with a flash of light bright enough to fill the universe.

"What the—!" I spluttered, staggering back. Gamon grinned at me. I'd never before seen that expression on her face, and I struggled to understand. It was proud, and it was fierce, and it was—directed entirely at me, her eyes shining with wonder, and something else too. Respect, I realized belatedly. Respect.

"Inanna," she said simply. "Is now reborn."

And across the cosmos, the rich and rolling voice reached me, at once intimately familiar and powerfully foreign. *"That was…very well done, Miss Wilde."*

CHAPTER TWENTY-NINE

I didn't even try to resist Armaeus's pull, and instead leaned into it, slipping through the millions of starbursts that lit up the night sky beneath Gamon's fortress, until I found myself in the familiar haze of neon that marked the Las Vegas Strip. A moment later, I slipped between the spires and turrets of Armaeus's Hall of Magician-ness and landed in a room that…surprised me.

Because I didn't recognize it.

Which shouldn't have been possible.

The room mostly resembled a medieval hut or hunting cabin, a simple chamber with a small fire burning in its center, the smoke escaping through a flue in the ceiling. Several blankets were spread out on the floor by the fire, and one was balled up beside them. I didn't miss the fact that the balled-up blanket was streaked with blood. I struggled to remember how many pieces I'd left Armaeus in and whether any of them were bloody, but that oddly wasn't my biggest concern in this moment.

"You know, I'd appreciate it if my abilities as Justice of the Arcana Council would settle the crap down," I muttered, peering into the darkness of the chamber. I could barely see the walls, given the smoke from the fire. "Because there's nothing that pisses people off more than changing magic rules, and I don't know this place. I shouldn't have been able to poof here. Beyond that, this whole setup is seriously not OSHA approved. You know that, right?"

Armaeus's laughter sounded from the darkness. "I'll be sure to take it up with management. But you're wrong, Miss Wilde. Your powers remain as they have since you ascended to the Council. You have the ability to translate any language, to capture those Connecteds who have used their psychic skills to commit crimes. You have the ability to use your third eye to identify the magical connections and circuitry that bind our world together. You can wield your magic in physical form to deflect danger, preserve life, wreak whatever damage you wish, and stop whomever you wish."

"Right," I said, wanting to keep him talking. Because I still couldn't see the Magician, and that struck me as…less than ideal. "Don't forget my ability to make a mean peanut butter and jelly sandwich."

"You also retain your ability to manifest that which you truly want, and you've extended that to include people, not merely items, which is…an improvement."

I nodded, circling around. "But corporeal travel kind of has a basic flaw," I protested, peering into the shadows. The room simply wasn't that big, and yet: no Armaeus. "I can't randomly pop in somewhere I've never been. And, again, I've never been here."

"So you know the logical answer to your question."

My irritation flared. "I'm not really in the mood for a lecture, Armaeus. And will you please stop with the magic trick? Because you suck at hide-and-seek."

Armaeus sighed, a long, lingering exhalation that sounded more like a moan than I wanted it to, and he gradually manifested into view.

I clapped a hand over my mouth, but didn't move for a moment, wanting to be sure of what I saw. Armaeus lay on the ground beside the fire looking...not at all like the Magician I knew. He was...younger, was the only way I could describe it. This was a little difficult to discern in an immortal—especially an immortal who was a master magician—but there was something ineffably different about the demigod lying on the ground versus the one I'd last seen exploding into a bunch of mini-Magicians in Myanya's pentagram. His hair was longer and fuller, his skin more darkly tanned, and he simply looked more...rested.

At least from the neck up.

From the neck down, which was made eminently more apparent given the fact that Armaeus was naked, he looked like the model for the invisible man, except the tracings of all his blood vessels were on the surface of his skin—and they were glistening with blood. A faint miasma of violet energy hung over him like a Snuggie, but it wasn't enough to mask the very real trauma overtaking his body.

"For gods' sake, Armaeus," I whispered. "What happened to you this time?"

"Myanya did," he said simply. "Or, perhaps more appropriately, you did."

"I didn't do this." I rejected that idea immediately. "I wouldn't hurt you."

Armaeus's laugh was quiet. "But I attempted to hurt you. You attempted to defend yourself, as is your right. As is anyone's right when faced with an unknown threat."

"No." I dismissed his response again. "Myanya did it, okay, I can take that. She...she's a little bent out of shape right now. I can't really hold her accountable, I don't think."

Again, Armaeus chuckled. "She surrendered to you, Justice Wilde," he said, and the slight variation on my name had me looking at him again askance. He was hissing with steam, the blood exposed to the open fire crackling along his open wounds, so I approached him slowly.

"Why aren't you healing yourself?" I asked him.

"Here, in this place, I am not who I am, but who I was. Innately magical, perhaps, but new formed, without training or experience or guile."

I looked around the rude hut, seeing it with new eyes that were still unimpressed. "You definitely were due for an upgrade. But that takes me back to my original question. How'd I find you here?"

"Because you can seek me out, Miss Wilde. I am as real to you as any location on this earth you have visited. I'm not only a person to you, I *am* a place."

By this time, I'd reached Armaeus. The up-close version of his wounded body was worse than the distance shot. "Well, you've definitely trashed my rental, I'll give you that," I muttered, dropping to my knees beside him. I lifted my hands, then hesitated as the heat from his body spiked beneath me. "Is it okay if I do something?"

"My dear, deliberately stubborn Miss Wilde. There is very little you can't do once you choose to do so. You have the energy of Inanna within you, and the Eye of Horus upon you."

"Well, Myanya is..." I narrowed my eyes at him. "Why did you call her Inanna? Did you and Gamon go to the same psychic reading? Because that business that she's an ancient Sumerian goddess—"

"Matches up perfectly to her incarnation as the prophesied strength-bringer," Armaeus said.

To shut him up, I bent over him, focusing on his body with my third eye. Speaking of stubborn, it seemed like every time I turned around, Armaeus was deliberately injuring himself. But this time was worse than most. The violet pink of his neural networks now were spiderwebbed with angry, fizzy strands of white gold that hissed and sparked as I moved my hands nearer to them. One lashed out, poking me with petulant fury, and the sudden, shocking pain was all it took.

Rage poured out of me.

Rage for Armaeus and his beautiful broken body, rage for Inanna or Myanya or whoever the hell she was, the fierce star-bright spirit who had endured so much to allow her power to burst forth, a dawn star in a bleak, unforgiving sky. Rage for Iskra, who tried so hard to preserve her family from a legacy she couldn't shake.

Rage for so many bright and dancing lights out there, whose stars were dimmed by those who would oppress them.

They would not oppress them anymore.

"Miss Wilde," Armaeus murmured, and I eased up slightly, but I didn't break from my task.

"You've got to stop doing this to yourself," I gritted out as I chased the furious, crackling energy around and through and over his nervous system, flooding Armaeus with white, protective light. "I need you, dammit."

"I know," he said, and that...

That did make me stop.

I lifted my hands like a surgeon needing to be gloved and stared down at Armaeus. He was once more pristine—his skin smooth, bronzed, unbroken. As it turned out, I hadn't managed to manifest any clothes along with the healing, but hey, a woman can only be expected to do so much.

Armaeus waited until I thoroughly inspected my handiwork. By the time I lifted my gaze to meet his, one side of his gorgeous mouth was curved into a half smile. I suddenly felt vulnerable, and I scowled at him, dropping my hands in my lap as I sat back on my ankles. "I mean, I don't need you a lot," I grumbled.

His smile stretched farther across his face. "You don't need me at all in the sense that most would use the term. But there is much that I can give you. My strength, my knowledge. My experience. My willingness to stand in front of the fire for you, wherever that fire may be."

"Right." I blew out a breath. "Well, yeah. I guess I need all those things. And maybe a few others." I wasn't going to name those, of course. It was like a whisper to the devil, and with my luck, the Devil would be hanging around close enough to hear me.

"What you don't seem to realize is that I need you too."

I glanced up, ready with a sharp comeback, but there was something in Armaeus's eyes that I didn't expect.

Tears.

"*Whoa*," I blurted. I shifted back onto my knees and scooted forward, lifting my hands to his face. His cheeks were wet, and I put my palm to his forehead, expecting a fever of malaria-level proportions. "What's wrong— what's happening to you? Did I miss something?"

The tears crested over his long, luxurious lashes and dripped onto his face, a new one forming as fast as I brushed away the last. "Dammit, Armaeus," I said tightly, feeling my own tears unaccountably surging in my eyes. "You even cry pretty."

"Sara," he whispered, and I was so startled at his use of my name that I froze, not moving even when he lifted his hands to cover mine and pull them gently away from his face. He held them against his chest instead, and I could feel the beating of his heart. It was — too loud, too fierce, even for the Magician. The heart of a young man in the first flush of his power, whom I'd helped heal.

"Ahh...Armaeus?" I offered, and his gaze fixed on mine. It was deep, black, and far too intense, and it never wavered from mine. "You feeling okay?"

"Inanna is not the only god who has been reborn with your actions tonight," he said. "You set her spirit free, her light over all the world. A light that has found its way to those who need it most."

"You need to stop with the Inanna stuff," I said, though the tiniest twinge of concern pinged deep in my heart. I'd dropped Myanya's medallion over the edge of Gamon's precipice, and it had set off its own little merry firestorm. Had that been the wrong thing to do? I needed to start being a little more careful with the artifacts I was flinging around.

Armaeus watched me with a smile on his face. "In this case, the artifact you flung around proved to be that which was most needed for more souls than you realize." He leaned forward, brushing my lips with his. "Including yours."

When I instinctively began to move away, uncomfortable with where the conversation was going, he tightened his hold on my hands. "No, you must listen to this." He flattened my hands over his heart, and I felt the gentle thud of it beneath my fingers, oddly reassuring in the strange, half-lit room.

"The first gift you gave me this day was to fight me, to fend me off when you thought I was a threat to you, but it wasn't your only gift. You also allowed me to reach back to a time when I was not the Magician at all, simply a man, a human. I needed to reestablish that link."

"This was really your house?" I asked, looking around. "Because no offense…"

Armaeus chuckled. "It was the eleven hundreds. At the time, this hunting cabin was more than sufficient for my needs."

"Did you actually hunt? Or were the rats sufficient quarry?"

"You're deflecting."

"It's a skill. I'm really good at it."

"This—is certainly true. However." He flattened his hands over mine more firmly, and I didn't miss the uptick in his heart rate. "You need to know that I'm not the only one whose connection to his source magic has been reborn. You've given that gift to any who are open enough to take it. Lost souls, newborn mages, cynical veterans. Everyone."

His smile shifted then. It was tender, almost painfully so. "Yourself."

I lifted one shoulder. "I hate to break it to you, but I don't feel any different."

Still, when he tugged me toward him, I didn't resist. I laid my head down on his once-again healed body and reveled in the strength of him, the mended perfection of, well, the scarred warrior. Though my magic had taken the surface of his skin and made it whole, there was nothing that could take away Armaeus's scars or the memory of his pain, his suffering. Those were his as truly as Myanya's had been hers, both her shield and her sword.

They were my shield and sword too, I thought distractedly, allowing myself to let my eyelids drift shut. For the first time in longer than I could remember, I felt truly at peace. With myself, my abilities, my role of Justice. Was this what Armaeus meant by being reborn?

Above me, Armaeus tightened his hold on me and chuckled, the sound deep and rolling in his chest. "Not...exactly, Miss Wilde."

CHAPTER THIRTY

The office was quiet. I picked up the case and turned it around in my hands, flicking my third eye open to see the locking mechanism when my regular eyes didn't catch it. With a quick turn of a lever, the case opened with a hiss, the scent of musty papers filling the room.

I carefully spread open the rolled-up sheaf of parchment, weighting the edges down with small bean bags, and leaned closer to peer at the tightly crabbed handwriting. Another complaint against a long-ago male witch, who might or might not be the village blacksmith. Sorrow wafted from the pages as it detailed the death of the complainants' beloved pets, and a suspicion of other affronts in the small town—a farm going bankrupt, a baby dying in childbirth, a husband forced into a war not of his choosing. So many crimes over the past millennia had been laid at the feet of Connecteds, it was easy to dismiss the cases out of hand.

But I couldn't do that. Each crime deserved its review, and my experience in the library of Justice at the start of this case, with some of the crimes in witchdom jostling for position while others leered down from on high, made me realize that there was more than a little malice lurking in the huddled stacks. It was odd to think of the cases themselves harboring ill will for their investigators, but such was the contradiction of being a Connected.

I closed my eyes and flattened my hands on the pages, unable to read its energy, exactly, but, as of very recently, able to do the next best thing.

"Speak," I murmured.

"It wasn't my fault." The voice was low, tortured, and ineffably sad, and I raised my gaze across the room, where a man in a long leather apron stood, gripping a pair of long, metal tongs. He looked like a man who'd once been broad-shouldered, robust, but who'd shrunken to a shadow of his former self.

And then there was the fact that he was dead.

Death's Eye of Horus tattoo on my arm burned hot as I regarded the man, taking in his pleading eyes. I didn't speak, and, like so many others, he rushed to fill the vacuum of silence. "The children died. The animals too. But I had no quarrel with my neighbors, and they none with me. But I was a witch. Everyone knew it, accepted it. And when things went wrong, well…they needed someone to blame. They ran me out of town, forcing me to barely make a living as a traveling smith, but when that wasn't enough, they—" He looked around. "They contacted you. You never came, though." His hangdog expression deepened. "I prayed you would. I wanted my name cleared."

"I'm sorry," I said, and I was. There were two sides to every cold case. The criminals who got away—and the wrongly accused who never got a chance to breathe freely again, who lived their lives with the weight of the allegations against them pressing them down, inescapable. But I could see the blacksmith clearly, and there was no silver mark at his temple, only the faint, purplish corona of the wronged around his slumped shoulders. "Rest in peace, Herr Smith. May your soul be light as you take the next step in the journey."

The spirit before me smiled in genuine relief, for all that the smile was rueful. "I'm grateful for your time, Justice. I am. But there's no more journeying for me, I'm afraid. For me, all that's left is…"

I pursed my lips as the spirit's eyes lifted and fixed on something over my left shoulder. His eyes widened, surprise and wonder lightening his whole face, and then—

And then he disappeared.

I leaned my elbows on the table, watching the pages of the case before me crackle with energy until they too faded out of existence. Only the case itself remained, destined for some utility closet deep in the heart of the library that only Mrs. French knew the location of. I sighed, weary to the bone, but satisfied as I blew the remaining parchment dust across my desk. "That's never gonna get old."

A sharp, irritated rap sounded in the reception area, and I smiled as I heard Mrs. French call out her reassurance that she would greet the caller. Still, it was past nine on a Thursday night. Nothing good ever happened after nine p.m. on a Thursday except football. And the season was over for the year.

For a moment, I thought it could be Nikki, but Nikki had made several new friends with the burly, brusque, highly skilled security team the Devil had handpicked to guard Lara's house in LA. Nikki was on indefinite leave at the moment.

"Oh! Well, my goodness, what a surprise, ah, miss, ah…ma'am. You make yourself comfortable, and I'll— oh! Please, there's no need for—"

A second later, a slender form filled the doorway to the inner sanctum, the woman's silhouette instantly recognizable in her black combat gear. Gamon, Judgment of the Arcana Council, gazed around my office with clear derision before flicking her gaze to me.

"Nice place," she said sarcastically. "Are you ever going to upgrade from Mid-Nineteenth Century?"

"I've discovered quite a fondness for Mid-Nineteenth Century."

Gamon snorted, but she didn't move from the doorway. Because my third eye was already open, I didn't miss the agitation in her energy field, the desperate humming of her circuits. Gamon had been a stone-cold killer in her day. She didn't get agitated, and she didn't do desperate.

"What happened?" I asked.

"Nothing happened. No, that's not true. You happened." She strode a few steps into the office, then pivoted as Mrs. French bobbed into the doorway behind her. "I'm not going to eat her. You can stop hovering."

"Well!" Mrs. French's huffy response made me smile as she straightened indignantly. "I was going to put on a pot of tea for you, but I will simply leave you to your conversation. Good night, Justice." She bobbed a curtsey, then spun on her heel.

I watched Gamon drop her body into one of my client chairs, her tension still wound tight, and waited for her to continue. It didn't take long.

"Something shifted in the Connecteds' energy field when you dropped that thingamajig off the precipice," she began. "I've looked for it, and it's gone. Do you have it?"

"The star of Myanya?"

"Inanna."

"Whatever. No, I haven't found it," I said. "And for the record, I wasn't the one who wanted to drop it. You practically shook it out of my hand."

"Well, ever since I did, things have—gotten weird. I don't like it, and I want to—" She flapped her hand. "Undo it. Somehow."

"Is there trouble?"

"No, no...nothing like that." Aggravated, Gamon pushed herself back out of her chair and stalked around the room, peering with distaste at the eighteenth- and early nineteenth-century oil paintings adorning the walls in ornate frames, the delicate side tables and the reupholstered coach. "Where'd you get all this crap?" she muttered.

Her problem wasn't with my sense of décor, however, so I waited her out. One of the benefits of immortality, time was always on your side.

Finally, she turned back to me, her arms folded. "I've been forgiven," she snapped.

Wasn't expecting that.

"Um—what?"

"You know something about my past. Not a lot. Not anywhere near everything. But I've done some things I do not regret. They needed to be done, and I did them."

She spoke with such a mix of conviction, pride, and self-loathing that all I could do was stare. Gamon wasn't looking at me, however; she was looking at the line of pneumatic tubes behind me, and she wasn't really seeing those either.

Gamon continued. "I've long since come to terms with my crimes. I'll be judged—or I won't—I really don't give a damn. But this..." She grimaced. "This is just weird."

"You say you were forgiven. By whom?"

"I don't know, exactly. But when I left my mark on a place, it was deep and wide. The energy shifted, and stayed shifted. Bleak, soulless, lost. For years and, in some cases, decades." She shifted her gaze to me, and her eyes were hard and cutting, as if daring me to defy her. "That's the way it needed to be."

"And now?"

"It's shifted back. I'm not saying it's healed. I did too much damage for that. But the collateral deaths and injuries, the innocents I harmed because they were in the wrong place at the wrong time, that energy should still be there. It's not. In its place is something new and different. Something...almost hopeful." She flexed her hands into fists. "I don't like it."

I bit my lip, struggling to keep a straight face. Only Gamon would decry the day when enough time had passed for some poor soul to pray for her forgiveness instead of her cruel and painful death. "What would you like me to do about it?" I asked evenly.

"Find that chunk of metal, wherever it got to, and destroy it," she said without hesitation. "It's clearly dangerous. It needs to go."

"I dropped it into *space*," I protested. "It probably burned up in the atmosphere."

"It didn't," she said darkly. "It's out there somewhere, and I worry it won't stop doing—" She flapped her hands. "Whatever it's doing. You're the great artifact hunter. You need to find it."

"I—I'll try," I said, forcing myself not to shade my voice too gently. There was something else going on with the star of Myanya, something Gamon was concerned about...something reborn? I didn't know, but I had no desire to poke what was obviously an open wound. "I'll look for it wherever I go. If it's causing that

303

much disturbance, I suspect it'll turn up sooner rather than later."

"It needs to be destroyed," she said again, but her voice wavered slightly, and she glanced away. "I didn't realize what its powers were before I had you throw it. I just wanted it away from me. That was clearly stupid."

She stood then, nodding sharply at me. "Justice," she said, and for the first time since she entered my office, her mouth slid into a half grin.

"Judgment." I stood as well. I walked around the desk and accompanied her out to the lobby, not missing her continued disapproval of my décor. For a woman who preferred her environment cold, utilitarian, and a million miles up in the sky, I didn't think she had any room to talk.

Mrs. French had apparently left for the night, and after I closed the door on Gamon, I turned back to my office. No matter how judgy Judgment was, I liked the place. It made me feel connected to past Justices, particularly Abigail Strand, whose life I needed to look into more deeply anyway.

I headed toward the library to do exactly that when I heard the familiar shuddering noise from my inner office, the sound of an incoming case—one arriving from some distance, from the sound of it. No matter how silly it felt, I truly enjoyed actually seeing a case land, so I changed direction and returned to my office. My desk was clear, but sure enough, the third tube to the right was vibrating in earnest now, preparing to receive a new canister—

Shhhhh-thunk!

But there was nothing there.

Frowning, I moved toward the wall of tubes, then peered into the velvet-lined trough that served as a landing pad for the more well-behaved canisters—as opposed to those that simply shot out into the room, clanging against the desk, the chairs, or the far walls. There was something there, but—it wasn't a canister.

My brows shot up.

I reached out and picked up a small silver pendant, no bigger than a nickel, swinging from a long metal chain. It was a fiery ball of flame, a shooting star, and as I held it in my hand, it warmed to the heat of my palm. Something light and buoyant danced across its surface, and I found myself grinning despite myself, my heart filled with unexpected joy.

Where it'd come from, who'd strung it on a chain, and why it had landed in my office, I couldn't begin to guess, but as to what I'd do with it...

I closed my hand around it and held it to my heart.

"I've got you, Inanna," I whispered. "A new day has dawned, and I've got you."

Then I turned out the lights of Justice Hall, and headed home.

~~~

A NOTE FROM JENN

Tracking down the Lost Queen eventually led Sara to the Queen of Swords, who represents the shrewd, often lonely, always cutting Queen in all of us! If you draw the Queen of Swords in a reading...brace yourself. Things are about to get real. Turn the page for an interpretation about the Queen of Swords!

ALSO: Interested in learning more about the Tarot, upcoming book releases, and other bits of arcana and mayhem? Get Connected (heh) and sign up for my mailing list at www.jennstark.com/newsletter!

The Queen of Swords

As you may remember from my previous book, THE RED KING, court cards are generally about people — the ones you know, the ones you'll meet, or possibly even yourself. The Queen of Swords, however, is quite unique in your world, so chances are, you'll recognize her immediately when you see her. Strong, incisive, and maybe a little cutting, she's very smart — with a razor-sharp wit and a keen sense of responsibility. She may not always be the warmest of friends or confidantes, but you can trust that she'll tell you what she really feels, and that her strategies will be dead on, particularly in conflict. In fact, in some interpretations, the card is thought to represent Pallas Athena, Greek goddess of wisdom and warcraft. Conversely, this queen can also seem quite lonely — the card has been termed "the widow's card" in other interpretations — but her alone-ness may well be by choice. Don't make assumptions when it comes to the Queen of Swords, or you may regret them! When this card does not represent a person, you are most likely involved with a project or issue that requires shrewd insight and sharp intellect to ensure your success, so put your thinking cap on. It's considered a card of wariness, strategy, and standing on your own two feet, so rest assured: you've got what it takes to tackle any challenge. When you see this queen in your reading, square your shoulders, lift your chin, and be prepared to put your mind and will to work. You'll amaze yourself and those around you with what you're able to accomplish.

ACKNOWLEDGMENTS

Writing THE LOST QUEEN has reminded me of why I fell in love with Sara Wilde in the first place, and I am incredibly grateful to my readers, who continue to allow me to write these stories. Thank you for the adventure, and I hope you enjoyed this tale! I continue to be endlessly grateful to Elizabeth Bemis for her beautiful work on my books and my site—especially my gorgeous series covers. My editorial team of Linda Ingmanson and Toni Lee kept me straight, as always. , Any mistakes in the manuscript are most definitely my own. I remain deeply grateful to Edeena Cross and Sabra Harp for their brilliant beta reads, and to Kristine Krantz, who survived this book with barely her sanity intact. And, of course, thank you, Geoffrey, forever and always. It's been a *Wilde* ride.

About Jenn Stark

Jenn Stark is an award-winning author of paranormal romance and urban fantasy. She lives and writes in Ohio. . . and she definitely loves to write. In addition to her Immortal Vegas and Wilde Justice urban fantasy series and Demon Enforcers paranormal romance series, she is also author Jennifer McGowan, whose Maids of Honor series of Young Adult Elizabethan spy romances are published by Simon & Schuster, and author Jennifer Chance, whose Rule Breakers series of New Adult contemporary romances are published by Random House/LoveSwept and whose modern royals series, Gowns & Crowns, is now available.

You can find her online at jennstark.com, follow her on Twitter @jennstark, and visit her on Facebook at facebook.com/authorjennstark.